W9-BRH-467

ON COPPER STREET

ON COPPER STREET

A Tom Harper Mystery

Chris Nickson

This first world edition published 2017
in Great Britain and the USA by
SEVERN HOUSE PUBLISHERS LTD of
19 Cedar Road, Sutton, Surrey, England, SM2 5DA.
Trade paperback edition first published
in Great Britain and the USA 2017 by
SEVERN HOUSE PUBLISHERS LTD

British Library Cataloguing in Publication Data
A CIP catalogue record for this title is available from the British Library.

ISBN-13: 978-0-7278-8696-5 (cased)
ISBN-13: 978-1-84751-805-7 (trade paper)
ISBN-13: 978-1-78010-869-8 (e-book)

All Severn House titles are printed on acid-free paper.

Severn House Publishers support the Forest Stewardship Council™ [FSC™],
the leading international forest certification organisation.
All our titles that are printed on FSC certified paper carry the FSC logo.

MIX
Paper from
responsible sources
FSC
www.fsc.org   FSC® C013056

Typeset by Palimpsest Book Production Ltd.,
Falkirk, Stirlingshire, Scotland.
Printed and bound in Great Britain by
TJ International, Padstow, Cornwall.

To Tom Maguire (1865–1895)
And my great-great grandparents, William (1823–1883) and
Charlotte Nickson (1827–1889)
All buried at Beckett Street Cemetery
Maguire quite justifiably has a headstone.
My great-grandparents share a common grave with many others.
May this be their memorial.

Oh! the wide outlook was dreary,
And my eyes were tired and weary,
For my hopes were burnt to ashes cold and white;
My heart was sick and faint,
And I felt the deadly taint,
Of the dull despair that hovers round the watches
  of the night.

But she's coming, coming,
I hear the fife and drumming,
Heralding the happy way
Turning night to light and day;
She's coming, coming;
The air around is humming
With the music of the silvery feet
Of Socialism Coming.

The Watches of the Night – Tom Maguire

ONE

T he brittle iron smell of the foundry. The noise of the hammers ringing in the air and the dark grinding of machinery, the blacksmiths of the industrial age. Even with his bad right ear it was impossible for Detective Inspector Harper not to hear the metallic music as he walked out along Wheeler Street, Sergeant Ash beside him, glancing around, eyes always curious.

The sound of their boots caught the factory rhythm, hobnails sparking on the pavement. A cold March morning with a hard wind: the month had come in like a lion. A boy in a shirt and a ragged pair of trousers ran along the other side of the road, a piece of paper clutched tight in his hand. On the way to the corner shop for his mam. Friday: the woman would settle her account later, once her husband was paid.

This was the Bank. He could feel eyes watching them from inside the houses, behind grubby curtains of cheap net. Suspicious of strangers, hostile to the police. Beyond Lower Cross Street, Upper Cross Street, and the houses grew even poorer, the bricks on the buildings all black from years of soot.

On the far side of Richmond Road the sounds faded into mild thuds. At the corner they paused for a moment, not saying a word, then turned down Copper Street. Boards papered over with advertisements covered a gap where a house had once stood. They passed a privy, the stench so strong it made them gag.

'Number thirteen,' Harper said.

It stood at the end of the terrace, identical to every other house round here. A back-to-back, two up and two down. Windows covered in grime. A front step that hadn't seen a donkey stone in too long. But then the owner had been in jail for the last six months; sentenced for receiving stolen items, thirty pounds' worth of silver in the suitcase he'd been carrying when he was arrested. However much they questioned him, the man had refused to say who'd given it to him.

The inspector had been waiting outside Armley Jail when Henry White was released the morning before. Out, free, the man looked fretful and scared.

'I said I'd give him twenty-four hours of freedom before I came calling,' Harper explained to the sergeant. 'And this time he was going to tell me everything.'

He bunched his fist and brought it down on the front door. It opened under his hand.

'Henry,' he shouted. Cautiously, he entered. Nobody in the front room. Someone had lit a fire, but it had burned down to ashes in the hearth. The room was cold, heavy with the smell of neglect.

He heard the sigh of the old wood as Ash climbed the stairs.

No one in the kitchen. A mug on the table with half an inch of cold, milky tea at the bottom. Part of a loaf on a cutting board, a wedge of cheese next to it.

Something was wrong here.

'Sir,' Ash shouted. 'He's up here.' A heartbeat's pause. 'He's dead.'

Henry White lay in his bed, under a blanket that was dark and stiff with his own blood. At least he seemed peaceful, Harper thought, all yesterday's strain and terror vanished from his face.

'It must have been quick,' Ash said. 'Doesn't even look like he put up a fight.'

'From the look of it, he was asleep,' Harper said. 'Someone came in and killed him before he could wake up.' He tugged back the blanket. White was fully dressed, only the boots gone from his feet. Two patches bloomed on the dull white of his shirt. 'Stabbed him twice.'

White had never been a large man, but time inside had left him thinner. Bony wrists poked out of his frayed cuffs like sticks. The jail scent still clung to him, a fragrance of pain and hopelessness, and his skin had the pallor of the cell. He'd always been shabby, the type to fade into the shadows, to cower away from a look. Now he'd never be able to hide again.

All his life White had skirted the fringes of the law, jobs that nudged the edges of legality, mixed with housebreaking and theft. Then someone made him carry that case filled with silver from a robbery. Someone scared him into not saying a word and giving up six months of his life.

And someone had come and murdered him in the night.

'God damn it.' Harper slammed his hand down on the iron bed frame.

It was his fault. He should have pressed Henry yesterday, outside the jail. Pushed hard and seen what happened.

Instead he had to be cocky. Powerful. To give White that taste of freedom, then pounce. Too bloody arrogant by half. Now he was staring at a corpse.

Harper looked around the room. Bare boards on the floor, only a single faded rag rug providing any colour. A table with a jug and basin. A shirt hung from a nail pounded into the wall. Harper glanced back at the body; White hadn't even enjoyed his full day out of prison.

Poor bloody Henry, he thought. Life's given you short shrift.

He left Ash to search the house and start talking to the neighbours, and began the trek back to Millgarth. Maybe that would calm him a little. He needed to get the corpse over to the mortuary in Hunslet, not that a post-mortem would tell him much he didn't already know. Get some bobbies out in the neighbourhood, hoping people might have seen something. Even more, that they might be willing to tell the police. But this was the Bank; many round here would rather let a murderer walk free than give a name to the rozzers.

'How long had he been dead?' Superintendent Kendall asked.

'Hard to tell.' There'd been some stiffness in White's arm when he lifted it. Rigor mortis. 'At least four hours. But it could have been eight.'

'Dr King should be able to tell us. I'll organize it.'

'I should have made him answer when I saw him outside the jail.' He needed to say it, like flaying himself.

'You couldn't know. You're not a fortune teller.'

'But—'

'No buts,' Kendall ordered. 'Find out who did it and make

them pay.' He stared out of the window for a moment, then back. 'I had word about something while you were gone.'

'What?' From his expression, it couldn't be anything good.

'Tom Maguire. They found him dead at home. You knew him quite well, didn't you?'

Knew him and liked him. Maguire had organized the unions. He'd helped them win their strikes, and he'd been there at the birth of the Independent Labour Party two years before. All that and not even thirty yet. But politics never paid the bills; he'd earned his money as the assistant to a photographer up on New Briggate.

'How?' The word came out as a hoarse croak. Surely no one would hurt him . . .

'Natural causes,' the superintendent said. 'The doctor's there now. I said we'd send someone over.'

'I'll go,' Harper said.

'A couple of friends called to see him this morning. Nobody had heard from him in a few days. The door was unlocked. They walked in and he was there . . .'

He knew Maguire had a room on Quarry Hill, no more than two minutes' walk away from Millgarth, but Harper had never been in the place before; they'd always met in cafés and pubs and union offices. It was up two flights of rickety, dangerous stairs in a house that reeked of overcooked cabbage, sweat, and the stink from the privy next door. How many others lived in the building, Harper wondered? How many were packed into the rooms? How many more had lost their hope and will in a place like this?

The door to the room was open wide. The table was piled with books and magazines and notebooks. Politics, poetry, all manner of things. A few had slid off, scattered across the bare wooden floor. No sink, just a cheap cracked pitcher with a blue band and a bowl. A razor and leather strop, shaving brush and soap. A good, dark wool suit hung on one nail, a clean shirt on another.

That was the sum total of the man's life.

The doctor was finishing his examination, wiping his hands on a grubby piece of linen. The inspector tried to recollect his name. Smith? That seemed right. An older man. Not uncaring, but hardened by the years. They'd met a few times before, always in situations like this.

'He's not one to trouble the police, Inspector.' Dr Smith closed his bag. 'Pneumonia. Sad at his age but nothing suspicious.' He said good day, and the sound of his footsteps on the stair slowly faded away.

Harper could feel the cold all the way to his bones, as if there'd been no heat in here for weeks. The hearth was empty, carefully cleaned, but not a speck of coal in the scuttle. He opened a cupboard. The only thing on the shelf was a twist of paper that held some tea. No food. Nothing at all to eat.

The bed was cheap, pushed into the corner. A thin, stained mattress. Maguire lay under a grubby sheet and a threadbare woollen blanket. On top of that lay a heavy overcoat to give more warmth.

Two bodies in their beds. So different, he thought with sorrow, but the ending was just the same. The doctor had covered the man's face, trying to offer a little decency against the brutality of death. Harper pulled it gently away. The policeman inside needed to see for himself. Maguire's skin was so pale it barely seemed to be there. His eyes were closed. No lustre in the ruddy hair.

A gust of wind rattled the window. Tom Maguire dead. No heat, no food. And no one to really care. Maguire had been ill; Harper had heard that. But this? How could he have died with nothing and no one around him?

Harper laid the sheet back in place. He'd liked the man. He was honest, he had principles and convictions that didn't bend with the wind or the chance to line his pockets. He'd believed in the working man. He'd believed in the power to change things.

Very quietly, as if a loud sound might cause the corpse to wake, Harper pulled the door to. He started the walk out to the Victoria public house in Sheepscar. He needed to tell Annabelle.

'Did you see him?' she asked. 'His body?' He nodded.

When he entered she'd been standing by the window in the

rooms above the pub she owned, gazing down at Roundhay Road. At first she didn't even turn to face him and he knew. The word must have spread like ripples across Leeds: Tom Maguire was dead.

His eyes searched around for their daughter, Mary.

'I asked Ellen to take her out for a little while,' Annabelle said.

He put his hands on his wife's shoulders. 'I'm sorry,' he said. He tried to pull her close but she didn't stir.

'I knew he was poorly. I should have gone down to see what I could do.' Her voice was tight and hard. Blaming herself, as if she could have kept him alive. 'I could have done something.'

What could he tell her? She'd known Maguire all her life. They'd grown up a few streets apart on the Bank, Annabelle a few years older. Life had taken them in different directions, then politics had brought them together again after she began speaking for the Suffragist Society.

Annabelle began to move away, ready to gather up her hat and shawl. 'I can go over there now. I'll see what I can do.'

Harper shook his head. 'Don't. There's nothing. Honestly.' If she saw how Maguire had lived and the way he died, then she'd never forgive herself. He put his arms around her, trying to find some words. But they wouldn't come, just thoughts of a barren, bitter room.

He stayed as long as he could. But Henry White's murder meant he had too much to do. And he knew her way by now; Annabelle's grief would be a private thing. She'd speak when she was ready, and she'd cry when the tears needed to come. At the moment she was blaming herself for not visiting Maguire. For not keeping him alive. Taking the weight of the world on her shoulders.

He thought back over things he'd heard in the last few months. Word was that the new Labour Party was pushing Maguire away, that he was the past, not the future. He'd been seen out drinking a fair few times, so far gone that people had to help him home. That wasn't the man he'd known, not the one he'd want to remember. It certainly wasn't the one he'd watched who inspired hundreds of labourers with a speech on Vicar's Croft and helped win them a cut in working hours. Not the man who led the gas strike like a general and beat the council. And definitely not the shyly humorous man he talked to in the café by the market. That was the Maguire who'd remain in his memory.

There was no need to return to the station. He cut through the back streets, across St Peter's graveyard, along the road with the ripe, wet smell of the paper mill in his nostrils. By the Malthouse, then beyond the factory at Bank Top until he was on Copper Street again.

A pair of uniforms were knocking on the doors and finding nothing from their frustrated expressions. Harper walked straight into White's house. He could just make out a murmur of voices from the scullery and followed the sound.

Ash must have found some coal. The range was pumping out heat, a kettle steaming on the hob. The sergeant sat at the table, and across from him was a woman. She had a pinched face, hair put up in a twist to show a creased, wattled neck, a heavy paisley shawl drawn around her shoulders. Forty, Harper judged, but it was impossible to be certain. The dress that covered her from throat to ankle was wool, good quality once but with its best days in the past. Scuffed button boots.

Not Henry's wife, he knew that; the man had never married.

'This is Rose Thorp, sir,' Ash said. 'Mrs Thorp. She's Mr White's sister. Lives just round the corner on Brass Street.'

He looked at her again, trying to pick out the resemblance but seeing nothing. Not even much sign of grief. Just a thin, pale mouth and sad brown eyes.

'I'm sorry about your brother.' It was all he could think to say.

She dipped her head slightly.

'Mrs Thorp said that Henry was at her house for his tea last night,' Ash continued.

'He needed something hot in him,' she explained. 'He were skin and bone.' There was a crow's rasp to her voice.

'How did he seem? Scared? Worried?'

'Did you know him?' she asked and he nodded. 'Then you ought to know what our Henry were like. Always scared. Jump at his shadow, he would.'

'And how was he last night?'

She shrugged. 'He didn't have much to say for himself. I'd

popped in to look after this place while he was inside. Said he could come over for his meals with me and my Peter while he got back on his feet. Once he'd eaten, he left. Said he was coming back here and going to sleep.'

'Anything else?' the inspector asked.

Mrs Thorp pursed her lips. 'He did say one thing that struck me. When I told him he'd need some brass he said, "It'll be all right now, pet." That was it.' She turned to stare at Harper. 'What does that mean? Who did it? Who killed him?'

'The same people who made him carry that stolen silver,' he replied, and he didn't doubt it for a second. 'He never told us their names.' He returned her gaze. 'Do you know who they are?'

She shook her head. 'He never said. I knew better than to ask.'

No doubt she did. Her father had spent his life as a bookie's runner, always dodging the police. The only good thing he'd done for his family was a win on the horses that let him buy the two houses he'd left to his children. But it was the only piece of luck old man White ever enjoyed. Henry hadn't even had that much.

'He didn't give any indication?'

'No.' She was a hard woman, Harper thought. No softness in her heart. God help any children she'd birthed. She'd said her fill; they'd get nothing more.

'Thank you for your time, Mrs Thorp. We'll let you know when you can bury your brother.'

She stood. The woman was taller than he'd expected, her shoulders straight and proud. She pulled the shawl tighter.

'What about the house? It's mine, by rights.'

'I'll see if Henry left a will.'

He doubted that White would have thought of such a thing. But the idea would leave her hanging for a little while.

The front door closed behind her. Harper heard it clearly; this was one of the better days for his hearing.

'Did you find much?'

'Not really had a chance, sir,' Ash said. 'I'd barely finished going through the bedrooms when she came knocking.'

'Did she see him?'

'They'd taken the body by then. If you want my opinion, sir, this place isn't going to tell us a blind thing.'

He agreed. White might not be too clever, but he wouldn't leave anything incriminating.

'I know,' he said with a sigh. 'It still has to be done. What about the uniforms?'

'Not heard a squeak from them.'

'Carry on, see what you can find. I'm going back to Millgarth to take a look at the notes I made when we arrested Henry. Maybe I missed something.'

He was clutching at straws and he knew it. If there'd been so much as a hint of a name he'd have pounced on it at the time. But for now it was all he had.

He didn't get as far as the office. Sergeant Tollman was waiting behind the front desk as he walked into the station, belly straining against his uniform. The same position he'd occupied since Harper had started out as a recruit, seventeen years before.

'You know how they say trouble comes in threes, sir?' No greeting, no how-are-you.

'Why?' Harper heard the urgency in his voice. 'What is it?' Surely not something else.

'That bakery Inspector Reed's wife owns in Burmantofts.'

'What's happened?' He felt a shiver of worry travel down his spine. Annabelle had sold the three bakeries she owned to Elizabeth Reed in 1893.

'I don't really know, sir.' Tollman shrugged. 'Just word of something bad.'

The maze of streets rising up from Mabgate were jumbled, higgledy-piggledy. Houses so dilapidated they looked ready to collapse. But sturdy enough for families trying to survive on wages that would hardly keep a single man alive. Elizabeth was standing outside the shop, talking to a constable who towered above her. There was fresh blue paint on the wood-work, a new sign on the window: *Reed's – Baker & Confectioner.* It all looked prosperous.

Her face was bloodless. As Harper watched, she seemed to shake slightly. At least she seemed unharmed. And he could spot no damage outside the shop.

'Report, please, Constable.' He reached into his memory for the man's name and couldn't find it.

'Wilson, sir.' He gave a small cough and stood to attention, as if he was in court. 'I was on Beckett Street, sir, by the cemetery, about an hour and a half ago, sir.' Get on with it, Harper thought. 'A lad came running up and said there'd been an attack here. When I arrived a boy was lying on the floor. It appeared that someone had come in and thrown acid on him. Some of it caught the girl behind the counter.'

Christ, he thought as he glanced at Elizabeth. Her eyes were closed, lips pushed tightly together.

'Where are they now?'

'At the infirmary, sir. I pulled over a hackney and had him take them.'

'Good thinking.' At least the man had some initiative. 'How bad are they?'

The constable took a deep breath before answering. 'The lad got the worst of it, sir. All over his face and chest and his right hand. The girl took some on her face.'

'Who's the boy?' Harper asked. 'What's his name? How old is he?'

'Arthur Crabtree.' It was Elizabeth who answered. Her voice sounded ancient, weighed down with pain. 'He's on the furnace at the brickworks. Comes in every day for bread and dripping so he can talk to Annie; he's sweet on her.'

'She's the girl?'

'Yes.' A small, loaded word. She looked bewildered. 'Annie Johnson. I was down at the Meanwood shop. I came as soon as I heard.'

'Do you have any idea—' Harper began, then a figure came out of the shop, limping as he leaned on a walking stick. There was fury on his face. Billy Reed. He was an inspector with the fire brigade now, their arson investigator, but once he'd been Harper's sergeant. A trusted friend back then, too. Bad blood had parted them; time had healed some of that, but the scar still ran deep.

'Tom.' He nodded and reached for his wife's hand, squeezing it lightly.

'Billy.' He hadn't heard that Reed had been injured. 'What . . .?' He glanced at the cane.

'A beam fell on my leg while I was on the job. It's mending.' He dismissed it. 'I've taken a look inside. The best I can tell, whoever did it pushed the door open and tossed the acid. Probably ran straight off.'

Harper turned to the constable. 'Any idea who'd want to hurt the boy?'

'No, sir.' He frowned. 'I know Arthur. He's only thirteen. Never a moment's trouble.'

'Ask around. I want everything you can find – and sharpish.'

'The same age as Annie,' Elizabeth said dully. She raised her head and looked at the men. 'Just children, aren't they?' She stared at her husband. 'I'm going to the hospital to see her.'

With Reed beside him, the inspector examined the shop. Where it hit, the acid had eaten at the fixtures and floor. Billy was right; this had been rushed. In and out. But deliberate. For God's sake, who'd want to throw acid at a boy?

'Do we have any witnesses?'

'I asked after I arrived. Two men who saw someone running down the street,' Reed said. 'Just his back. Not much use. I've got their names.'

'I'll need them. How bad's the leg?'

'Improving,' he answered. 'At least nothing's broken.' He grimaced. 'I'm off for another week, until I'm firm on my pins again. I'll give you a hand with this if you like.' His eyes flashed. 'After all, I have an interest.'

Harper considered the offer. Billy had been a good detective, one of the best; he knew what to do, the ways to find answers. And with the White murder, the inspector and Ash had ample on their plates.

'It's yours,' Harper said, holding out his hand. Reed shook it. 'If you need something, anything, just ask.'

'Don't you worry about that.' He grinned. 'It'll be better than sitting at home all day.'

He spent another half-hour at the scene, going over everything, visiting the two witnesses Reed had found. The running man had been tall. He'd been short. Stout. Thin. Wearing a cap. Bare-headed. The pair couldn't agree on a single thing. Typical. Useless.

'Have there been problems at any of the shops?' he asked Reed. 'Tangles with customers?'

'Not that Elizabeth's told me. They're all doing well. She's started

selling confectionery and the wives all seem to go for that.' Harper
noticed Billy was wearing a new suit. It was good tailoring, not
from Barran's, and more than he'd be able to afford on his
money from the fire brigade. 'They weren't going after the shop,
that's obvious.'

Reed watched as the inspector walked away, hands in the patch
pockets of his coat, his soft felt hat pulled down over his forehead. It was hard to believe they'd once been close friends. But
that was before Annabelle, before Elizabeth. When things had
been so different. His own life had been a tangle then. Drinking
every night, temper always on edge.

Those days had gone. Both of them had changed. He'd met
Elizabeth, a coal miner's widow with four children to support. He'd
never expected affection, never looked for it. But it had happened.
He was a family man now, he'd finally found contentment.

And he was damned if he was going to let anything ruin that.
Elizabeth had worked herself to the bone since she'd bought the
bakeries. She'd built them up; each one took in more than when
Annabelle Harper owned them. Between the profit and his wages
they didn't have to count pennies any longer.

Yet reputations were precarious things; he knew that. So hard
to earn and so easy to lose. He needed to find out who'd thrown
that acid and why, before folk began thinking something was
wrong at Reed's Bakery. Justice for the boy and the girl. But he
was really doing it for Elizabeth.

The lad's parents would be at the hospital now. He'd go and
see them tonight. They only lived a few streets away. He'd talk
to Annie's mam, too, although he doubted the girl was involved
at all. She was simply in the wrong place at the wrong time.

He could begin to clean up the shop. Mop the floor and arrange
for tradesmen to come and fix the damage. The sooner they were
open again, no sign of what had happened, the quicker gossip
would die down.

TWO

Mary was quiet as she ate. It worried him. Normally she was so full of life and eager to recount everything that Harper kept looking across the table at her. His daughter kept her head lowered, moving the food around before spearing it on her fork and raising it to her mouth.

She must have sensed the mood, he decided, the way the room felt so subdued. But at three years old, how much could she understand? The world was still a huge, strange place to her.

Annabelle had barely said ten words since he came home. Lost in her thoughts and sorrows. He'd tried to play with Mary, to follow some complicated game she'd invented, but the little girl had run off to the table as soon as the meal was served.

'Mam?' she asked. Her voice seemed unnaturally loud in the silence. Three, and with a head full of questions.

'What is it?'

Mary cocked her head. 'Has Mr Mageer gone to heaven?'

How did you answer a question like that, Harper wondered?

Annabelle was smiling at her. 'Yes, love, he has.'

'But isn't that a good thing? Isn't heaven beautiful? He won't need to be sad any more.'

'No,' she agreed. 'He won't. But people miss their friends when they're gone. Even if it's to heaven.'

Half past seven. He tucked Mary into bed. A story from *The Blue Fairy Book*, watching her face as she fought sleep. He stroked the hair away from her face. Simply being with her lifted his worries and made him forget the job for a short while.

Annabelle was sitting by the fire, a heavy woollen shawl over her shoulders, as if she was still cold. A book lay unopened on her lap. He rested a hand on her shoulder and she moved hers to cover it.

'Heaven,' she said quietly. 'I don't know where she hears it.'

'Let's hope she's right.'

'Yes.' Annabelle was silent for a long time. 'I went down to

Maguire's room in the end. I had to. I didn't take Mary,' she added before he could speak. 'She stayed here with Ellen.' She paused, staring into the flames. 'How could he live like that, Tom? There was nothing.'

'I know.'

'If he'd said something . . . he knew I'd have helped him.'

Perhaps Maguire had been too proud, Harper thought. Or perhaps he simply hadn't cared any more. If politics didn't want him, what was left? No wife, no woman in his life apart from his mother living up on the Bank.

'What are you reading?' he asked after a while. There were books all over the room. Politics, law, philosophy; she always had one or two on the go.

Annabelle held it up so he could see the spine. *Machine Rooms Chants, Tom Maguire.*

'His poems.' It was enough of an explanation. He'd been publishing his verses in magazines for a few years. 'He sent me a copy a fortnight ago.' She looked up and tried to smile. 'Tell me something. Please. Take my mind off all this.'

But what did he have to offer? Murder and acid attacks? He tried to think.

'I saw Bill Waters when I was coming through the pub.' He was a councillor for Chapeltown, as conservative as they came. 'He was gabbing to Jeb Smith.' Smith was a union man, too far to the left even for the Labour Party. Odd companions. But even a nugget that juicy didn't spark a response. Annabelle sat, preoccupied.

The bar was busy, men with their wages ready for their pleasure, the end of the working week just a day away. Others, wearing better suits, watching, listening. He poured a glass of gin and took it back upstairs.

'Drink that,' he told her.

It helped a little. She cried, clinging on to him, letting the tears come. For Maguire, for her own helplessness, for the past. Harper held her until it all subsided. And when she was drained, he kept his arm around her as they went into the bedroom.

She was still sleeping when he left in the morning. A quick peek to see Mary, only her hair visible above the covers, burrowing away from the cold.

Saturday morning. The air in the café by the market was thick, steamy. He sat with a cup of tea. How often had he and Maguire talked in here over the years, crime and politics, this and that? He could still hear the gentle humour of the man's voice as he spoke and see the twitch of his moustache when he laughed. Once they finished, they'd go their separate ways: the inspector to Millgarth, Maguire back to the union on Kirkgate.

Time to leave, he thought, and raised the cup in a short, silent toast. He'd miss the man.

Ash was already in the office, going through Henry White's file. Harper had pored over it yesterday, noting names, places, anything at all. Somewhere to start. To try to dig out a killer.

'Any luck at the house?' he asked.

The sergeant sniffed. 'Not so you'd notice, sir. Doesn't look as if Henry was much for possessions.'

'Nothing hidden away?'

A quick, sharp smile. 'I was very thorough, sir.'

Harper passed across the first page of the list he'd made. 'Get started on those. Henry knew them all. Someone made him carry those goods.' A constable had stopped him at the railway station, looking suspicious and worried as he waited for the train, a ticket to London in his pocket. As soon as the suitcase was opened, he was under arrest.

'Yes, sir.' He glanced at the writing. 'One or two familiar names on here. I'd trust them as far as I could throw them.'

'Push them all hard.' He chose his words carefully. 'That murder was in cold blood. I want the man who did it.'

'We'll find him, sir.'

He hoped so.

Reed knocked on the door. He'd made sure it wasn't too early, although they wouldn't have slept a wink. He didn't bring his fist down too hard; no need to scare the people inside. A back-to-back house, like everywhere around here. Smoke rising from the chimney, neatly kept, the front step proudly scoured.

No answer. There'd been none when he called last night, either. But someone was definitely at home. Then the click of a key in the lock, a squeak of hinges and a man was staring at him.

'Mr Crabtree? I'm Inspector Reed, sir. I'm so sorry about your son. Do you mind if I come in?'

He'd been waiting when Elizabeth returned the evening before. Sat her down, made her a cup of tea with three sugars, saying nothing until she'd finished it and the colour returned to her cheeks. Then, 'How's Annie?'

'Poor love.' Just the two words and a long pause. 'She's going to have the scars as long as she lives.' Elizabeth stroked across her cheek and up into the hairline. 'Right there. About the only blessing is it missed her eyes.'

'I told Tom I'd look into it. I have the time.'

She nodded, frowning. He wasn't even certain she'd heard him.

'Why, Billy? That's what I kept asking myself on the tram. Why would anyone do that?'

'I don't know.' He was damned if he could see a reason.

'I told Annie and her mother that she'd always have a job with me. Doesn't have to be behind the counter if she doesn't want.'

'That's something.'

'I went to visit Arthur afterwards. It caught him full in the face. He's never going to see again.' Reed couldn't help himself; he shuddered. 'His parents were there.' Her face crumpled. Sobs punctuated her words. 'All I could do was tell them I'm sorry. Why, Billy? Why would anyone . . .'

He held her, feeling her body shake with anger and fear.

Harper took the second page of the list, ten men to talk to about Henry White. He was about to leave when Kendall called his name. The superintendent was sitting behind his desk, hair greyer than ever, thinning on the top. His cheeks had grown hollow; after so long in the job he was beginning to show his age.

'Come back later and tell me what you've found.'

'Of course.'

'I want a word with you about something else, too.' He smiled and drew the pipe from his pocket. 'This afternoon.'

Curious, he thought as he walked through the outdoor market. Never mind; he'd find out later. Harper squeezed between the wives and servants, eyes open for pickpockets. Out on Kirkgate he climbed the worn stone steps between two buildings that led to Waterloo Court. It was a dank, airless place, mortar crumbling between the bricks of the buildings, weeds edging through cracks in the flagstones, half the windows missing their glass.

Adam Godfrey had a room at the top of a house, up two treacherous flights of stairs. At seventy-five, the miracle was that he could still manage them. But he was spry, as light on his feet as a dancing master, with a twinkle in his eye, constantly amused by life.

'Mr Harper.' A smile crossed his face as he opened the door. 'Come in before you let in the winter.'

The room felt no warmer than the outdoors. No hearth, not heat of any sort. Godfrey picked a pile of blankets from the bed and wrapped them around himself as he sat and cocked his head.

'Now, what brings you here?'

'Henry White.'

The old man looked up at him. His gaze was clear and bright. 'Got himself killed, didn't he?'

'I know. I found his body, Adam.' He leaned forward until his face was just a foot away from the old man's. 'Think about it for a minute. Not even out for a day and he gets a knife in the chest.' He let the words stick to Godfrey's imagination. 'Six months in jail and that's his payment for keeping his mouth shut. Does that seem right to you?'

'Course not.' There was indignation in the man's voice. Godfrey had served enough sentences in Armley in his time; everything from fencing goods to being caught climbing out of a window with a pocket full of jewellery. But there'd been no word of him doing anything wrong in the last few years. Either age had put him on the straight and narrow, Harper thought, or he'd finally become good at hiding his tracks.

'Then tell me who set him up, Adam. Who had him too scared to speak?'

'I've no idea, Mr Harper, and that's the truth.'

'You knew Henry. You taught him half of what he knew. Come on,' he said, half-pleading, half-threatening. 'Doesn't he deserve that?'

'I'm out of that game.' The way he said it, the inspector believed him. A mix of wistfulness and triumph. 'I hadn't seen

him in a long while before it all happened. I told you all this
when you arrested him.'

'You might have heard a whisper.'

But Godfrey simply shook his head. 'Part of the problem with
living at the top of the stairs. Whispers don't reach this high.'

'Ask around. If you hear anything . . .'

'You know what Henry was like, Mr Harper. Wouldn't say
boo to a goose. What they did to him was wrong.' It was as close
to a promise as the man was going to make.

Jonas Fox, Tobias Johnson – both of them claimed to know
nothing, and he believed them. By dinner he could feel frustration starting to burn in his gut. He was close to Whitelock's First
City Luncheon Bar. John Whitelock had done a good job on the
place; it was pulling in trade. Noon on a Saturday and it was
full. Men in good suits, escaping shopping with their wives.
Working men, caps and tired eyes and a deep thirst, their week
just ended. All and sundry.

The tables were busy so he stood at the bar, eating a sandwich,
a glass of beer in front of him. He was lost in his thoughts.
Making his plans. More inquiries, then talk to Ash. See what
Superintendent Kendall needed that was so important. Out to
Burmantofts to visit Billy Reed and learn what he'd discovered
about the acid attack. And if he was very lucky, not too late
home.

Maguire's death had hit Annabelle hard. She was taking the
blame on her shoulders, as if she could have stopped it. They
were friends, no doubt of that, with a history that ran all the way
back to Leather Street on the Bank. But she couldn't see that
Maguire had kept her at arm's length, the way he had with
everyone else. He would never have let her come close enough
to save him.

'White had to go. That's what Willie said, that's what he was
told.'

He caught the words at the very edge of his hearing, but even
with his bad ear he was certain he'd made them out properly.
Harper jerked his head around, looking for the speaker. Just a
press of men in the small room, chatting in twos and threes. No
faces he knew from his work. No one glancing about furtively

or trying to slide away. Everyone innocent and nobody noticed him. Desperately, he strained, trying to pick out that voice again. Anything to identify the man.

Nothing.

He knew how bad his hearing had become. But he was sure of what he'd heard. Those exact words. They seemed so clear, so sharp.

Finally, Harper pushed his way through the crowd, out into the cold air of Turk's Head Court.

Could he have imagined it? Twelve short words.

He looked over his shoulder, through the window and into the place. Maybe it was another White, he thought; the name was common enough. The reference could have been meant something entirely different.

Could. Maybe. Perhaps.

Not the kind of words a policeman wanted to hear. But deep in his gut he felt the truth.

More people to talk to during the afternoon. Plenty of questions but no more answers. Folk had liked Henry White; no one had a bad word to say about him. Men who'd go to his funeral and take a drink to remember him. Yet not a single one of them willing or able to say who'd been behind the robbery that put him in jail, or his murder. And Harper believed that none of them knew.

'Who's Willie?' he asked. Blank responses, shakes of the head. One or two ventured names the inspector immediately dismissed. Another mystery.

It was after five when he returned to Millgarth. Ash was still out. That meant he'd learned nothing; any information and he'd have been back quick enough.

Harper knocked on the superintendent's door. Time to see what the man wanted. He'd been too preoccupied to give it any thought.

'Close it behind you, Tom.'

Just the two of them, the noises of the station muffled. Kendall puffed on his pipe, staring out of the window.

'Tell me something – what do you want to do?' he asked.

'Do?' He didn't understand. Do? 'What do you mean?'

'In the force.'

'I don't know.' The question took him aback. He had to scramble for an answer that made sense. 'The same as now, I suppose. Solve crimes. Why?'

'Because someone's going to have to run all this after I leave.'

'Leave?' Harper stared at him blankly. Kendall was part of the place. He'd trained Harper as a detective, guided him. He was the officer who commanded at Millgarth.

The superintendent gave a weak smile. 'You're supposed to be the detective, Tom. Use your eyes. *See*.'

He looked again, and in a moment he realized. For God's sake, how could he have failed to notice? The pale skin, the hollow cheeks. The haunted eyes.

'I—'

'Don't start with sympathy,' Kendall warned. 'I've had enough of it to float a barge. I've already talked to the chief. I was back at the doctor. Turns out it's worse than they thought. Going faster than they expected, so I'm leaving next Friday.' He shook his head. 'For whatever that's worth, anyway. Maybe it'll give me a little more time with the wife. But he asked me who I thought should take over here.' The superintendent's gaze was steady.

'Me? But . . . come on, sir.' The brass would never accept him. A parcelful of reasons. His political sympathies for the working man rather than the bosses. His background, growing up in a terraced house in the Leylands. Married to an outspoken woman, a publican, a Suffragist speaker . . .

'You,' the superintendent told him. 'Before I talk to him I need to know if you want it, Tom.'

He knew what the job involved. Countless hours behind a desk. Meetings with political men who'd forgotten what real crime was, if they ever knew at all. He wouldn't be a copper any longer, not the way he liked to be. He'd become a manager, sitting behind that desk and shifting piles of paper around.

And yet . . .

He could make changes here. He knew how Millgarth worked. All the ins and outs. He could improve things. He could fight.

Then there was Annabelle. What would she say?

THREE

'Well?' she said, eyes wide. 'What did you tell him?' For the first time since she'd heard of Maguire's death, there was a spark in her eyes. Her face had fallen when he told her about Kendall's illness, the short time he had left. But now she leaned over the table, eager to know, her meal half-eaten and the plate pushed aside. Mary watched the pair of them, intent and curious. He let the moment linger.

'Honestly, Tom, if you don't say, I'm going to throttle you and it won't matter!'

'I told him to put my name forward,' he said finally.

She gave him the widest smile he could remember.

'I'm so proud of you. Superintendent Harper.' She rolled the title around. 'It has quite the ring to it.'

'It doesn't mean it'll happen,' he reminded her. 'The chief will never go for it.'

Before she could answer, Mary said, 'Da? What's a supa-indendent?'

'Well, you know I'm an inspector now?' he began, and she nodded solemnly. 'Superintendent is the next rank up.' His mind raced for a way to make it clear. 'It's like one rung higher up the ladder.'

Mary looked at him, confused. 'Will you have to climb ladders, Da?'

'No.' He laughed. 'I hope not. Most of the time I'll be sitting on a chair.' He tousled her thick hair. 'Anyway, it probably won't happen.'

Later, when the little girl was asleep, he and Annabelle sat by the fire. She'd been leafing through Maguire's book of poems, stopping here and there to read one. Her other books, all the political volumes and suffragist pamphlets, stood in a tottering pile by the chair, ignored for a few days.

'Maguire and Kendall . . .' She closed the cover and stared

into the flames. 'It makes you realize how fragile everything is, doesn't it?'

'Yes.' But he hadn't been thinking of them. His mind was on Henry White again. Ash had brought nothing back with him, no thread they could pull. And neither of them knew anyone named Willie who ran a criminal gang.

'The only one I can think of is Willie Binns, sir,' the sergeant said eventually. 'And he'd be hard pressed to lead himself, never mind anyone else.'

He must have misheard. Some other White, not Henry at all. That had to be the explanation. Still, he turned it over and over in his brain.

After Millgarth he'd gone up to Burmantofts. As he passed, he saw two men working in the bakery. Reed was at the house, in his shirtsleeves, no collar or tie, braces dangling at his sides. He'd put on a little weight in the last few years, the inspector thought. Not portly, but filled out. It suited him.

'Found much?' Harper asked once they were settled in the kitchen. A copy of the *Leeds Mercury* was folded on the table, Henry White's murder the glaring headline.

'You've heard how bad the attack was?' Reed said. He took a cigarette from a packet of Capstan and lit it.

'I saw the report. The lad's blinded?'

'He is. Poor Arthur.' He sighed and shook his head at the hopelessness of it. 'I sat down with his father this morning. I could hear the mother crying up in the bedroom. Too upset to talk.'

'Was he able to tell you much?'

'Not really. He was still in shock. You can imagine.'

Harper knew how he'd feel if someone hurt Mary. He'd rage for revenge; he'd destroy whoever was responsible. From the determination on Reed's face, he felt the same about Elizabeth's children.

'Did he have any idea at all why it happened?'

'No. He just looked baffled.' He smoked in silence for a moment. 'Elizabeth was down at the infirmary. That girl who works for her is going to be disfigured. Scarred for life.'

'It couldn't be anything to do with the girl, could it?' Even as he spoke he knew it was a waste of breath; Reed was already shaking his head.

'Not a chance. I talked to her mother. Annie has nothing to do with it.'

'Then what do we have to go on?'

'I'm not sure yet.'

'Mistaken identity?'

'I've considered that. I just can't see it. The attack was too precise.' He shrugged. 'But I've barely started digging.'

'Let me know what you turn up.'

He didn't mention Kendall's illness or the possibility of his own promotion. No need. The word would pass soon enough. Instead he walked quickly back to Sheepscar and home.

After Harper left, Reed stared out of the kitchen window at the small yard. He exhaled, a wreath of smoke billowing around his head. There was one thing he hadn't mentioned. It seemed too small, too hard to put into words. But he had the feeling that something wasn't quite right, quite true, when Arthur Crabtree's father talked. Maybe it was just his imagination. He was rusty on investigations like this. But he'd find out.

'You're miles away, Tom.'

Annabelle was standing by his chair, holding out her hand. He took it and rose, seeing that she'd banked the fire for the night and locked the door. He'd been drifting in thought.

'I went over to the Bank this afternoon,' she said as they settled in bed. Her head was against his chest; he seemed to feel her voice as much as hear it. 'I wanted to see Maguire's mother. She remembered me from all that time ago, can you believe it? And she made a right fuss of Mary.' He could sense her smile. 'Did you know he supported her?'

'No.' He'd known little about the man's life. Giving money to his mother might explain why he lived with nothing.

'The coffin will be there on Monday. Lying-in, and the funeral a week tomorrow.'

That would be big, he thought. Plenty of working men in Leeds owed Tom Maguire a debt. He'd fought hard for them, won them time, money, respect. They'd come out in their hundreds to pay their respects.

*   *   *

Morning. Harper scraped the frost from the inside of the window.
A clear sky outside, brilliant blue, the sun pale as lemon above
the horizon.

A heavy coat, gloves, muffler, and finally his soft felt hat,
pulled down by his eyes.

Sunday, and the world was quiet. All the factories were closed.
The bellowing roar of machines was silenced for a day, the only
sound in the morning the click of his hobnail boots on the
pavement.

The only life was in the Leylands, where the Jews made their
home. Their Sabbath had ended the evening before. Now they
were back to work, the buzz of sewing machines coming from
the sweatshops as he passed.

Ash was already at Millgarth, poring over an old file. The ink
had faded but the copperplate script was clear enough.

'Henry White's father, sir,' he said. 'I went down and dug it out.
Looks like he was a bit of a character in his time. Made a little
money and lost it, that seemed to be the story of his life. I just
wondered if he might have created some enemies.' He raised an
eyebrow. 'People who might have seen Henry as a target.'

'And?'

'All I've found is ancient history,' he answered with a smile.
'But there might be something. A few pages to go yet.' Ash gave
a small cough. 'There's been a little talk, sir.'

'Oh?' Harper perched on the corner of his desk.

'The word is that Mr Kendall's leaving.'

'Is that right?'

'And that you might be taking his place.'

Where in God's name did they hear all this? The door had
been closed when he and the superintendent spoke. The only
person he'd told was Annabelle. But the rumours were running
wild around the station.

'It's true that he's going. Friday will be his last day.' The
inspector picked his words with care. 'He's ill. Very ill, it turns
out. He probably doesn't have too long left. But I don't know
who'll be running this place after that.'

It was hardly a lie. He had no idea who'd be in charge. His
name would be one of several, probably men with far more
experience and less abrasive personalities than his. It wasn't as

if he expected the job. Right now all he wanted was to find Henry White's killer.

'First things first,' Harper said. 'Let's keep looking.'

But Sunday was never a good day for searching. Businesses were closed, none of the beer shops or gin palaces open until evening. By ten he felt as if he'd wasted hours scuffling around Leeds for no result. Finally, as the clock sounded the hour at the Parish Church, he crossed Crown Point Bridge into Hunslet.

Dr King was the police surgeon, widowed, in his eighties, but still with a reputation as a ladies' man, always flirting and paying court. He worked when he chose these days, but he was usually in the mortuary and laboratory under the police station on Hunslet Lane. His place. King's Kingdom.

The smell of carbolic was strong, and other chemicals made his throat feel raw as Harper pulled open the door at the bottom of the stairs. Whistling, meditative and off-key, came from a room at the end of the corridor.

'You took your time, Inspector. I expected you yesterday morning. Lost your eagerness?'

What remained of King's hair was white. The jowls of his face grew larger and ruddier each year.

'The body that came in on Friday,' Harper began.

'What do you want me to tell you?' He put down the glass vial he'd been watching. 'If you've seen him, you know how he died.'

'Stab wounds.'

'Two of them in the chest,' King said. 'One slipped between his ribs and pierced the heart. No signs of resistance that I found. Attacked in his sleep, perhaps?'

'He was in bed.'

The doctor nodded. 'That's what I thought. What else? He was malnourished, looked as if he'd spent a great deal of time indoors.' He reached across and picked up a piece of paper covered in the scratch that was his writing and sucked on his lower lip. 'If I had to guess, I'd say he was a prisoner.'

'He came out of Armley the morning he was killed.'

The doctor gave a brief smile of satisfaction. 'Good, I haven't lost my faculties yet. But that's all I can tell you, Inspector. It's as straightforward as anything you've sent me.'

If only that were true, Harper thought. Henry White's death was anything but plain and obvious.

'Nothing else at all?'

'What do you want? I can't make up facts. All I can say is what I've observed and examined. For what it's worth, the knife blade that killed him was probably six inches long and an inch across at its broadest point. A vicious weapon. Doubled edged.' He raised a bushy eyebrow. 'A deadly weapon, in every way.'

It wasn't much, but each tiny scrap helped.

'Thank you.' He glanced around. 'Where's the body?'

'You're too late,' King told him. 'A relative took him yesterday.' He peered through his spectacles, checking the notes again. 'His sister. Mrs Thorp, I think?'

'That's right.' He remembered the woman he'd met in White's kitchen.

'I daresay he'll be in the ground tomorrow. But don't worry, Inspector, there was nothing more he had to give us, anyway.'

'Thank you.'

He was at the door when King spoke again. 'I see that your friend has passed on. My condolences. I never met Mr Maguire but he seems to have been a very successful advocate for the working man.'

'Yes,' Harper replied. 'He was.'

The dead and the dying. For now, his world seemed to be filled with them. In a curious way, that made the acid attack even worse. There was no end for them: Arthur Crabtree and Annie Johnson would have to spend years living with what happened. It would be there every time they looked in the mirror, touched their faces, saw someone staring at them. Just the same suffering, day after day after day.

Kendall wasn't in his office. Ash had gone out. The old file on Terence White, Henry's father, lay on his desk. Harper opened it and began to read.

In and out of jail for carrying bets. He hadn't been a lucky man. Nor a clever one. There'd been that single piece of good fortune, the two big winners at the races. Each one gave him enough to buy a house on the Bank. One on Brass Street for himself and his family and the other close by, Copper Street, rented out to bring him an income. It looked like the only intelligent decision the man ever made.

Harper glanced through the list of offences. One caught his eye, from 1875: handling stolen property. Not silver, but a pair of enamelled snuff boxes taken in a robbery. He'd been stopped by the bobby on the beat who searched him for betting slips. What he found was even more valuable, reported stolen a month earlier.

No one suspected Terry White; he didn't have the nous for that. All he ever admitted was buying the boxes from a man he met at the Pack Horse inn. Three shillings for the pair and he thought they'd make a pretty gift for his wife. Instead, they brought him three months in jail with hard labour.

He saw the name of the arresting officer: PC Kendall. An old tale, back when the boss was still in uniform.

Did any of it mean anything? Probably not. And he couldn't spot anything else worthwhile in the file.

The door opened. Sergeant Tollman.

'I've just had Inspector Reed on the telephone. He's at the infirmary and wants you to meet him there.' Harper felt his stomach lurch. 'He says it's to do with the acid attack, sir.'

'That's fine.'

He strode quickly along the Headrow, almost the only person around. No swell of voices on the pavements or carts jamming the road. A tram passed, just two passengers inside.

Harper cut through Oxford Place, next to the Town Hall, and along Great George Street until he reached the hospital. Reed was standing outside, a cigarette cupped in his hand. The old soldier's trick to keep it hidden from view. It made Harper smile, the way some actions became so natural. Long before he'd been a copper or a fireman, Reed had served with the West Yorkshires, fighting in Afghanistan.

'Billy,' he said. 'You wanted to see me.'

'I came in to talk to Annie. She remembered something.' He led the way back into the building, up a flight of stairs and along a corridor with the overpowering smell of disinfectant.

The ward had high windows that let in the bright light. It allowed him to see the girl's face all too clearly. The left cheek and jaw were livid and puckered, contorted. Part of her hair had been burned away by the acid and there was an awkward twist to her mouth. As he stared, Harper struggled to keep all expression from his face.

'This is Inspector Harper,' Reed told the girl. His voice was gentle, patient, with warmth in his eyes. 'I told you about him; he's a good policeman. Will you tell him what you told me, Annie?'

She squirmed away in the bed, turning her head to try and hide the damage before she spoke. Her eyes glistened, on the edge of tears. How many nights in the future would she cry herself to sleep, he wondered? In one moment her whole world had changed. He couldn't do anything for her looks. But he could try to bring her some justice.

'It were only a second.' Her voice was tentative, small and fragile. 'Just while he opened the door. Then he was throwing something and it were burning so bad.' She brought her knees up under the blanket, huddling in on herself.

'It's all right, love,' Reed said. 'You can tell him.'

'All I remember is he had a cap on his head. He looked just like Dan Leno, you know, from the music hall. I seen a picture of him on posters. I wondered what someone like that was doing, coming into our bakery.'

'Is there anything else?' Harper asked. He didn't want to press the girl too hard and scare her. She shook her head. 'How old do you think he was?'

'Old, mebbe. Forty. More.'

'Was he tall? Short?'

'Normal,' Annie replied after a moment. He needed more than that.

'Fat? Thin?'

'He were wearing a coat. A long coat. He weren't fat,' she said, then added, 'Not really.' She began to blink, to try and hold back the tears. Reed inclined his head; enough.

'Thank you,' Harper told her.

'Elizabeth will come down to see you later,' Reed promised the girl. 'You try to get some rest.'

They paced along the corridor, then out into the light without speaking. Cold air, alive, fresh.

'Dan Leno,' Harper said slowly.

'I thought you'd want to hear it.'

'Do you know anyone like that? He must be someone local to Burmantofts.'

'No, I don't.' Reed lit a Capstan, pulling a strand of tobacco off his tongue. A carriage passed on the road, curtains closed, drawn by a sleek brown horse, the driver with his back straight, wearing a dark suit and bowler hat. 'I'll start asking around.' He sighed. 'Poor thing. She was a bonny lass before this, too.'

'You see what you can find. Let me know if you need anything.' A quick handshake and he walked away.

Reed stood, smoking. Dan Leno, he thought. Ever since the girl first told him he'd been going through every face in his mind. No one seemed to come close. But he knew all too well that her idea of Leno might be very far from his; they'd see two different things in the same man.

Still, it was a place to start. And Elizabeth might have a few ideas. He raised an arm to wave down a hackney carriage.

'Go home,' Harper told Ash as the hands on the clock turned to four. 'We're not going to solve this today.'

The last two hours had been filled with frustration. Names pulled from the files and the past, every one with some connection with Henry White. Some were in jail. A few had left Leeds. One or two had died. Their list had dwindled to twigs.

'We only have two left, sir. We could get to them easily enough.'

'Tomorrow,' he said. He felt weary, drained. White, the girl, Maguire. And the Superintendent. Cancer, Kendall had confided, and not too long for this world. How could he have failed to see all the changes? They'd happened right in front of his face. Maybe that was the reason. When you saw someone every day, it all became so gradual. Natural. Still, he should have noticed. He should have known.

And maybe he should have realized what was happening to Maguire, too. The man had been under the weather for so long that it was impossible to know what was normal. A summer cold, a touch of this or that, but he'd always insisted he was fine. He'd become quieter and thinner, slowly disappearing right in front of their eyes.

'It'll wait. You go and spend some time with your Nancy. She doesn't see enough of you.'

'I'm not sure she'd agree, sir.' But Ash's grin was broad under his moustache. 'Especially when she says I'm getting under her feet.' He gathered up his battered bowler hat and said goodnight.

The inspector sat, lost in his thoughts for a few minutes. Then he shrugged on his coat and left.

The house stood off Chapeltown Road, the last building in a terrace of impressive villas, three tall storeys. A small garden at the front, a much longer one behind. The kitchen and quarters for the cook-servant in the cellar.

He knocked on the door and heard a scamper of footsteps, then a girl in a black and white uniform turned the handle, her face red from running up the stairs. At the entrance to the parlour she announced him, then he was ushered into a room where the fire blazed hot in the grate.

Kendall sat in a heavy leather chair near the fireplace, a newspaper open on his lap. His wife was at the table, spectacles on her nose as she leafed through a heavy book.

'Tom.' The superintendent didn't stand, just looked at him in surprise. 'Has something happened?'

'No,' he answered. That was certainly the truth. 'Nothing at all. We're getting nowhere. I wanted to come and talk for a few minutes, that's all.'

Kendall glanced at his wife. She didn't seem to notice, but still she gathered her things and stood, beaming at Harper as if there wasn't a thing wrong in the world.

'I'll leave you two to business. I'll have Sarah bring you some tea.'

'Sit down, Tom. You're making me worried, standing there.' He took out his pipe and lit it, smoke billowing into the air. 'They told me I should stop, you know. I said I'd keep my pleasures.'

'I should have seen what was happening . . .'

'You didn't, and I didn't say a word.' He shrugged. 'What was the point? It couldn't change anything.'

Kendall had taught him how to be a detective. As the super-intendent at Millgarth he'd reined in the worst of Harper's excesses and turned a blind eye to others. He owed the man more than he could ever repay.

'Even so . . .'

'It doesn't matter.' He waved it away. 'I've put in my recom-mendation for the job.'

'They won't want me. You know I don't make a secret of my politics. Annabelle's a suffragist . . .' That was just the tip of the list.

'And you're a damn good policeman.' The doorknob turned: the maid with a tray of tea and biscuits. They waited until she left. 'If I didn't believe you could do the job, I wouldn't have asked you.'

'Thank you.'

'Don't worry too much about the other things. The chief constable isn't a fool. I know you don't care too much for him, but he's capable of seeing beneath the surface. And he wants what's best for the force.'

That was it. From there they moved to idle chatter about the station, tales of a few of the characters. It was only later, walking home in the growing chill, that Harper realized the man had been giving small pointers and hints.

FOUR

Slowly, the heat of the fire seeped through to his bones. He sat in the chair with Mary on his lap, tired after the long day spent in the cold.

'And then we went to church,' his daughter said.

'Church?' He sat a little straighter, not sure he'd heard her properly. She nodded her head.

'Maguire's mother asked when I saw her yesterday,' Annabelle explained as she set out the knives and forks. 'I couldn't really say no, could I? The service was for him.'

'Where was it?' Harper asked, although there was only one place it could have been held.

'Mount St Mary's,' she answered. 'Where else? Walking in that place made me feel like I was five again.' Other than weddings and funerals, she hadn't set foot in a church since he'd known her.

'What did you think of it?' he asked Mary.

'The smell made me sneeze,' she answered very seriously, and he smiled.

'It's the incense,' Annabelle said. 'It gets in your throat.' She smiled at him. 'Don't you worry, I'm not going back any more than I have to. The funeral next week and that's the lot.' She looked at Mary. 'For both of us.'

'You should have told me,' she said to him later. Evening noise came up from the bar, a low carpet of sound.

'Told you what?'

'What happened at the bakery.' He could hear the disapproval. Stupid of him. Of course she'd want to know, those places had once been hers.

'I'm sorry. There's just too much on my mind. And you were thinking about . . .' About Tom Maguire.

'Someone mentioned it, they assumed I knew.' She raised an eyebrow. 'We popped over to see Elizabeth after church. She's beside herself with worry. Thinks it's all her fault.'

'But that's—'

'I know. Doesn't stop her thinking, though.' She smiled. 'I gave her a talking-to.'

'Was Billy there?'

She shook her head. 'Out looking for whoever did it, she said.'

'He's on the sick list, and I need the help. He knows the area.' He took her hand. 'I'm sorry. I should have said.' He sighed. 'Things just seem to be piling up, one, then another, then another.'

'It doesn't matter.' She squeezed his hand. 'We deal with it and carry on.'

She was right. That was life. Keep on moving.

He stood by the door of the superintendent's office, Ash sitting on the chair. Kendall had listened, nodding here and there and smoking his pipe. Finally he sat back, watching the others.

'I'd forgotten I ever arrested Terry White. He was one of those people you could never take seriously.'

'Henry was the same,' Harper said. 'He must have had some steel in him, though. He never gave up the names of the people who made him carry the stolen silver.'

'Steel or fear, sir?' Ash wondered.

The inspector considered the question. 'Fear, more likely.'

'Was there anyone else outside the jail when you met Henry, sir?'

'I don't know.' He stopped, trying to frame the picture in his memory. 'I didn't look. I was thinking about him, what I'd say.'

Ash stroked his chin. 'It seems to me that someone must have known you were going to see him the next morning, sir.'

'Go and talk to his sister again. Maybe he mentioned something to her.'

'Yes, sir.'

As he closed the office door, the inspector kept wondering if Kendall would call him back. But what else was there to say? Five more days of work. All the men at Millgarth would go out on Friday evening and toast the man, wishing him a long retirement and good health. And he wouldn't have the time to enjoy either.

Harper drifted through the open market: only a handful of traders today, none of the storytellers or entertainers. No Indian chiefs, no feast of snakes to delight. He stopped at the café for a cup of tea, half-expecting Maguire to slide in and stop for a short conversation. Maybe a tip on where to look for Henry White's killer.

But all those strands that connected him to the past were being snipped away. He sat and drank and found no inspiration in the steamy room.

What about the voice he'd heard in Whitelock's? The more he worried at the words, the more he doubted himself. Misheard, perhaps, or a reference to someone else. It had to be. He hadn't managed to find a meaning for it.

He pulled out his pocket watch to look at the time, then marched along Kirkgate. The window of the Labourers' Union office wore a surround of black crepe. A notice in beautiful copperplate read: *We mourn the loss of our brother, Thomas Maguire. Whom the Gods love die young.*

A wonderful sentiment, Harper decided as he dodged between

a handcart and a tram on Briggate and through the small, hidden opening into Turk's Head Yard.

Polished wood, glittering brass, not a single smudge on the mirrors. The tiles on the floor still shone from the mop. Behind the bar a man with his shirtsleeves rolled up was laboriously writing out the menu.

'Anything good today?'

'Good every day.' There was an edge to his voice, but it turned to a laugh when he raised his head. 'Mr Harper. How's that wife of yours? We haven't seen her at the Licensed Victuallers' lately.'

'She's as busy as ever. I was in here on Saturday. You're doing good business.'

John Lupton Whitelock shrugged. He worked hard. He tried new things, and he was astute; most of them paid dividends.

'I've only just started. I'm looking at putting in electricity as soon as I can. Then we'll have some real light in here.' He cocked his head, frowning at the hissing gas mantles. 'You're not here for my plans unless you're spying for Annabelle, and you're definitely not one for an early tipple.'

'I'm after some information.' He recounted what he'd heard two days before. 'Any unusual characters in here on Saturday? Somewhere around noon.'

'No,' Whitelock answered with a slow shake of his head. 'No one I can pick out, anyway. Some regulars, some strangers. The usual mix.' He shrugged. 'I'm sorry, Mr Harper.'

'It doesn't matter.' Nothing ventured . . .

What else?

Henry White would have needed to buy a few things for the house. There had been some tea and sugar. His sister might have left them for him. But he might have purchased them in a shop.

It wasn't that far up to the Bank, climbing Richmond Hill, in the shadow of Mount St Mary's church. Between White and Maguire, he couldn't escape the area at the moment.

Two small shops, each one on a corner, goods displayed on dusty shelves in the windows. The first was neat enough inside, plenty of tinned goods, cheese under a bright glass dome, a marble board for cutting. The owner stood behind the counter, a genial smile on his face, side whiskers growing like a forest.

'Can I help you, sir?'

An honest man, Harper decided. He'd have sniffed out a policeman quick enough otherwise.

'Do you know Henry White? Lives on Copper Street.'

The shopkeeper's face dropped. 'I do. But if you're looking for him, he's dead.'

'I know,' the inspector said. 'I'm with the Leeds police. I'm looking into his murder.' He saw the man's mouth form an O. 'Was he in here on Friday?'

A brisk nod. 'In the morning. He bought a quarter of tea . . .' He thought. 'Sugar, some salt.'

'Did you talk to him?'

'Of course I did, he's a customer.' The smile returned. 'We all knew he'd been in prison. You can't keep that a secret round here.'

'Did he have much to say for himself?'

'Not a lot.' The man wiped his hands on his long apron. 'Surly, you might say.'

'Anything at all?'

'Just what he wanted, then counting out the money.'

'Was he on his own?'

'Yes.' But there was a flicker of hesitation in the voice.

'What?'

'There was someone outside, waiting for him.'

'A man?' He waited for the shopkeeper to nod, then asked, 'What did he look like? Was he with Henry when they arrived?'

'I don't know.' The man was starting to look a little worried. He gestured over his shoulder, at a curtain to another room. 'I was in the back when the bell went.'

'Did they walk off together?'

'Yes.' The smile returned. 'I saw that. It took me by surprise to see Henry again. He looked so pale.'

'Did you happen to see what the other man looked like?' He tried to make the question sound like a throwaway, as if it didn't matter. That often helped, he'd found. It seemed to spur the memory. No such luck this time.

'Not really. I just glanced at his face, that's all. Dark hair, and he had a cap on. He was taller than Henry, two or three inches.' He shrugged. 'That's all I can remember.'

Still, it was something, and much more than he'd had when he entered.

'Thank you.'

Harper drifted along the street and past White's house. He could feel eyes watching him, the air of distrust all around. He'd had more battles on the Bank than anywhere else in town. It was as if the people here felt that the rule of law should stop at the bottom of the hill. That wasn't going to happen, though. Leeds was a modern city. A place for empire and industry. And real justice.

He had one solid piece of information now. On its own it was worthless. That description didn't narrow things down. He needed more. Someone else who'd seen Henry and the other man together. And on the Bank it wouldn't be easy to find anyone who'd admit to that.

From Copper Street he cut through to Leather Street. Where Annabelle had grown up, and where Maguire's mother still lived. The black crepe of mourning in the window. Inside, the body would be on display for anyone who came to pay their respects.

He spotted two familiar figures in the distance and began to run. The woman turned as he grew close, then smiled, saying something to the child. She looked, then began to dash towards her father, tiny legs pumping hard.

Harper picked Mary up and swung her round until she began to giggle, then carried her towards his wife.

'Visiting?' he asked as he bounced the girl in his arms.

'I wanted to see if there was anything I could do to help.'

'Was there?'

She shook her head. 'The old women are taking care of it all. Honestly, I think they relish someone dying, it makes them feel useful.'

'And what about you?'

A long moment passed before she answered, looking down at the ground as she spoke.

'A bit lost, I suppose, if you want to know the truth. It just seemed like he'd always be there to look after the politics.'

'And his age?' He was younger than her.

'That too,' she agreed. 'It's like when Harry died. Not as bad, but I feel at sixes and sevens. Seems like the world's gone upside down a bit.' Annabelle had been a widow for three years when

Harper met her. Her first husband, Harry Atkinson, who owned the Victoria, had been much older than her. His death had been sudden, unexpected.

'I heard things weren't too good between the Labour Party and Maguire.'

'They'd have worked it out. They needed him, he was popular.' She spoke with the certainty of a believer; he wasn't going to try and change that. And certainly not here, and not now.

At the bottom of Steander he lowered Mary to the ground, feeling the ache in his back; she was growing so fast. A quick kiss to the girl's forehead, another to Annabelle's cheek, and he was gone. Too many things to do.

Ash was waiting in the office, writing in his notebook.

'Did you see Mrs Thorp again?'

'For what it was worth, sir,' he replied with a sigh. 'From the way she talks, getting anything from Henry must have been like blood from a stone. Either that or she's just not saying, and I'm not sure which it is.'

The inspector recounted what the shopkeeper had told him, but Ash simply shook his head.

'It's nothing, sir, is it? I'll get back up there, see if anyone else saw him with this man and might give me a description.'

'Depends if they like Henry more than they hate us.'

'I wouldn't put any money on that, if I were you,' Ash said as he settled the battered bowler hat on his head.

At the infirmary, Billy Reed waited to see Arthur Crabtree. The boy's face was swathed in bandages, only the nose and mouth uncovered. The poor lad would never look at his reflection again, but maybe that was a blessing. He'd caught a glimpse when they were changing the dressings. Whatever he'd looked like before, now his face would scare people away.

How could anyone do that?

Finally the nurse told him he could go in. Arthur was lying in bed, face wrapped, along with his right hand and wrist. It reminded him of the pictures he'd seen of the mummies they found in Egypt. He pulled out a chair.

'Hello, Arthur, I'm Inspector Reed.'

The boy struggled, turning his head towards the sound.

'Hello.' It was a child's voice, one that hadn't broken yet, tentative and afraid of the world.

'Are the nurses looking after you?'

'Yes, sir.' A subdued, formal answer. That wasn't what he needed from the lad. He had to know exactly what he remembered. Arthur must have played it out, over and over. No choice, the very last things he'd seen. Reed wanted every tiny detail.

It took the best part of an hour but he put the boy at ease. He told tales of the army. His time in Gibraltar and Afghanistan. None of the true horror, but little things that had made him laugh back then.

Finally, Arthur seemed more cheerful. Reed drew in his breath.

'When it happened,' he began, 'what do you remember about the man who threw the acid?'

'I didn't know him,' Crabtree replied. 'I'd never seen him before.'

'You're sure of that?'

'I'm positive, sir.'

Slowly, he teased out a description. Older, fair hair under a cap, hate in his eyes. A thin, pained face. Tall, skinny, a long coat and trousers. The kind of description that fitted thousands of men in Leeds. Like Dan Leno, the way Annie thought? It didn't seem that way.

Why would someone throw acid at a boy who'd never seen him before? Arthur was telling the truth. He had no reason to lie. It was mindless. It was tragic.

Was there a madman out there? Someone who'd do this again? Without cause, without reason? It was every policeman's nightmare.

'Never seen him before at all?'

'That's what he said. I believe him.'

Harper sat back in his chair and ran a hand through his hair. It couldn't be. No one was as insane as that. But he knew it was possible. Anything could happen, he'd learned that much. And it terrified him.

'What do you think, Billy?'

'Honestly,' Reed said, 'I don't know. There's absolutely no reason for the attack that I've been able to find.'

'Begging your pardon, sir,' Ash interrupted. 'But are you sure everyone's told you the truth?'

'As far as I can be.'

Harper saw Reed straighten his shoulders and frown a little. 'If it's a madman he's going to be almost impossible to find,' he told him.

'That's why I came to tell you,' Reed said. 'You need to know.'

'Thank you.' But all he could do was pray it wasn't true. 'I'll send bobbies around the chemists.'

They'd find some names of people who'd purchased acid. There were plenty of other places to buy it, though, and giving a false name was the easiest thing in the world. Anyone could lie.

Yet what else could they do?

'What do you think, sir?' Ash asked after Reed had left.

'I hope Billy's wrong.'

'I think he must be,' the sergeant said thoughtfully. 'I can't imagine anyone walking around with a bottle of acid then picking out a lad at random, can you?'

'No.' Put that way, it seemed unlikely. But in the mind of someone who wasn't sane, maybe there was some odd logic to it.

Even worse if there was a cause and they missed it. He trusted Billy, but the man was rusty as a detective. His instincts were blunt. If it happened again, and the newspapers discovered a fireman had been investigating the crimes instead of the police . . . Dammit, he thought, he was thinking like a politician, not a copper. Still, the fact remained.

'I want you to work with Inspector Reed,' he told Ash. 'Go over everything again, the pair of you. Talk to all the people.'

'Yes, sir. What about Henry White?'

'Leave that to me for now.' After all, if he hadn't been so arrogant, giving White a day to sweat before questioning, the man might still be alive. His fault, his guilt.

He had one lead, the brief description from the shopkeeper. More would have been better, but it was a start. The first layer.

Harper stood on the corner, outside the shop, imagining the way White would have taken to his house. Along Mill Street,

Richmond Road, then down Copper Street, with the door key heavy in his hand. Did the stranger go all the way there with him?

With a sigh, he started to knock on doors. Asking the same questions over and over to all the suspicious women who answered: had they seen two men walking along last Friday, one shabby and pale, the other with dark hair?

Everyone claimed not to remember. He believed most of them; the words didn't spark a light in their eyes. He'd almost finished with the houses on Mill Street when four men appeared in front of him, blocking the pavement. Big men with vicious faces and cold, dark eyes. One had an old scar down the length of his cheek.

'You're asking questions,' he said.

'That's right,' Harper told him. It had taken them longer than he expected. 'I'm going to keep on asking them, too.'

'Not up here, you're not.' The man sounded adamant.

'I'll ask them where I want. I'm Detective Inspector Harper with Leeds Police. I'm looking into the murder on Copper Street. *That* gives me the right. I don't care if you like it or not.'

He stood, not giving an inch. A copper didn't turn tail and run from threats. And these men knew what would happen. They might win a fight, but then the police would return in force, truncheons drawn, breaking heads to make sure of their revenge. It had happened up here often enough before.

The moments passed. He counted them slowly, one, two, three, all the way to eight. Then the man warned, 'We'll be watching you.' He turned on his heel and strode away, the other three following. No backward glances, no threats. Harper waited until they turned the corner before he exhaled slowly. So close to a fight and he'd have been the certain loser. He kept his fists clenched and pushed them deeper into his pockets, standing for a minute before he carried on.

FIVE

A minute to compose himself and Harper was knocking on doors once again, turning on to Copper Street. The bobbies had done their house-to-house along here but it never hurt to ask again. People remembered things. And they treated a man in a suit differently from a man in a uniform.

He found the truth of that at number five. The woman must have been about fifty, hair in a severe bun. She had her sleeves rolled up, traces of bread dough clinging to her fleshy forearms, an apron covering a black cotton dress, scuffed clogs showing under the hem. Her eyes flashed with suspicion.

'Rozzer,' she snorted. He smiled and introduced himself. 'About Henry White, is it?'

'That's right.' Not that difficult to guess.

'Feckless as they come, that one. Allus was.'

'Did you see him on Friday?'

'Only day I could see him, wasn't it?' She put her hands on her hips and stared at him. 'Dead the next morning, wasn't he?'

She knew something. He could see it on her face. And she was challenging him to worm it out of her.

'What do you know about his death?'

She cocked her head, assessing him. 'Same as everyone else around here.'

He shook his head. 'No, you don't. There's something more than that. Did you see Henry with a man on Friday?'

His question took her by surprise. Her mouth puckered, then she raised an eyebrow and he knew he'd struck gold.

'Go on, then, how did you know that?' she asked after a moment. 'Do you read the tea leaves or summat?'

He tapped the side of his nose. 'Coppers often know more than you think. The man he was with, what did he look like?'

'Nowt special,' she answered without hesitation. 'You'd not give him a second look, would you?'

'You didn't know him?'

She shook her head. 'Not seen him before. But Henry had been gone a while.' Her eye was sharp on him. 'You should know that. Your lot put him away.' She continued to stare, chewing on her bottom lip. 'Harper. Is it your missus who grew up round here?'

'On Leather Street.'

'That's right. I remember now. Nice lass when she were little. Always a smile.' Her face brightened. It was as if he'd passed some test. 'That man with Henry, I didn't like the look of him. He were greasy.'

'Greasy?' he asked.

'Oil all in his hair. What I could see of it was all shiny.' She made a disgusted face. 'He was chattering away nineteen to the dozen, and Henry was trudging along with a face as long as a fiddle, just like always.'

'Could you hear them?'

'Didn't have much more of a glimpse as they went past, did I? Oh,' she remembered, 'and he had front teeth that stuck out a bit. You know, like a rabbit.'

That was something he could use.

'What was he wearing?'

'Cap. Jacket. Same as all of them round here. Nothing good, that's certain. I'd have noticed that.'

She'd given him what she had. And would the woman have done it if Annabelle hadn't been born a few streets away? Not as much, he felt sure of that. Harper tipped his hat to her and carried on.

It was the only luck he had. Still, one more piece to add to the puzzle.

He had a copy of the key to White's house and let himself in. There was a thin layer of dust on the mantelpiece and a smell of disinterest in the place. It felt musty. But Henry hadn't been back long enough to air it out. He glanced in the kitchen then went up the stairs.

Ash's search had been careful but neat, everything left tidy. The inspector wasn't looking for anything in particular. Hoping there might be some small item to catch his eye, to offer a hint. Nudge him in one direction or another.

But a few minutes going through the place didn't bring any new ideas. Nothing more than an underlying sorrow at the sparseness of Henry's life. There didn't seem to be anything in the house that might give him pleasure. Not a book, an old magazine, no games, not even a pack of cards or a set of dice.

It had been empty for six months, but even so . . . He thought of Maguire. No food, no coal, but he had his books and would never burn them for warmth. He'd stayed surrounded by a life of the mind until the end.

As he was leaving, just turning the key in the lock, a voice called out. Mrs Thorp, White's sister, gathered her skirts around her as she bustled down the street.

'Someone told me they'd seen a man going into the house.' No greeting, no asking if the police had found her brother's killer yet. She stopped, her shrew face looking him up and down. 'Did you take anything?'

'No.'

'Just make sure you don't. Not without telling me.' She glanced up at the house with hungry eyes. 'Soon as the will goes through, this is mine.'

'Henry left a will?' That was astonishing.

'Course he did,' she said with a satisfied smirk. 'Me da drummed it into the pair of us. Make it legal and nobody can take it away from the family.'

'What else did he have to leave?' Harper asked.

'Don't know.' She shrugged as if the thought had never occurred to her. But she only had eyes for the bricks and mortar and the money it could bring her. 'He couldn't have had much, could he?'

'No,' the inspector agreed. 'Who's the lawyer?'

'Mr Cockburn on Commercial Street.' Suddenly she seemed worried. 'Why? It's all done proper. Our Henry's left it to me, all above board.'

'I'm sure it is.' He smiled. 'I just wondered.'

The roads on the Bank had been quiet, the cobbles empty. In the middle of Leeds he was engulfed by the relentless bustle of trams and carts, pavements filled with people. Women in their gowns and capes and wide hats. Men wearing caps and bowlers, a few with shiny toppers. And every one of them with a purpose. Business behind their eyes.

Harper waited for a small gap and ducked across Briggate as a hackney took off, the driver cracking a whip over the horse. Commercial Street was no better, so jammed with traffic it was impossible to navigate. Two men unloaded a dray. A young lad lazily changed the display in the window of the Irish Linen shop.

He found the building he needed and climbed the stairs to the third floor. It was quieter here, perched high above the relentless noise. Beside a polished wooden door a brass plaque read: *James A. Cockburn, Solicitor*. The inspector knocked once and entered.

A clerk perched on a high stool, copying a document. A high collar and black tie, a tight dark jacket. The clothing was long out of fashion but still something lawyers wore every day.

Cockburn's office looked down over the street, light from the wide window shining down on to his desk. Mutton-chop whiskers, the hair thinning on top and going grey, bags under his eyes. An anonymous fellow, easy to lose in a crowd. But from the papers in front of him, he was a busy man.

'The will's begun its journey through probate,' he said when Harper asked. An odd phrase, he thought. It made a simple procedure sound so grand.

'Do you expect any problems?'

'Not at all. It's perfectly straightforward,' Cockburn told him. 'I reviewed it when Mrs Thorp came in.'

'I'm curious what Henry had to leave.'

'Oh?' The solicitor cocked his head. 'And why is that, Inspector?'

'You know he was murdered last Friday night.'

'Of course.' A small nod.

'There might be something in his will to help me find his killer.'

'I don't think so.' A quick smile. 'It's a very basic document. The only item of value is the house.'

'And that goes to his sister. She told me. What else is in there?'

'Nothing that can help you, Inspector.'

'I'd like to make up my own mind about that.'

Cockburn shook his head. 'Unless Mrs Thorp gives her

permission, I can't show it to you.' He paused. 'As I said, though, there's nothing in there to help your investigation.'

He squeezed and pushed his way through the people on the street, moving up Briggate then into Lockhart's Cocoa House. Away from the bustle he had time to think as he sipped a cup of hot chocolate.

Something he'd learned early on – never trust a lawyer. Their words were as slippery as fish, darting this way and that. Cockburn wasn't about to help him, and greed was the only thing on Rose Thorp's mind, the rent from the house on Copper Street.

Maybe the solicitor was right and the will wouldn't tell him anything at all. There was certainly nothing worth having in the house. Not unless Henry had hidden it very carefully indeed.

He turned his thoughts to a greasy man with protruding teeth, the one who'd been seen with White on the Bank.

'There's something that doesn't add up, sir,' Ash said. He'd listened to everything Reed told him. The mystery man with his bottle of acid. Arthur Crabtree and Annie in the shop.

'I know. No reason to it.'

'I don't believe it's a madman,' the sergeant said slowly.

'Why not?' It appeared as plausible an explanation as anything else.

'I'm not saying it impossible, sir, but very unlikely. You have to admit that.'

They were standing in front of the bakery. It had re-opened that morning, all the traces of damage vanished. Elizabeth had hired a man to walk around Burmantofts wearing a sandwich board to advertise the place and bring in custom. Special prices on bread and fancies.

'We'll get the ghouls out shopping,' she said with disgust. 'They'll be asking for all the details and looking for any signs of what happened. Won't buy much.' She sighed. 'Still, a day or two and maybe that'll pass.'

Reed hoped she was right. He'd only counted seven customers in the last half-hour.

'Fine,' he snapped at Ash. 'If it's not someone insane, then who did it?'

'You said it's nothing to do with the lad.'

'How can it be? He's only thirteen, for God's sake. I've talked to his father.'

'Plenty have gone bad by that age, sir. You know that better than I do. It doesn't mean the boy's done anything wrong, just that we have to look at it.'

'Yes,' he agreed slowly. Reed had to admit it, Ash had a point. He'd seen it often enough in the past. But Arthur Crabtree? No. He'd been sloppy; that thought should have been in his mind from the start. Instead he'd made assumptions and tried to fit everything into them. He'd grown too used to thinking of fires, where things were absolute.

'I can ask around if you'd like, sir. Or you, if you'd prefer.'

'I'll do it.' He'd asked Tom to give him responsibility for the case. But he'd been too slack; he hadn't thought everything through. Now he needed to go back and do the work properly, to make it right.

'And you're certain no one could have been coming after the girl?'

'Positive.'

Ash turned to stare at the shop, as if he was trying to imagine the scene when it happened. He rubbed his thick moustache. 'Someone must have followed the boy here.'

'He has a job at the brick works.'

'That's what, about a quarter of a mile away?'

'Something like that,' Reed agreed.

'Five minutes' walk. If someone wanted to attack him, that's plenty of time.'

'But he'd be moving, walking.'

'True.' Ash nodded. 'Still, it's worth asking around the brick works to see if they remember anyone loitering.'

Reed hated being schooled by a sergeant, but Ash was right. He should have already done all this. He wasn't just out of practice, he'd become a liability as a detective.

'I'll take care of that, too.'

'One last thing, sir. I know the bobbies have been talking to the chemists, but it might be worth paying a visit ourselves.' He gave a small, polite cough. 'You know what the uniforms are like.'

*   *   *

They were all basic things. He knew them; used to know them, at any rate. And he should have thought of them without prompting. Still, better late than never. It took him a couple of hours, but he discovered that Arthur Crabtree was as good a lad as he'd suspected. No complaint against him. Not even any real childhood mischief, let alone worse.

Down at the brick works they were eager to help. Arthur had been well-liked there. But no one remembered anyone around on Friday, and nobody recognized the faint description the boy had given. Dead ends. Ones he should have explored long before. Damn it.

He was no further along, though. Time to try the chemists' shops.

'Does he sound familiar to you?'

'Protruding teeth and greasy hair?' Kendall shook his head. 'There must be dozens like that. But no one springs to mind.' He puffed lightly on the pipe and began to cough, lifting his hand as Harper started to rise. 'Don't, Tom. I'm not a bloody old woman.'

'I've talked to Tollman about this fellow seen with Henry White. He had four names off the top of his head, but none of them sound likely. Forger, pickpocket . . .' He shook his head. 'He's going to see if there are more. I daresay Ash might know a few.'

'Keep pushing. What's going on with this acid case?'

'Billy Reed's looking into it; he's off work at the moment and it's his wife's shop.'

Kendall grunted. 'Is he getting anywhere?'

'Ash is giving him a hand.'

'I'd like that wrapped up soon. It always looks bad when children are involved.'

'I'll have a word with them.'

'Good.' He ran the back of his hand across his mouth. 'I talked to the chief this morning.' Harper waited. 'He thinks the same as me: being in charge of the station could be the making of you.'

He wasn't sure how to reply. 'That's very generous of him.'

Kendall pulled the pocket watch from his waistcoat. 'He's in front of the watch committee in about half an hour. We'll have a decision tomorrow morning.'

'I'm not going to hold my breath.' The watch committee would never agree to promoting him; he'd made enemies of too many of its members.

'You might be surprised. They want someone in the post before I go.'

Harper stood. He'd known the superintendent too long. He didn't want to think of him no longer here, dying.

'I'd better get back to work.'

Nothing more by the time he caught the tram, watching the shops on North Street go by. What did he have? Hints. A man with Henry that they couldn't identify. Words overheard in a pub. Nothing he could even knot together.

He walked through the bar of the Victoria. A fire burned in the grate to warm the place, but there were few customers. Their money was all gone; they were scraping by on nothing until Friday and the wages were paid. Over in the corner old Charlie Crowder played dominoes with Harry Fisher, the sound of knocking tiles the loudest thing in the pub. He waved to Dan and went up the stairs to their rooms.

Books were spread across the table in a jumble, along with a paper and a pen. But Annabelle knelt on the floor, playing a game with Mary and a doll. He kissed them both on the top of their heads. For a moment he tried to listen, but his ears were tired and his hearing wouldn't co-operate. In the kitchen the teapot was still warm and he poured a cup, standing and looking out over the yard and across Sheepscar.

Another few months and he'd have lived here for five years. Married, happy, settled in the pub. Roundhay Road, Manor Street, Holroyd Street; they'd become home. Faces he knew, people he liked. He'd become part of the fabric of the area. Accepted in spite of being a copper, because he was Annabelle's husband.

With so much suddenly changing, he needed some things in his life to remain the same. He had an anchor in this building. And he had Annabelle, and Mary, although she was growing so fast that sometimes she seemed like a different girl from minute to minute, shifting like quicksilver.

Superintendent Harper. It appealed; impossible not to. But the prospect terrified him. As an inspector he was only responsible for his investigations, along with a sergeant. Maybe a detective constable too, if he was very lucky. A promotion meant he'd look after everything in Millgarth: uniforms, plain clothes, even the horses.

'Penny for them.' He sensed the rustle of her gown, felt her hands around his waist, the press of her body against his back.

'Probably only worth a farthing.' He told her about the watch committee.

She hugged him and kissed the back of his neck. 'I'm proud of you, Tom.'

'Why? I haven't done anything.' Nothing more than the job he was paid to do, and he was having no success with that.

'Kendall and the chief constable don't see it that way.' She seemed about to say more when Mary shouted, 'Mam!' from the other room.

Later, once the child was in bed and asleep, he sat by the fire, staring at Annabelle as she worked.

'You're back to it.'

She put down the pen and smiled. 'I decided that moping wasn't going to solve anything. I was probably feeling sorry for myself as much as I was for Maguire.'

'He was a good man.'

'He was,' she agreed sadly. 'And he deserved better. From all of us.'

'There'll be a good turnout for the funeral.'

'That's why they're having it on Sunday,' she pointed out. 'Everyone will be free to go. Miss Ford has sent a letter round to the Suffrage Society, the Labour Party wants members there. The unions are organizing something.'

'And what about you?'

'They've asked me to speak at the service.'

That explained the books, he thought. And the determined look in her eye. She had a purpose again after drifting for a few days.

'What are you going to talk about?'

'Something that's not politics. There'll be plenty ready to go on about everything he's done. I'll tell them what I remember.

I'm going to talk to a few others who knew him when he was a boy.' She held up one of the books; he recognized the spine. Maguire's poems. 'I'll read one of these, too. You know, I'm not sure I ever saw him happier than when the publisher sent him the first copies.'

He sat for a moment, hesitating, then said, 'He was drinking a lot. That's what I heard.'

'I know. People told me, too. I have eyes and ears, Tom.'

Of course she did. And she kept them open.

'I'm not saying he was perfect or some sort of saint,' Annabelle continued. 'But I should have done something. I didn't, and it's too late now. About the only thing left is to make sure he's remembered. I've put in a guinea towards a headstone.' She sighed. 'Sometimes I wish the pub didn't run itself so smoothly. Work's a good way to distract yourself, isn't it?'

He had to laugh. She knew that half the time he was thinking about cases and investigations.

'I don't think you'll ever want for something to do.' She kept herself busier than anyone he knew.

'That's because there are always things that need to be done.' Her face turned serious then she gave a weak smile. 'Sorry. I'm not preaching, honest. But there's a meeting next week that Miss Ford wants me to address. I have to prepare for that, too.'

'Where this time?'

'Wortley. We had a good crowd there in December. It's growing, Tom. It's really beginning to take hold.'

She believed in suffragism. She spoke for it, she fought for it. But Annabelle was enough of a realist to know that votes for women wouldn't come soon. Maybe not in her lifetime. But Mary, she'd have it. Everyone would have the vote then, all men and women.

'You can keep all those things Maguire believed in alive.'

'I plan on it,' she said, and he didn't doubt her for a moment.

'Be back here for noon,' Kendall said as he prepared to leave.

'Noon?' Harper asked.

'To find out if you're the new superintendent. I told you, the decision's this morning.'

He hadn't forgotten. He'd simply tried to push it out of his mind, to focus on more pressing things: Henry White's murder, the acid attack. More immediate.

'I will.' He pulled the watch from his waistcoat pocket and checked it against the clock on the wall. A few hours yet until midday.

Ash was outside, talking to a constable in uniform. He raised an eyebrow to the inspector, a silent request to wait. Another minute and they were done, and Ash fell into step next to Harper.

'You learn something new every day, sir.'

'What's that?' He was going over to Kirkgate with nothing specific in mind. No one special to see.

'Did you know Henry White had a lady friend?'

'What?' He stopped in the middle of the pavement. He'd never heard a whisper about it. The only woman to visit him in Armley was his sister; she'd gone once.

'That's what Hodgkins was telling me when you came out. Seems he knows the lass's sister.'

'Who is she?' He thought of Henry. Hard to believe any woman would find him irresistible.

'A married woman. Mrs Parkin.'

Someone's wife. That would explain the secrecy.

'What do we know about her? And Mr Parkin?'

'He's a clerk, evidently. They have a house on Bayswater Mount.'

He could picture the street. A row of through terraces, no more than fifteen years old. Very respectable and definitely not cheap. Parkin must be doing well for himself, a senior clerk at least.

'We need to talk to her,' Harper said. But police on the doorstep, especially in plain clothes, that would be the talk of the neighbourhood. Her husband would hear. No need for her secret to be revealed. 'Do we know the house number?'

'Indeed we do, sir,' Ash said with a grin.

'I have an idea.'

The café was a few yards away from a tram stop in Harehills. Far enough from Bayswater Mount that no one would recognize Mrs Parkin. If she carried a basket, she would appear to be shopping on the parade. He'd sent a boy to her house with a note. Now he had to wait and see if she'd come.

He sat alone, a cup of tea undrunk in front of him. Ash occupied a table by the window to keep watch on the main road. Finally a woman entered, looking around quizzically. She had the dowdy look of someone who dressed to avoid being noticed. He probably wouldn't recall her face tomorrow. Mrs Parkin was thin. Bony, her face all angles. Somewhere around forty, he guessed, and showing every year of her age.

Harper nodded his head and she sat across from him, ordering tea from the waitress. She looked around, nervous as a rabbit.

'I hope you'll forgive me,' he began. Politeness would be vital here. She'd need to know he was discreet. 'I believe you knew Henry White.'

As soon as he mentioned the name her face seemed to collapse. No tears, but she pulled a handkerchief from her sleeve and dabbed at her eyes. She was wearing decent clothes. A heavy, black wool coat against the March weather, a hat from a good milliner. But somehow she made them all anonymous.

'I did.' She took a small, neat sip of the tea then looked him in the eye. 'I loved Henry. And I can't tell a soul about it.'

She spoke the words in such a matter-of-fact way that it took a moment before he understood the ocean of pain behind them. She'd carry it all inside for the rest of her life, locked away, unable to grieve for him.

'I'm trying to find out who killed him,' Harper told her and she nodded. 'Do you know who he'd been involved with?'

'Did I know he was bad? Is that what you mean?' She hissed the words. 'Of course I did. It didn't matter. But he protected me from all that side of his life. He told me it was safer.' A wistful, sad smile crossed her face. 'But there's no safety, is there?'

'Did Henry ever tell you any names?'

'No.'

'Did he tell you why he was carrying that stolen silver?'

She shook her head. 'I didn't even know what happened to it until I read that he'd been arrested.' Her shoulders slumped. 'We'd seen each other once a month for the last five years. Kept it all quiet as mice. I knew he was getting out last Friday. I was desperate to see him again. And then I read about the killing on Saturday. I've not been able to sleep properly since.'

'Mrs Parkin—' he said, but she carried straight on.

'I loved him the way I didn't think anyone could love. I don't expect you to believe that, but it's true. I'm not going to see him again this side of heaven. If I knew who'd done it, I'd kill them myself.'

She pushed the chair back, took a deep breath, and marched out of the café. No one paid any attention.

'No luck, sir?' Ash asked as they waited at the tram stop.

'Grief,' Harper said, then corrected himself. 'Nothing but grief.'

SIX

'What now, sir?' Ash said.

'We need to find this man who was seen with Henry on Friday morning. He's the best lead we've got so far.'

'I can't believe he left a will. He always seemed too feckless.'

'The solicitor insists there's nothing of interest for us in it. But he won't let me see it.'

'If you ask me, that's suspicious,' Ash said.

'Don't you worry.' Harper winked. 'The day I take a lawyer's word is the day they pension me off.'

They parted at Vicar Lane; Ash back to Millgarth, the inspector walking along the Headrow towards the Town Hall. He dodged between carts, pulling back as a hackney galloped along. The loud clang of a bell warned him as an electric tram approached.

Past the square outside the art gallery and the library, across the street, then up the wide stone steps and between the lions outside the Town Hall. The building was big, on a massive scale, but badly weathered; the stonework was black, coloured by years of smoke and soot. Inside, though, the grandeur was on full display. Marble floors and columns, flights of stairs that rose up and up, rooms with high, ornate ceilings.

He knew the office he wanted. At the back of the second floor, hidden away down a dusty corridor. Two clerks in a room with a view over Great George Street. The same men had been here for years, as if they existed in this separate little world.

One of them glanced up as he entered, his serious face breaking into a wide smile.

'Mr Harper. Haven't seen you in a long time.'

'How are you, Geoffrey? You too, Stephen.'

Geoffrey Gordon never seemed to age. He'd been bald as long as Harper had known him, just a monk's fringe of hair around the sides of his head that blossomed into broad, bushy sideboards. Portly, he moved in a waddle but always seemed happy with his lot. The other man, Stephen Kesey, was quiet, with a long, permanently disappointed face.

'Fair to middling, same as ever,' Geoffrey said, wafting away all the cares of the world. 'Something must be important to bring you all the way up here.'

'I'm looking for a will. Entered probate in the last day or so.'

Geoffrey adjusted a pair of spectacles. 'We always have plenty of those, Mr Harper. People dying like flies.' He grinned at his own wit. 'What's the name?'

'Henry White.'

'Henry White,' Geoffrey repeated. 'Do you hear that, Mr Kesey? Can you be a good fellow and look for a copy?'

The other man shuffled off into a back room. For a few minutes the inspector talked to Geoffrey. He was a grandfather again, and full of the joys of it; his daughter had given birth for a fourth time the month before.

Five minutes passed until Kesey silently returned with the papers. The will was dated 1893, two years earlier. No amendments or codicils. All the usual phrases – of sound mind and body – but he passed them by. He wanted the meat of it: what had been left to whom.

Rose Thorp would receive the house on Copper Street, exactly as she'd said. She'd receive most of the contents, too, for whatever little they were worth. A pottery figurine to Mrs Parkin as a token of their friendship. That was one way of phrasing it, but he wondered what the woman's husband would think. Tiny bequests to relatives. No money, but Henry had never had two brass farthings to rub together. And finally, words that jumped out at him.

To William Calder, a good and true friend across the years, I leave my keys, except for that which opens my house. One is important. He will understand.

William Calder. Willie. The name he'd heard in Whitelock's. He wasn't one to believe in coincidences. And keys. He'd never given them any thought. He pictured the house, slipping through it room by room in his mind. No boxes with locks.

William Calder. He tried to place the name, but all that came into his head was John Calder, a detective sergeant in B Division. Still, someone would know the man. He made a few notes, jotting down the exact wording from the document, and pushed it back to Geoffrey.

'Worth your time, Mr Harper?' He beamed.

'Yes,' he answered with pleasure, 'I do believe it was. Good day, gentlemen.'

As he came out into the cold air, the inspector looked at his pocket watch. Above him, the Town Hall clock boomed half past eleven. Plenty of time to get back to Millgarth.

He chose the long way, down East Parade, past the grand offices of the banks and insurance companies, all the way to the Post Office at City Square. The grit and smudges floating from the railway stations landed on clothes and flesh, and darkened the stones on the buildings. Back along Boar Lane, with its headlong rush of traffic, then across Briggate, darting and diving and taking his life in his hands. By the Corn Exchange and finally through the open market. It was a circuit that reminded him of what Leeds had become. Rich and poor, cheek by jowl, and each month the divide between the two seemed greater.

Kendall was sitting at his desk, talking to someone with shining silver hair. Harper could make out the man's back. Square shoulders, a pale neck, a stiff celluloid collar on his shirt. The superintendent waved him in, and he found himself facing Chief Constable Webb. Without even thinking, he stood to attention.

'At ease, Inspector.' He gestured to the empty chair in the corner. 'Sit down.'

Back straight, pulse racing, he perched on the edge of the seat. The chief must have come to give the news to Kendall, he thought. He'd arrived too early.

'Tom,' the superintendent said with a smile, 'you look as if you're scared the ceiling's going to fall on you.'

'Sorry, sir.'

'You might as well stop with the sir nonsense,' Kendall told him. 'Not that you remember it most of the time, anyway.'

Webb was staring at him, eyes showing nothing.

'Tell me something, Inspector,' he said after a moment. 'Do you think you can run this station?'

'Yes, sir,' he replied. 'I believe I can.'

The man's mouth curled into a slow smile.

'I'm very glad you said that. Because after Friday you'll have your chance.' He extended a hand. 'Welcome, Superintendent Harper.'

For a moment he sat, dumbfounded, convinced his hearing had failed him again. Yes, they'd talked about it. He'd been put forward for the job. But . . .

He took a deep breath. 'Thank you, sir.'

Webb stood. 'I'll leave you two to work out the details.' His hard features softened. 'I told the watch committee this morning that they'd made the correct decision. I'm sure you'll be an excellent commander here, even if you have big shoes to fill.'

'Congratulations, Tom,' Kendall said once they were alone. 'Not that I ever doubted it. They've picked the right man.'

Harper still couldn't believe it. He'd convinced himself that they'd turn him down, that his name had only been on the list to make up the numbers. Now all of this would be his, taking care of every man, of every detail.

'There's plenty to learn,' the superintendent continued. 'You'll be doing most of it on the job.' He brought a sheaf of papers from his desk, neatly bound with a black ribbon. 'Notes about the place from everyone who's been in charge here since it opened. Mine are on the bottom. When you have the chance, read them.'

'I will.' He felt dazed. Overwhelmed. 'I still have cases, though.'

'I know. You already have the general idea of how everything's run here. You've done it before.'

He had, when the superintendent was ill or busy elsewhere.

But only for short periods. 'I'll learn,' he said with a startled smile and stood. 'I'd better get back to work while I still can.'

'Annabelle will be pleased,' Kendall said.

'Over the moon.'

'Should I salute you, sir?' Ash asked with a grin.

'Give over.' He settled on his chair. 'I suppose everyone knows.'

'It's all through the station. No secrets here.'

When had it ever been any different? But there was more urgent business.

'Tell me, what do you know about a man called William Calder?'

Ash pursed his lips. 'Not a thing, sir. Have you tried Sergeant Tollman?'

'On the way in. He only knew that sergeant from B Division.'

'That's a different Christian name. Why do we want to know about him?'

Harper explained about the will and the key.

'Key to what, though?' Ash asked.

'We'll have to ask Mr Calder when we find him. You see what you can discover. I'll go and get that key from Mrs Thorp.'

'It worries me that we're not familiar with an associate of Henry's, sir.'

'Maybe he knew a few honest people. He's full of surprises – there's Mrs Parkin, after all.'

Ash laughed. 'True enough. Who'd have thought of Henry White as a Romeo? I'll see what I can dig up, sir. And everyone at the station is glad you'll be in charge here.'

'Thank you.' It was a vote of support he'd value, and it would make the new job easier.

She had the keys, a ring of them. Seven, shiny and dangling.

'Which one is for the house?' Harper asked and she pointed at the biggest key.

'That.'

He removed it and placed it on the table. 'I need to take the rest of them, Mrs Thorp.'

She eyed him with suspicion, as if he was trying to rob her of something. 'Why?'

'I'm trying to solve your brother's murder,' he reminded her.

'Go on, then,' she said reluctantly. 'But I want them back when you're done.'

She hadn't bothered to ask about the investigation. She wasn't dressed in mourning. No grief on her face. At the door he turned back to face her.

'Did your brother ever mention someone called Willie Calder?'

Rose Thorp frowned. 'No,' she replied. But it was obvious that she was lying. Later, he thought; he'd find out the truth later.

On Leather Street he tapped lightly on a front door. A wreath of black leaves hung on a nail. A man let him in, a face he'd seen around the union office, dressed in a suit and tie, so closely shaved that his cheeks seemed to shine.

No words; none needed. Right in front of him, in the centre of the parlour, the coffin lay on a table, the lid propped in a corner. Maguire, hands crossed over his breast. Wearing his good suit, red hair combed, moustache waxed. The undertaker had done a careful job. The man looked better than he had in his bed at Quarry Hill. No longer so gaunt or hopeless. If anything, he seemed to be at peace, and Harper hoped that death had at least brought him that.

There was no one else in the room. For a moment he was tempted to tell Maguire about his promotion and imagined the man chuckling.

'I'll have friends in high places now, Superintendent. That might prove useful if I ever need a character reference.'

But there was no voice, only the echo through his imagination. He stood for a few minutes then went through to the scullery. The man sat at the table, reading a newspaper. Next to him was an old woman, tiny, hunched over. She had the faintest traces of red among the thin grey hair. Her hands were gnarled, moving slowly and painfully as she knitted.

'I'm sorry for your loss,' Harper said. 'I admired your son.'

She raised her head, looked at him and nodded. 'Thank you.'

Just two words but he could hear the brogue.

Outside, the wind began to swirl. He buttoned up his coat and walked back to Millgarth.

*   *   *

'We're off out,' Annabelle told him. 'We're celebrating. You've got ten minutes to wash and change. I have a hackney booked for six.'

'You've heard, then?'

Annabelle rolled her eyes. 'Of course I've heard, you daft thing. Everyone in Leeds has probably heard by now.' She looked at him and smiled proudly. 'Superintendent Harper, eh?'

She was wearing a new gown, as pale as a summer sunrise, with leg-of-mutton sleeves, a wrapover skirt and a deep waistband, along with the yellow shawl he'd bought her a year or two before. Her hair was up in some elaborate coiffure and he could smell her scent as she held him close.

'Mary wanted to know if all the policemen have to live here now you're in charge.'

He laughed. 'You should have told her yes.'

'I was tempted. She's up with Ellen. Get a move on and you can tell her goodnight before we go.'

Powolny's. She definitely wanted to make it an occasion, Harper thought as he escorted her up the wide, carpeted stairs to the restaurant. A table for two, attentive service, good food. Things he never found elsewhere. This was how the other half lived.

'It doesn't feel real, you know,' he told her as he pushed the empty plate away. 'None of it.'

'I hope that changes soon,' Annabelle said with a smile. 'Since you're going to be doing the job before you know it.'

'It scares me,' he admitted after a minute.

'It should do,' she said. 'You'd hardly be human if it didn't. At least you've done it before.'

'Only for a day or two while Kendall was away.'

'Doesn't matter,' she said. 'You've done it. It won't be any different.'

But it would. Everything would rest on his shoulders, and he wasn't certain they were broad enough. Still, he'd imagined that before, first when he made detective sergeant, then after the promotion to inspector. And he'd managed. He knew that he'd fill this role in time. She was right, though; it was good to be nervous. It kept him alert.

He was going to need a new inspector to handle investigations.

'Tom.' Her voice brought him back.

'Sorry.'

'Let's keep it just us tonight,' Annabelle said softly. 'Leave work behind, eh?' She reached across the table, over the crisp white cloth, and took his hand. 'I really am proud of you.'

'I'm glad.'

'You know, when I was little I'd never have imagined marrying a copper, let alone one on his way to being chief constable.'

He laughed. The idea was so ridiculous, so impossible. And he'd never want that job.

'Look at the pair of us.'

'Why?' she asked, confused. 'What's so funny?'

'You grew up on the Bank. Now you go out and give speeches, you hobnob with councillors, people do you favours, you have money.'

'That's just luck,' she told him.

'No, it's not. Not all of it,' he pointed out. 'And me. Born on Noble Street and now I'm going to be running Millgarth. That's why it doesn't seem real. From there to here.'

She nodded. 'It's true enough, I suppose. All of it. Funny thing is, I doubt we've come two miles between the pair of us from where we both started out to the Victoria.'

He chuckled. 'We sound ancient.'

'You speak for yourself.' Her eyes flashed. 'There's plenty of life in me yet. You too, I hope. I have plans for you once we're home.' He stared, seeing the sly smirk on her face. 'You didn't think you were going to get away with just a meal for a celebration, did you?'

For once he didn't want to stir with the morning. Annabelle's arm lay over his chest. Her hair was wild over the pillow, tickling his face. He was warm, cosy. Happy. He surfaced very slowly, shaking off dreams and sleep before easing himself out from the blankets and into the cold room.

If early birds got the worm he'd go hungry today. The tram was filled with men in suits and ties, on their way to work in the offices. The factory hands were already at their jobs, chimneys spewing smoke into the air.

Ash was busy when he arrived, leafing through a small pile of folders.

'Getting ready for bankers' hours, sir?' he asked with a grin.

'That and the long luncheon,' he answered. 'What's that?'

'Couldn't find any William Calder in the records, sir, so I pulled everyone called Calder that we've arrested in the last twenty years.' He put a large hand on the files.

'Any luck?'

'Just got started. No one with the middle name or nickname of William so far.'

Harper hung up his coat. A thought came to him.

'Detective Sergeant Calder in B Division – isn't he from a large family?' He had a faint recollection of the man laughing about it over a drink once.

'I've no idea, sir. I've never really talked to him.' He looked sharply at the inspector. 'You don't suspect him, do you?'

'No, nothing like that.' He'd never heard that John Calder was anything but honest. And he'd have caught a whisper if there'd been one.

For the next hour he sat with Superintendent Kendall, listening to procedures until his eyes began to glaze and his mind drifted.

'Tom,' Kendall said with a smile.

'What? Sorry.' He almost blushed.

'This White case?'

Harper nodded. He knew he had bigger things on his plate. A whole station to run. But he'd put too much into this. He wanted to see it through to the end.

'Yes.'

'Then go and look after it. Worse comes to worst, you'll learn all this on the job. If I managed it, you can.'

He didn't need a second invitation. He was already out of the chair.

SEVEN

A sh had left a note on top of the records with a single word: *Nothing*.

No William Calder.

Back to the beginning. But perhaps there was something. An idea had blossomed as he listened to the numbing details of running a police station. Maybe Detective Sergeant John Calder had a brother named William. A little quiet digging . . . who knew where it could lead?

It took much of the morning, sending clerks at the Town Hall to work through old, dusty records and delving through birth certificates and wedding certificates. But finally he had the information.

William Calder existed. Thirty-eight, two years younger than his brother on the force. Married with no children, his occupation listed as a clerk in the city directory. He lived on the border of Kirkstall and Headingley, edging into respectability.

The man seemed like someone quite ordinary, probably not the Calder mentioned in Henry White's will or the Willie he'd heard mentioned in Whitelock's. But a few questions wouldn't go amiss. He'd make sure he discovered the truth.

He should learn a little more about Detective Sergeant Calder, too. But he'd be careful to tread very lightly. Not a single word, not a breath that could get back to the man. No shred of doubt or suspicion without something solid to back it up.

His first stop would be the beat bobby who patrolled by William Calder's house.

'Never had cause to talk to him, sir,' PC Goodland said as he shook his head. They were standing on the corner of Kirkstall Lane and Cardigan Road, out of the breeze, in the lee of a brick wall.

'Do you know him by sight?' Harper asked. 'Any idea where he works?'

'Not really, sir. Round here, half of them toddle off to their offices every morning. They're all out and back at the same time, not a sign of trouble. I might have seen him but that's probably it. I haven't a clue where he works. Somewhere in town, I expect.'

'What about his wife? Do you know her?'

'I don't, sir.' He sighed. 'Sorry if I'm letting you down, but that's how it is round here. From the address I can picture the house just fine. I know the girl who's a servant there. To say hello to, like. But not the mistress.'

'I'd like you to ask around a little, very discreet. See what anyone knows about Mr Calder, then tell me.'

'Yes, sir,' he replied doubtfully. 'I wouldn't expect much, though. Do you mind if I ask why?'

The inspector simply tapped his nose. 'Just keep it quiet.'

The first seed planted.

'I don't understand it,' Reed said. 'I can't make head nor tail of it.'

He was sitting in the back room of the bakery in Meanwood, his hands around a mug of tea. Elizabeth stood by the desk. He'd spent the morning going around Burmantofts and asking more questions about Arthur Crabtree. He'd found several of the boy's friends, talked to people in shops all around the area.

Not a soul had anything bad to say about the lad or his family. They lived quiet lives. There was some talk that the father had been wild back when he was young, but that was years ago. He taught Sunday school now, at the Baptist church they all attended each week.

The more he searched, all he found was no reason at all for the acid attack. And no sign of anyone buying acid at the chemists' shops in the area.

'Could you have missed something?' Elizabeth asked.

He'd asked himself the same question coming here on the tram. What had he forgotten? What had he overlooked? It *had* to be there.

Billy Reed shook his head. 'I don't think so.'

'Maybe you're looking at it the wrong way,' she suggested.

'What other way is there?' He couldn't see one.

'I don't know,' she admitted after a while. 'But you've been away from the police for a long time now.'

He looked at her. Was she saying he couldn't do the job? He could feel his skills returning with every question he asked.

'I'll find whoever did it,' he promised.

'You heard about Tom Harper?'

He had. A beat bobby he knew had been full of the news that morning. Even with their history and the ending of a friendship, it was impossible to begrudge the man his promotion. He was capable. He was ambitious. The men liked him. And he was a good detective.

'Good luck to him.'

'Annabelle stopped by this morning,' Elizabeth told him. 'She wanted to order ten dozen bread cakes.'

'Why? Are they celebrating his promotion?'

'No. There's some funeral on Sunday and she's going to have the people at the Victoria afterwards. That political chap she knew.'

Maguire. Reed had read about his death in the paper. Twenty-nine, no age at all. He knew Annabelle had grown up with him on the Bank and that Tom Harper liked him; that was it. None of his business.

'What I need is to find the man who threw that acid.'

'You'll do it, Billy love.' She smiled and stroked his cheek. 'You know I believe in you. I did from the moment we met.'

'I'd better make sure I take care of this, then.' He stood and stretched, taking hold of his walking stick. 'I'll be home later.'

Harper knew he had to make his choices carefully. He wanted to know about Detective Sergeant John Calder, but he had to do it without the man knowing. Who could help him? Everything completely unofficial, not a single word written down.

He drifted across Crown Point Bridge and into Hunslet, where Calder was stationed. He kept his distance from the police station, hugging the back streets, popping his head into public houses in a search of any familiar face.

At the Royal Oak he found one. Peter Hope. It wasn't a name he carried well. Hopeless would be more apt. Almost forty, he'd been in and out of jail for petty offences since he was old enough to be sentenced. If he held a job, it never lasted long. Now he was sitting with a hangdog look, staring at the glass of beer the inspector had bought him.

'Sergeant Calder,' Harper prompted.

'He only arrested me once,' Hope said. 'Caught me stealing some lead from a roof.'

'When was this?'

The man shrugged. 'Don't know. He was still in uniform so it must have been a while.'

'Who else has he arrested, Peter?'

'Plenty, I suppose. Jed Cartwright, I know that.'

'Who's he?'

'A bad lad.' He gave a toothless grin. 'In Armley right now. Caught breaking into a house. It was Mr Calder who took him in, I remember that.'

'How long ago was this?'

'A month?' Hope replied. 'Happen a little longer.'

'How was the sergeant with you?'

'Fair.' He turned his head to stare at Harper. 'As fair as any of you lot can be, any road.'

The jail was loud, every sound magnified and echoing around the walls. He waited patiently in the interview room until a guard brought Jed Cartwright.

He was a scarecrow of a man, gaunt as death and almost as pale. Teeth brown, cheeks sunken, eyes haunted, Cartwright looked like a man who wasn't long for this world. But he moved fluidly and settled himself on a chair with a smooth movement. First impressions could be deceptive, Harper decided.

'You got a cigarette?' Cartwright asked.

'I don't smoke.'

'Then why should I talk to you?' He folded his arms.

'I can always have a word with the wardens and the governor. It's interesting the range of privileges a prisoner can have.'

The man had two months of his sentence still left to serve. Hardly his first time inside, Harper had seen that in his record. It wouldn't be his last, either. Cartwright was an old hand at prison; that meant he appreciated the little things that could improve a man's life.

'What do you want to know?'

'Sergeant Calder arrested you.'

'That's right.' Cartwright frowned, mystified. 'What about it?'

'Was he a fair man?'

'He nicked me, took me in, gave his evidence. That's it.'

'Did he offer you a deal?'

Cartwright laughed, a raw, rasping sound. 'Oh aye, and what could I give him?'

'The names of your fences, who hired you.'

The man simply shook his head. 'Everybody knows who the fences in Hunslet are. And no one hired me. I saw a house and took a chance. That's it. Why?' His gaze hardened. 'Someone been saying something about me?'

'Not a word.'

'Just as well.' He tried to sound threatening, but there was no fire behind his words.

'What do you know about the sergeant?'

'He's a rozzer. What's to know?'

'Any rumours?'

'Someone told me he was a hard man, but he was fine with me.'

Nothing. But that fitted. No whispers or doubts about his honesty. He'd ask around a little more, just to be certain.

By the end of the day he was convinced that John Calder was straight as a die. In the office he found a note from PC Goodland, the beat man who patrolled the area where William Calder lived.

There was some talk along the street of men visiting the house from time to time. Always after dark. Suspicious-looking men. But, as Goodman pointed out, round there the words didn't mean much; anyone unknown was suspicious.

There was no real substance, but it was something. He'd need to think about it and decide what to do.

A pile of papers waited on his desk. *Take these home and read them. Kendall.* One thing about running a station – the work never stopped.

Annabelle had her books scattered across the table in the parlour. Now he had his papers. She laughed as he put them down.

'How about all this?' she said. 'Anyone would think we were a right pair of clever clogs.'

'Homework,' he explained as Mary took him by the hand and led him into her bedroom. Sitting next to him on the bed, her expression as serious as an adult, she asked, 'Da?'

'What, sweetheart?'

'Will you be in charge of every po-eeseman in Leeds?'

'No, love, I won't.' He smiled. Where on earth did she get these ideas? 'Only the ones at Millgarth, where I work. You've been there. And it'll only be when they're doing their jobs. Why?'

'Ellen said that you had to pay them all out of your money.' She stared up at him, cocking her head, with the same quizzical expression her mother wore at times. 'But if you do that, how will there be any money left for us?'

Dear God, he thought. He needed to talk to Ellen. First, though, he took time to calm Mary's worries. She was at an age when she still believed him without question, nodding as he explained. Soon enough she slipped down on to the floor and pulled a doll from the toy chest, content and distracted.

'What's Ellen been saying?' he asked Annabelle, and told her about Mary's question.

'You know Ellen; she'd never say that unless she was teasing. Mary must have misunderstood.' Annabelle was sorting through a pile of clean clothes, picking out everything to be mended. A shirt that needed a new button, socks and stockings to be darned. A sheet that could use a patch. A few minutes' stitching and there'd be another year or two left in it.

'I hope she did.'

'I'll have a word with her.'

He sat and started to work through the papers. At times his hearing problem was a blessing. The buzz and noise of daily life faded to nothing and let him concentrate. Figures and budgets were never riveting but he needed to make sense of them.

'Tell me something,' Annabelle said later. Mary was fast asleep, only closing her eyes after three stories. He was back with his papers, the only sounds in the parlour the crackling of coal on the fire and the scratching of Annabelle's nib on paper.

'What?' he asked.

'Do you remember when you were little?'

He looked at her curiously. 'I don't know. I've never thought about it.' He put down the papers. 'I can recall some of it. Why?'

'Did you ever think about who you'd grow up to be?'

'I had hopes, I suppose,' Harper said after a moment. But back then, life seemed a straight line. School for a few years, then work for the rest of your life. The same as his parents and their parents before them. It was the way everything was. He wanted to be a copper but that was a dream and dreams weren't for the likes of them; he knew exactly what his future would be. He'd taken it all in with his mother's milk. 'I suppose I knew what would happen. Everyone did. A job at the brewery. I was lucky; I managed to escape it in the end. Why?'

'This piece I'm writing for Maguire's funeral,' she said, as if that was an explanation. 'I was talking to people who knew him when he was young. He didn't have a thought about politics until about a dozen years ago. Funny how things can change, isn't it?'

'Is that true?' he asked in surprise.

'That's what they told me.'

He was astonished. The man seemed as if he'd always been a firebrand, that it had been in him from the time he was born. The turns a life could take were odd. His own was enough. Who'd have imagined that grubby boy from Noble Street would end up in charge of Millgarth police station? Certainly not the lads who started at Brunswick Brewery when he did.

'Good for him,' Harper said finally. 'He found what he wanted to do.'

'Not for long enough,' Annabelle said. 'Come here and give me a cuddle, Tom.'

EIGHT

'William Calder,' Harper said.

'Found much, sir?' Ash asked. 'I've certainly had no luck.'

'I found a possibility.' He knew it wasn't more than that.

But still, he'd take a closer look. He recounted what PC Goodland had discovered.

'It's not a lot, is it?' The sergeant frowned.

'Thin as gauze,' the inspector agreed. 'But it's all we've got. Let's see what else we can come up with.'

'Yes, sir.'

'Anything more on the acid case?'

'I saw Mr Reed late yesterday. I think he's stumped, truth be told.'

Harper rubbed his chin. 'What do you suggest?'

'Honestly, sir, I don't know.' He pursed his lips under the heavy moustache. 'It's not a madman, I'm certain of that.' He shrugged. 'I can't find hide nor hair that makes a reason.'

'Do you want me to take a look? A fresh pair of eyes?'

'If you have the time, I think it might be a good idea, sir.'

'What about Inspector Reed? How do you think he'd react?'

A small, polite cough prefaced the reply. 'You know him better than I do, sir.'

'Maybe I did, once upon a time, anyway.' Harper smiled. And now? Who could tell?

'It's not my place to say, sir.'

That was as much of an answer as he was going to get, the inspector saw.

'Write it all up and leave it on my desk. Then follow up on this William Calder as a fence. It would definitely fit with Henry White.' He took the keys from his desk drawer. 'He left one of these to a William Calder. I'd be very curious to know what it unlocks.'

'I'll do my best, sir.'

He read the sergeant's report on the acid attack and sat back, recalling what he'd seen at the shop the Friday before. Bad things came in threes, that was what they said, and he'd had them. Henry White's murder, this, and Kendall leaving the force so he could die. Four, if you counted Maguire's death. Enough, Harper thought. More than enough.

Billy Reed was walking down the street as the inspector arrived, a firmer, surer stride, barely leaning on his stick. It was a bright morning, even the promise of some sun later once the early mist vanished.

'You're looking better.'

'Back to work on Monday, the doctor says. I'll still need to watch myself, but . . .'

'That's good news.' Harper paused for a moment. 'You know why I'm here.'

A small nod. 'I think I bit off more than I could chew, Tom.'

He could see how much it pained Reed to admit it. That he might have failed. The old Billy – the detective sergeant who'd worked for him – would never have been able to say it. Instead he'd have spent the evening hidden in a pub, getting drunk.

'We can work together,' Harper offered. 'I can give it what time I have.'

'The way I hear it, you won't have much of that.'

'Kendall wanted me to apply for that job. I never expected to get it.'

'You didn't turn it down.' He grinned as he spoke.

'Would you? I don't think Annabelle would ever have forgiven me.' He looked around. 'Where's the nearest café?'

'There's one by Beckett Street Cemetery. Why?'

'Let's sit down, have a cup of tea, and try to sort out what's going on here. There must be something we've all missed.'

Reed lit a cigarette and blew out a slow stream of smoke.

'I've been over it every which way. Up and down, in and out.' He knew he'd examined everything. Looked into the boy *and* the girl. Made his enquiries about their families and turned up nothing at all. 'I can't find a scrap of sense behind it, Tom. I'm sorry.'

'Right. Go through everything. Every single detail.'

He talked, and Harper listened attentively, head angled to make sure he heard. It was easy to see his hearing was worsening, Reed thought. It took more effort, and he asked for a few things to be repeated.

Billy signalled for two more cups of tea, wet his throat, and continued. Harper had questions; he answered where he could. There was no point trying to pretend he knew everything.

'Well,' he asked finally. 'What do you think?'

'You've been thorough,' Harper said approvingly, and Reed felt the relief. He hadn't made mistakes. 'But if you've eliminated someone going directly after the boy or the girl, it means we need to look for something else.'

'I've gone into the families. What else is there?'

'That's what I don't know, Billy. We need to cast the net wider. The only acid attack I can recall was about ten years ago. That had something to do with revenge.'

'What could anyone want revenge for here?' He leaned forward, his face set. 'For God's sake, Arthur and Annie are children. They haven't done anything.'

'Then it must be something to do with the families.'

'I've asked questions.'

'Perhaps we need to go back and ask some more, Billy,' Harper told him.

'What if it was all a mistake? That he was looking for someone else?'

'Then there's nothing we can do.' No. The action seemed too deliberate, too certain. 'But I don't think it was.'

'I'll look again,' Reed said warily. 'I just don't think there's anything to find. The Crabtrees are good, churchgoing people.'

'Everyone has secrets, Billy. You ought to remember that. *Everyone*. I'll leave you to it.'

Reed watched him leave. Time to start over.

Another hour with Kendall, going over the correct procedures for complaints and discipline.

'I warned you, Tom, most of this job is looking at forms. That and going to meetings. Your first one's on Monday, by the way.'

'Monday?' He hadn't heard anything about this. He thought he'd have time to become accustomed to the new rank first.

'Official promotion and introduction to the watch committee. Think of it as Daniel in the lion's den.' He raised an eyebrow. 'Well, maybe not quite that bad. But you're going need to hold your own with them.'

'I will.'

'I mean it,' the superintendent warned. 'Right from the very

start. If you let them walk over you once, you'll end up fighting
for every single thing. Let them know straight off that you won't
be cowed. I had to learn the hard way.'

'Maybe I'd be better off staying an inspector,' Harper said
ruefully.

'You'll be fine in the job. And you're taking on a good bunch
of men.'

'Mostly.'

'There are always one or two bad apples,' Kendall agreed.
'But you know this place inside out. You can get rid of the rotten
ones. And they know you. That helps.'

'I'll do my best.' A thought came to him. 'Have you ever heard
anything about John Calder in B Division?'

'No,' the super answered thoughtfully. 'Should I have?'

'Not really. Let's finish this before I go out again.'

'I might have something on William Calder, sir.'

'Oh?' Harper had just returned from the market café. A quick
dinner of tripe and tea to keep him going. Ash had been waiting,
sitting and writing up his report for the file.

'A chap called Kirk claims he's taken stuff there. Only once
or twice, but he swears to it.'

'Taken things to Calder's house?' It seemed almost too good
to be true.

'Even gave me the address and described the place.' He was
grinning.

'Did you get a statement from him?'

'Right here, sir.' He pulled a folded sheet of paper from the
inside pocket of his heavy wool jacket. 'He signed it, too.'

'Excellent.' Finally they were moving ahead. Harper could feel
his blood surging. He took the watch from his pocket and checked
the time. After three already. Where did the days disappear? 'Calder
should be home by six. We'll go and see him then.'

'Are we arresting him, sir?'

'Oh yes,' Harper said with a twinkle in his eye. 'I think we
will.'

There was a time he wouldn't have bothered with protocol; he'd
simply have pushed ahead and believed he was right. Now, with

his new post so close, Harper knew he had to follow every rule.
Dot every i and cross every t.

Superintendent Mills pointed to a seat. He was in charge of
B division, out of the station on Hunslet Lane. Close to fifty, his
thick sideboards were turning grey, the hair receding on the top
of his head.

'I'll be sorry to see Bob Kendall go, especially under the
circumstances. But at least they've made a good choice to replace
him.'

'Thank you, sir. I appreciate it,' Harper said.

'Don't.' He waved it away. 'Bar the shouting you're already
a superintendent. Call me Peter. Now, what can I do for you?
You're hardly out making your afternoon calls.'

'I wanted to tell you I'm going to be arresting Sergeant Calder's
brother this evening. I've got evidence he's fencing stolen goods.'

'John's brother?' Mills sat back, frowning, hands laced behind
his head. 'Are you sure?'

'We have a statement. I wanted to let you know. If you could
tell him after six o'clock, I'd be grateful.'

'You're not implying my sergeant's involved in this, are you?'
He could sense the man start to bristle. 'He's as honest as they
come.'

'No,' Harper assured him, 'nothing like that.'

'Good.' Mills eased a little. 'I've worked with John for a long
time. I have a lot of respect for him.'

'I wanted to make sure he learned through the proper
channels.'

'I'll do that for you, lad.' Mills's voice was gruff, tired. 'He'll
be torn apart, but . . . always a black sheep in the family, isn't
there?'

'Always.' He stood and shook hands with Mills.

'Good luck to you. You have some big shoes to fill, but you
know that better than I do.'

'I'll try.'

'Why? I don't understand.' William Calder blinked behind a pair
of thick spectacles. He sat in the hackney, wrists cuffed, Harper
next to him, a burly bobby opposite. 'Why do you want to arrest
me? You know my brother's on the force.'

'Save it for the interview,' the inspector said. 'You can tell me you're innocent then.'

He'd left Ash to search the house and fight off the yelling of Mrs Calder. She'd been silent when they arrived, sitting by her husband and holding his hand. But as soon as Harper produced his handcuffs she began to shout and screech.

The man was guilty. He could smell it on him. And he was terrified. Now to let that fear simmer a little before the interview began.

'How did you know Henry White?' he asked casually as the carriage clattered over the cobbles on Woodhouse Lane.

'Henry?' Calder sounded surprised. 'I—' He stopped himself. Too late; he'd already given an answer.

At Millgarth he watched as Calder was escorted down to the cells. Just leave him for an hour, or until the morning? In the office he looked at folders. Morning, he decided. That would give Ash all the time he needed to search the house; they could challenge Calder with what he found.

Things were rolling. About bloody time, too.

He was about to leave for the night when a man entered the office, a bowler hat clutched tight in his hands. He wore spectacles, a watch chain on his waistcoat. At first glance he was unprepossessing, hair glistening with pomade, nothing remarkable or memorable about his face. But that helped make him a good detective.

'Good evening, sir,' Detective Sergeant John Calder said.

'Sergeant.'

'The super told me.'

'I'm sorry. It must be a shock to you,' Harper said.

'It is,' he replied slowly, then raised his head, his expression confused. 'Are you sure there's no mistake, sir?'

'We've got a statement from someone who sold him stolen goods. Gave us details about the house, everything.'

Calder's face fell. 'I see, sir.'

'It's hardly your fault, Sergeant. We can't choose our family.'

'I know, but . . .' He pushed his lips together as he searched for the words. 'We were all so proud of him. He seemed to be doing well for himself.' He leaned against the door jamb. 'I should probably have seen it.'

'No,' the inspector told him. 'He kept it very quiet. It was sheer luck we found out.'

'How did you discover it, sir?'

Harper explained about Henry White's will.

'I see.'

'Following a trail. You know how that is, Sergeant.'

'Of course.' He gave a small, sad nod. 'Do you think I could see Will?'

For a moment he weighed the idea. What harm could it do? Maybe Sergeant Calder could shame his brother into confessing and make their job easier in the morning.

'Yes. Tell him it'll go better if he admits everything.'

Calder gave a wan smile. 'I will. Like you said, sir, nothing to be done. Congratulations on your promotion, by the way.'

'Thank you.'

'Where's Mary?' he asked as he looked around the parlour. He was so used to the sound of little feet running as he came in that the silence felt strange and worrying.

'Do you know Maisie Tyler?' Annabelle asked as she glanced up from the books surrounding her on the table.

'No,' he answered in surprise. He'd never heard the name before. 'Who is she?'

'Lives on Manor Street. Her husband's a brickie. She has a little girl. Mary's round there to play and I'll have her lass here next week. It gives me a chance to work.'

He kissed the back of her neck and felt her small shiver of pleasure. She put down the pen, turned her head and kissed him tenderly.

'Tom,' she began, stretching out his name the way she did whenever a question was coming, 'apart from me and Mary, how many women are there in your world? Ones you talk to every day?'

He'd never given the idea a moment's thought. The force was all men. Almost all the criminals he met were male. Plenty of shop assistants were women and all the housewives, of course. But none of them were people he talked to day after day. Perhaps the closest was Ruby who worked at the Market Café, and she just took his order for tea and food.

'None,' he replied after a long time. 'Why?'

'I'm putting together my talk for the suffragists. I got to thinking how men are always in groups. At work, in the public house. It's the same with women, if they're with anyone apart from children. The only time women and men are together is at home.' She looked at him and he nodded; he understood and agreed. 'How can women ever be equal when we're separated all the time?'

'What about women who work?' he asked. 'There are thousands of them.'

Annabelle raised an eyebrow. 'They're all together, working in mills or below stairs, with men in charge. And they end up paid much less than men, even if they're doing the same job. You know that.'

'But don't some jobs need men?'

'Do they? Think about it, Tom. Do you honestly believe there are jobs women can't do? Even mining, if push comes to shove. Women are strong.'

'I don't know.' He felt tiredness rising through his body. It had been a long day and he didn't feel up to this. Not now. She was clever, she could think on her feet. She'd wipe the floor with any argument he made. 'You're probably right.'

'Of course I am.' Her voice was firm but she began to grin then gave him a gentle kiss. 'You ought to know that by now, Tom Harper. There's a meat and potato pie between two plates in the oven.' She glanced at the clock. 'I'd better go and collect Mary. She'll be chattering nineteen to the dozen on the way back; enjoy your peace while you still have it. And think about what I said.'

Mary burst through the door, words tumbling and falling over themselves as she tried to tell him everything she'd done. She climbed on to his lap, hugging him tight. He kept her to his left so he could make out every word. She took a final deep breath.

'And we had bread and dripping for our tea.'

He laughed. The week before Mary had pushed the same food away. Now she made it sound like a feast.

It still made him smile as they settled down in bed. Mary had been asleep for hours, worn out from an afternoon of play. He pulled Annabelle closer, her hair loose, tickling his cheek and his neck.

'She's becoming a real Sheepscar girl, isn't she?' he said.

'Nothing wrong with that. It's good enough for the likes of you and me.'

'I know. I'm not complaining.'

NINE

'Come on, Willie, everyone knows you're guilty. Why don't you just admit it?'

'I haven't done anything.'

They'd gone round and round for half an hour. A night in the cells hadn't broken Calder. He was unshaven, smelling a little, but quietly defiant, standing on his dignity.

Harper lined up the items on the desk. A silver snuff box, a hairbrush with a silver back, and a gold signet ring with the initials AWD. Ash had found them pushed to the back of a desk drawer, wrapped in brown paper and hidden behind some ledgers.

Mrs Calder insisted she'd never seen them before; she had no idea how they'd come into her house. Now she was in prison, too, charged as an accessory, booked into the Bridewell and sharing a cell with a girl who picked pockets. In the afternoon she'd go before the magistrate, along with her husband.

'These didn't fall from the sky, did they? You had them neatly hidden away, Willie. That's not going to look good to a jury.' Harper stared at the man. 'With your brother on the force, they'll destroy someone like you in prison.'

'I don't know where they came from. Your man must have planted them there.' But he was sweating as he spoke, forehead shiny, staring down at the table.

'Is that what you think? Accusing one of my officers? I can tell you exactly where they came from.' The inspector leaned back in his chair. 'A robbery last week up at Headingley Lodge. There were a few more things, but these will do for a start.'

'They're nothing to do with me,' Calder insisted.

Harper slapped his palm down on the wood.

'Let's stop playing silly buggers. You're a fence. I've got a statement that says so. And we've got the goods.' He paused. 'You'd do best to make a clean breast of it, Willie. Or we could charge you with burglary as well, since you don't seem to know how they ended up in your house. You'd be looking at a fair few years behind bars. Your wife, too.'

When Calder didn't respond, the inspector reached into his jacket pocket and drew out the set of keys he'd taken from Henry White's sister.

'One of those belongs to you.'

'Eh?' Willie Calder jerked up his head, confused. 'What are you on about?'

'Henry White. Good old Henry left you something in his will. A key.'

'Who?'

'Don't play daft.' Harper's voice hardened. He was tired of games. 'You know exactly who I mean. You fenced some things for him before he was put away. You probably even know who he was working for.'

'I've never heard of him.'

'Willie.' The inspector shook his head and sighed. 'He's dead. Happened last Friday night. You must have read about it. It was in all the papers. He was murdered.'

'Maybe that's why I recognized his name last night,' Calder said hopefully.

'And you know the moon's made of green cheese because you read it in a book. Come on. Why did he leave you a key?' He pushed them across the table. 'Which one is it?'

'I don't know.' He didn't sound angry or outraged. Just not quite ready to concede defeat yet.

'What does the key open, Willie?' he persisted. 'What's inside?' No answer. He watched as the man kept his eyes on the keyring. 'I want whoever killed Henry. I might be willing to forgive a lot in return for information that helps me find a murderer.'

Harper gathered up the keys and the silver. 'Why don't you have a think about it? I'll be back in a little while.'

A little silence could bring plenty of clarity.

*   *   *

'Has he admitted it, sir?' Ash asked.

'Not yet.' He was surprised. Calder seemed a weak man; he'd expected him to crumple quickly. This could take a while. 'Why don't you have a go at him?' Harper suggested. 'Let's see if that works. You've done a sterling job on all this so far. Remind him he'll be up before the beak this afternoon.'

Kendall was in his office, sorting through the drawers and pulling out a few items: a cut-glass inkwell, a cigarette case, a heavy leather tobacco pouch.

'It's funny how much there is,' he said as Harper entered. 'I've already filled one box.'

Tomorrow would be the superintendent's final day. Thirty-one years of service on the force. From walking the beat to all this. And he probably wouldn't live long enough to see in the new year. Cancer. Bloody cancer.

'You won't miss spending every day here.'

'Probably not,' Kendall agreed with a regretful smile. 'Maybe I'll sleep a little more, too. Don't be surprised if I pop in from time to time, Tom. Just to keep an eye on things.'

'You'll always be welcome. You know that.'

'Don't worry, I'll keep out of your hair for a while.' He glanced around. 'You need to make your mark on the place. How are you getting along with that fence you brought in? Broken him yet? I'd love to have the White murder wrapped up before I leave.'

'He's not doing us any favours yet. Ash is with him.'

'Let's hope for the best. The pair of you have played this exactly right. Now we just need that little bit of luck.'

Luck. The thing that solved so many cases, Harper thought. It had been luck that he'd overheard the remark in Whitelock's. Luck that had put them on the path to Calder. Just a tiny bit more, he hoped, and they'd crack this. Maybe Billy Reed would have some luck of his own, too, and find some answers about the acid.

Another hour, not long before William Calder was due in court. Ash came into the office, rubbing his cheeks with his palms.

'He's admitted being a fence.'

'That's a start. What about the rest?'

The sergeant shook his head. 'Still insists he's never met Henry White and doesn't know anything about a key or a will.'

And if he stuck to that he was in the clear. They had absolutely nothing to tie the two men together. A name on a will proved sod all; he wasn't the only William Calder in England.

'We have enough to get him sentenced.'

'He did tell me who brought him that silver, sir,' Ash said with a smile.

'Anyone we know?'

'Oh yes. The uniforms are on their way to his lodgings now.'

'Good job. Well done.'

'I saw Sergeant Calder outside. He said he'd like to go down to court with his brother.'

'If that's what he wants. We've bought ourselves a little time now. Let's see if we can come up with a connection between Calder and Henry White. It's there, I can feel it in my water.'

'Yes, sir.'

'And sergeant?'

'Sir?'

'Have you ever considered applying to become an inspector?'

Harper spent the rest of the day going around his informers. Plenty of them knew Henry White, but the name William Calder seemed to mean nothing. Then, just as he was close to giving up, Nancy Ross leaned heavily on the table in the Golden Cock and asked, 'Do you mean Willie Calder the fence?'

He could feel his heart beating a little faster. 'That's the one. You know him?'

'You've used him, haven't you, George?' She nudged her husband. He had a sly, feral look.

'I did,' he agreed. He wasn't a man of words; his wife usually spoke for him. The inspector had no idea how old Nancy Ross might be; she'd looked close to fifty for all the years he'd known her. Plump, her skin very pink, hair grey and wiry. Most of the time she had a clay pipe in her mouth, smiling to show cracked, brown teeth. Now she was sitting with a glass of gin in front of her.

'And you knew Henry?'

'Course we did, luv. Shame what happened to him.' She

frowned, the lines showing deep on her face. 'He kept himself to himself, but I never heard anyone say a bad word about him.'

'What do you know about him and Willie Calder?'

'I saw him there once,' George said.

Harper turned. 'Where? When?'

The man shrugged. 'At Calder's house. I don't know. Could have been a year ago. Maybe two. He was on his way out. I ran into him at the door.'

'What did he have to say?'

George Ross shrugged again. 'I don't remember. How do you do? Hello? Something like that. Nothing important, like as not.'

'You only saw him there once?'

'That's right.'

'Did you ever see Henry with anyone else?' He had them sitting here; it was worth asking.

'Not really. We'd just spot him here and there, wouldn't we?' Nancy said. 'Why?'

'It doesn't matter.' The moment had passed; he could feel it slipping away. Nothing more to learn here. He placed two shillings on the table, enough to keep the pair of them drinking into the evening.

At least he had a connection now, although he'd never dare to drag George Ross into court. Any competent solicitor would tear him to shreds. Still, he had a small wedge to use on Calder now.

He hadn't forgotten the remark he'd overheard in Whitelock's. Willie and Henry. It might have been nothing, but it felt as if it had weight. He just didn't have any evidence. Yet.

'I've known the Crabtrees for years,' the woman told Reed. Her face was prim, shocked that anyone even needed to ask questions. 'They're a lovely couple.'

He'd gone back and done what Tom suggested: ask about the family. No matter what he tried, everyone gave him the same answers. Not a stain on their characters. Regular chapel goers for as long as anyone could remember. Jack Crabtree had been involved with the Band of Hope and he ran the Sunday school. As upright as it was possible to be. He'd worked for the same company since he left school, promoted to foreman.

Some of the older folk had tales about Jack's father, the kind of gambling drunkard Reed had encountered so often when he was still on the beat. But after he'd grown out of his youthful wildness, Jack had always been one for the straight and narrow and his wife was exactly the same. One child, Arthur, and now he was blind from the acid.

'I don't know why the Lord is punishing them that way,' the woman continued. 'But I can tell you this – He wouldn't test those who couldn't stand it.' She sniffed and held a small hand-kerchief to her nose.

It was a street of through terraced houses, a large step up from the back-to-backs no more than a hundred yards down the road. The windows all shone; the women used vinegar and newspaper on the glass, and the steps were scrubbed clean twice a week. People took pride in their homes and wanted everyone to know it. The Crabtrees lived at the end of the terrace, a place as spick and span as all the others.

'Have you met Dorothy Crabtree?' the woman asked.

'Yes.' He remembered the small confused woman he'd briefly seen. She'd been overwhelmed by everything, and who could blame her? Her husband had been the stoical one when they met, but even he looked as if his faith was being tested.

Neighbours had helped. Meals cooked and left for them so they could spend time at the hospital. After two days Jack Crabtree had gone back to his work. Never a question about it. That was what a man did. His wife was the one who passed her days and evenings at the infirmary with Arthur.

'Jack was never one for idle chitter-chatter,' the woman answered when Reed asked. 'Dun't talk about himself, thinks that's the sin of pride.'

He thanked her and moved on, hearing the door close softly. After being on his feet for hours, his leg and his back were aching. But he'd keep pressing. He wanted a solution before he returned to the fire brigade on Monday. He wanted to succeed. He'd had failures before, but he was the one who'd requested this case. He'd admitted he was getting nowhere, but Tom had offered only suggestions and support. Damned if he was going to show himself up now.

Finally, halfway through the afternoon, Reed walked down to

the factory by York Road. Three large stone buildings with windows set high in the walls, all set around a cobbled courtyard. A smaller brick building off to the side. And everywhere a noise like striding into an inferno, with engines rattling and humming and men shouting at the top of their voices to be heard. The heavy hiss of steam burst like punctuation in the air.

He had to ask twice, and was pointed in a new direction each time until he found Jack Crabtree tapping a gauge at a boiler in the brick shed and looking worried.

'I need to talk to you. About what happened to your son.'

'I'm working.' Crabtree barely bothered to glance at him. 'It'll have to wait.'

'No,' Reed said, 'it won't. This is police business.'

'All right.' The man set his jaw firmly. 'Wait a minute.' He waved a young man over and gave him instructions, pointing to different controls. Eventually he seemed satisfied and turned away. 'In the yard.'

He led the way to a far corner that was sheltered from the wind. Crabtree stood, arms folded, waiting.

'Now,' he said, 'what do you need?'

'What do I need?' Reed said in disbelief. 'Why do you think I'm here? I want to talk about whoever threw that acid at your son.'

'God will get us through it.'

'Maybe He will. That's between you and Him,' he said, his voice sharp. 'But I want the man who did it.'

'I don't know. I've told you that before.'

Reed took out a cigarette and lit it. He didn't bother offering one to Crabtree. The man was chapel; he wouldn't smoke or drink.

'You must have thought about it, though.'

'Of course I have. Every minute.' Crabtree raised his eyes and for a second the pain showed. 'My wife, too. But we can't change it. We'll come through, and we'll be stronger for it. All of us.'

The man's willing acceptance of it all, the weakness inside that he tried to disguise as strength, disgusted Reed.

'And while you've been thinking, have you come up with any idea why it happened? Or who might have done it?'

The man shook his head. 'I said the last time you asked me. I've no idea. I still don't.'

'And your wife?'

'She doesn't, either,' Crabtree said with certainty. He opened his mouth to say more. A sudden roar drowned him out. It seemed to begin underground, making the whole yard shake beneath their feet. Then it grew. Deafening, metallic. Painful. The feeling that the air was being sucked out of his lungs.

Reed didn't need to think. He ducked, covering his head, and pulled Crabtree down to the ground with him. All the training, the constant repetition, paid off. A heartbeat of complete stillness, then the sound returned, louder than before as the explosion came. Metal and glass flew through the air.

They were lucky, hidden away round the corner. But he felt the blast. He knew more debris would come in a second. Splinters of wood, fragments of stone and metal poured down like rain.

It couldn't have taken more than five seconds. In his head he knew that. But it still felt like forever. A century. An age. Cautiously, Reed exhaled. He stood, feeling all over his body for injuries. A few cuts on his hands and face, nothing major. Nothing broken. Crabtree was stumbling to his feet, dazed and terrified, a deep gash on his cheek bleeding heavily.

'Are you all right?' The man didn't seem to notice. But he was upright and moving; he couldn't be too bad.

Reed ran across the yard, broken glass crunching under his feet. The shed with the boiler had simply disappeared. There was just a space where it had once stood. A few twisted, jagged shards of metal and a broken concrete floor were all that remained. The rest was strewn everywhere.

He stopped. Sniffed. Gas. Christ.

A few men began putting their heads tentatively around the door of the main factory. All the windows had been blown out, but the building looked safe enough.

'Get back,' Reed yelled and waved. His ears were ringing; he could hardly hear a thing. The men started to duck away. 'There's gas.' His voice hardly seemed to be there. 'Call for the fire brigade.'

Crabtree was coming towards him, a rag pressed against the cut on his face.

'Charlie . . .' he began, staring around. 'Charlie was in there.'

'You can't do anything for him now,' Reed said, not even sure if the man could hear. His voice seemed to be underwater, muffled, muted. He put a hand on Crabtree's arm, pulling him into the factory. It was like handling a scarecrow, soft and strange.

A manager stood inside, a tailor's dummy in his neat suit and tie, looking utterly lost.

'Gas,' Reed said. The man simply stared at him. 'We need all the gas off. Everywhere. Now! Do you understand?' For another second the manager stared at him dumbly, then nodded and dashed away.

All around, men were talking, on the verge of panic. He could see the desperation and fear in their eyes. The thick stone walls of the factory had shielded them from the blast. A few injuries from falling glass, but nothing bad.

'I'm Inspector Reed.' He shouted the words, then repeated them, waiting until they gave him their attention. He could still barely hear himself. 'I'm with the Fire Brigade and Police. I need you all to stay in here. You're safe for now. Is anyone hurt?'

Men shook their heads. A few looked down at the ground. Others chattered away, prattling, relieved to be alive and unin-jured. Someone had put Crabtree on a chair in the corner and put a cup of something in his hand. He was going to need to talk to the man. Later, much later. Once everything had been cleared.

Reed shook his head and swallowed, trying to clear his ears. A thought flitted through his mind: this must be how Tom Harper felt all the time. Cut off. Disconnected.

He grabbed at a man going past. 'I need a count of everyone here, and how many reported for the shift.' The man nodded, then turned on his heel.

In the distance, on the edge of his senses, he believed he could make out the bell of a fire engine. Good. Get the lads here, taking care of everything.

This was what he did. He was trained for situations like this. He knew how to handle them. As the firemen dismounted from the engine and stretched out the hoses, Reed joined them in the yard. The smell of gas seemed to have dissipated. The manager must have done what he asked. For the first time, he could look around properly. With all the rubble – bricks, heavy timbers, metal sharp as spears – it was a miracle that the cobbles weren't strewn with bodies. Absolute bloody luck.

'Not much for us to do here, sir,' Sergeant Wilson said after half an hour. The men had been thorough, checking the gas was off and combing through the remains of the boiler house. They'd found a body fifty yards away, battered, broken, hardly recognizable as the man Crabtree had left in charge. 'I'd say they got off lightly, all things considered.'

No fires to extinguish. No real danger. It had been an easy call, Reed knew that. He'd served with every one these men, he knew he could trust them. He knew they'd been surprised to find him here, leaning on his walking stick and directing them all over the place. But they obeyed without question.

'You're right,' he agreed. 'It'll be a little while before they're making anything again, but they'll survive. Good work. Thank you.'

The sergeant smiled and saluted. 'Glad to help, sir.'

It could have been so much worse. A single death. A few more injured by flying glass, none of them serious. Crabtree looked shaken and quiet, as if he'd retreated into a little world of his own. But he was the man in charge of the boiler; it was all his responsibility. Another minute or two and he might have been the one blown up.

Reed thought back. When he walked in, Crabtree had been tapping a dial and looking worried. Was there a problem? He'd find out. But not now. Let the man ponder his mortality. Once that shock had passed, there'd be time. In the morning.

An envelope was waiting on his desk when he returned to the office, *Inspector Harper* written on the front in Ash's neat, clipped penmanship. He tore it open and pulled out a newspaper cutting.

A woman was killed in an accident with a tram yesterday on Vicar Lane. It is believed that she stepped out between vehicles into the path of the electric tram. An ambulance was called but her injuries were too severe and she died at Leeds General Infirmary. She has been named as Mrs Gertrude Parkin of Harehills.

Accident, he wondered? Or grief? He was never going to know. One more casualty from all this. Like ripples slowly moving out across a pond.

TEN

'You were there?' Harper asked. Reed nodded.
'I was lucky. We were round a corner, away from the blast. But now I have to look into it for the Brigade.'
'Yes, of course.' He was their arson investigator; this was part of his job. 'So no more on the acid.'
'There won't be much chance, Tom, I'm back to work. I definitely have quite a few questions for Crabtree about the boiler. He didn't look happy when I first saw him, before it all happened. I wanted to let you know what was going on.'
'Did you talk to him about the acid?'
'Only for a minute. He says he doesn't have a clue, but I'd swear there's something he isn't telling me. Everything happened before I had the chance to press him.'
'Where else should we be looking?'
Reed let out a long, weary sigh. 'Honestly, I wish I could tell you.' He gave a shrug. 'I'm sorry. I thought it was going to be simple.'
'I've given up hope of anything being easy. But you were lucky.' He reached across and felt the broad hole in Reed's coat.
'The lads on the engine pointed that out when they arrived.' He grinned and barked out a short laugh. 'I hadn't even noticed.'
'Elizabeth will be glad to see you in one piece.'
'She'd be happier if we could get this solved.' He took a deep breath. Time to say his piece, the reason he'd come down to Millgarth instead of going straight home. 'I don't want to, but I'm going to have to throw it back to you. I'm officially back to work on Monday. But I'll be starting on the explosion in the morning.'
'Keep asking questions about Crabtree if you get the chance.

Talk to him – with someone dead, this is bound to have shaken him up. See if anything comes up.'

'I will.' He hesitated a moment. 'No promises, but I'll do what I can.'

'That's all I can ask.'

'I've been worried sick about you, Billy Reed.' He was barely through the door when she appeared, her glare turning into a look of horror when she saw the cuts on his face and the tear in his clothes. 'Are you hurt?'

'I'm fine,' he said with a smile, putting his arms around her. 'Honestly. I was there when it happened, but I was safe.'

He told her all about it, sitting at the kitchen table and sipping hot, sweet tea.

'Luck doesn't hold forever,' she said when he finished. 'That injury to your leg was bad enough.'

'It's my job.' She knew that; they'd talked about it often enough before. Yes, the work was dangerous. They were careful; they weighed every risk. The fire brigade rarely lost a man. The only things you couldn't account for were accidents.

It had been a good do, Harper decided as the hackney carried him back to the Victoria. The kind of send-off people remembered with a warm smile. The chief constable had come and given a speech, the heads of all the divisions were there, each of them wishing Kendall a long, happy retirement.

Everyone in the room knew he was dying, but no one was about to ruin the evening by saying so. Instead there were jokes and laughter, tall tales and plenty of beer. The whole time the superintendent looked relieved, as if a heavy weight had been lifted from him.

Harper moved from group to group, accepting their congratulations on his promotion. Before he left, though, he settled next to Kendall, watching the others. He was tired, his ear ached from straining to hear so many conversations, but he needed this moment.

'Do you think you'll miss it?'

The super toyed with his glass, the pipe in his mouth. 'Every day,' he answered with a wry smile. 'For a while, at least.'

'It won't be the same without you.' Kendall had taught him how to be a detective, always there from the first day Harper began working in plain clothes. And now that would become his role. Everything changed, it all moved on.

'You're good enough for the job, Tom. You've learned.'

'Let's hope so. I'll start finding out tomorrow.'

'You'll be just fine.' He raised his beer in a toast. 'Good luck to you.'

'And to you.' Like everyone else, he was skirting the truth. But if there was one night when that was acceptable, this was it. 'Thank you for all you've done.'

'At least you made it interesting.' Kendall laughed. 'You have a knack for doing things the hard way. But you get them done. Come and visit us, you'll always have a seat by the fire. Annabelle and your daughter, too.'

'I will,' he promised, meaning it. How long would the super last, though, away from Millgarth?

'You look like that job's already worrying you and you don't even start until tomorrow,' Annabelle said.

'It's not that.' Harper was sprawled in the chair, legs stretched out towards the fire. 'I was just thinking about Kendall. He loved the work. It's . . . I don't know. And someone else died today, too.' He told her about Mrs Parkin and the way she'd felt about Henry White.

'Poor love,' she said. 'Do you think she . . .?'

'I haven't a clue,' was all he could tell her. He reached across and took hold of her hand, needing the contact, the warmth.

'Are you going to look into it?'

He shook his head. Accident or suicide, it wasn't police business. In a day or two they'd hold the inquest and next week the woman's body would be in the ground. He didn't even know if she had children. With a low sigh, Harper roused himself. It was late and he needed to sleep. Tomorrow was going to be a big day.

Millgarth looked exactly the same. No bunting, no flags out to welcome him. Tollman was on duty at the front desk, treating him the way he had every other day.

It felt strange to pass by the desk that had been his for so long, then into the office that would probably still smell of pipe tobacco a year from now. He settled into the chair, looking around, then pulled the first paper from the waiting pile. Time to make a start.

At eleven Harper walked out of the station. He needed some air. He needed to talk to people. He was a detective, not a damned glorified clerk. And he was still determined to solve Henry White's murder. He'd started this case and he'd see it through. Ash was out, trying to find anyone else who could connect Henry with Willie Calder.

Time to go back to the source.

Voices echoed around the prison, bouncing off the walls. The place smelt of old boiled cabbage, urine, and too many lost hopes. The eyes looking out from the cells held a mixture of hatred, desperation, and pain. Harper marched along the corridor, close on the heels of one of the uniformed guards, a young man with a moustache and a cocky smile.

'In here, sir,' the lad said. 'We'll have him along for you in a minute.'

The window was too high to look out, but it brought some pale light into the interview room. Two chairs and a scarred wooden table. He'd been there five minutes when he heard the sharp clicks of boots in the corridor, then the door opened and Calder appeared.

'How do you like Armley jail, Willie?' Harper said. 'Have a seat, I want to talk to you.'

A police nick might not have broken him, but a real prison had damaged his spirit. Calder hadn't even been here a full day but already he looked like an old lag. Hunched shoulders, folding in on himself as if he was trying to disappear. His face was so pale it seemed haunted, and the dirt was ingrained in his skin.

'Bit different from Headingley, isn't it? No servant to come round and take care of you.'

Calder didn't raise his head or reply. Harper pulled out the set of keys and tossed them on to the table.

'Which one is it, Willie? Which one did Henry leave you?'

Silence filled the room. Somewhere in the distance a voice screamed, a stream of words he couldn't make out. Calder didn't move. But Harper knew he'd get his answers.

'Which one?' He pushed them towards the man. 'Show me.'

Very slowly, timidly, Calder's fingers crept along the table. He touched the smallest of the keys on the ring, a shiny piece of steel. Good, Harper thought; that was progress.

'What's it for? Give me some good information and you could end up spending less time in here.'

'For a box.' His voice was a croak, as if the spark had gone from it. 'In a bank.'

A box in a bank?

'A deposit box, you mean?' he asked and Calder nodded. 'Which bank?'

'I don't know. He never told me.'

Harper took a deep breath.

'Let me get this straight. Henry White left you a key in his will, even though you insist you don't know him.' Calder shrugged; one lie dismissed. 'You know it fits a deposit box in a bank, but you've no idea which bank. Is that right?'

For a moment the man glanced up and nodded. 'Yes.'

'What's inside the box?'

'Don't know.'

Frustration was beginning to rise inside him. 'You're not much help, are you?'

'I'm telling you the truth.'

'Then you'd best tell me all of it,' he warned.

Calder gave a cough and leaned forward as if he was passing on a secret.

'Henry said he had something for me in his will, a key to a box. Said I'd have to find out which one for myself. He was laughing when he said it, like it was the funniest thing he'd heard.'

Harper stared at him. 'You seriously expect me to believe that?'

'It's the truth. I swear.' He blinked behind his spectacles. 'That's what he said. I thought it was a joke.'

'But you picked out the key without a problem.'

'He showed it to me. When he told me about it.'

'And you never asked what was in the box?'

'Course I did,' Calder replied. For the first time there seemed to be some fire in his voice. 'But he wouldn't say. It'll be a surprise, that's what he promised.'

Harper was thinking, trying to fit the small fragments together and coming up with nothing.

'Did he give you any kind of clue as to which bank?'

'No. I asked but he wouldn't tell me.'

'I see.' Harper stood, sweeping the keys back in his pocket. He'd learned everything he could here.

'What are you going to do to help me?' Calder said. Fear filled his face. 'I've told you everything I know.'

'You're going to have to wait and see. But if you want my advice, plead guilty when you come to trial and ask for all your offences to be taken into consideration. That often makes the judges more lenient.'

'I—'

But Harper was already leaving, waving the guard through to return the prisoner to his cell. He'd knew he'd taken long enough from his new job simply to come out here. He didn't have time to waste bartering over scraps with Willie Calder. The man had gone free for years; let him face some justice now.

Ash stared at the key and rubbed his chin.

'And we've no idea which bank, sir?'

'None,' Harper told him. 'It's probably one in the middle of town, though. I can't see anywhere past there having deposit boxes. If you describe Henry, that should help. There can't be many as down-at-heel as him leasing one.'

The sergeant grinned. 'That's true enough.' He started to rise.

'Did you give any thought to what I said?'

Ash cocked his head. 'Sir?'

'About becoming an inspector. We're going to need one at the station. I think you'd be ideal.'

The sergeant kept a hand on the doorknob. 'I talked to my Nancy about it . . .'

'What did she say?'

'She thinks if you believe it, then it's a good thing. So yes, sir, I'm interested.'

Harper smiled. 'I'll have a word with the chief next week. But that means we're going to need a new sergeant.'

'Conway, sir,' he replied without hesitation. 'He's a detective constable over at D division. We trained together. He has a sharp mind, he deserves the chance.'

'Sound him out, see if he'd be interested.'

'I will, sir. And thank you.'

D Division. It covered Wortley, Armley, Kirkstall. Plenty of crime. Anyone who'd worked there would be well-seasoned. One more thing to consider when Monday rolled around. He took the watch from his waistcoat. After four and he still had plenty to keep him busy. Back to the grind.

He climbed the stairs at the Victoria and opened the door to the parlour to find Mary standing two feet away. Her back was as straight as any new recruit, eager to please. As she gazed up at him, she brought up her right hand in a salute, her expression serious and intent.

'Soo-tend-unt.'

From the kitchen he could hear Annabelle trying to stifle her giggles. He wanted to smile but forced himself to keep a straight face. Carefully he raised his own hand and saluted back. Only then did the girl relax.

'Mam said that was how we could celebrate,' Mary said.

'Your ma can be very strange, can't she?' He picked the girl up and twirled her around until she began to shriek with pleasure, then carried her through to stand by the kitchen door.

Annabelle was still softly laughing, dabbing the tears of joy away from her eyes.

'Honestly, Tom . . .' She shook her head and tickled Mary under the chin. 'If you could have seen your face when you walked in. Then the two of you saluting each other. I'm going to remember that as long as I live.'

'I will, too,' the girl said, squirming down from his grip and running off to her bedroom.

'Did you really like it?' Annabelle asked.

'Yes.' He kissed her. 'How did you come up with it?'

'Blame your daughter, it was her idea. All I did was show her how to salute properly.' She winked. 'One thing about having

the barracks nearby. Those soldier boys are always ready to show
a girl a real salute.' A chuckle, then she said, 'You look all in.'

'Trying to do too much,' he told her.

'Never mind. You'll get used to it.'

ELEVEN

Nine o'clock on Sunday morning and Harper was back at
Millgarth, wading through a pile of papers as a mug of
tea turned cold by his hand. The sun played hide and
seek with the clouds, light flooding in through the window.

He was in his black suit, ready for Maguire's funeral at noon.
He'd arranged to meet Annabelle at Mount St Mary's church. A
service with full mass, then a procession up to Beckett Street
cemetery for the burial.

But there was time to do some work before all that, to keep
his head above water with all the tasks.

He'd been busy for an hour when Ash arrived, tapping on the
door before entering.

'Any luck with that key?'

The sergeant raised an eyebrow. 'It was Saturday, sir. None
of the banks were open.'

Of course. Harper shook his head. Stupid; he should have
remembered that.

'You've got a smile, though. You must have found
something.'

'Another link between White and Calder, sir. Do you remember
Christian Simms?'

With a name like that it was impossible to forget the man.
Especially when he was the most irreligious, foul-mouthed man
Harper had ever met.

'You wouldn't call him a reliable witness.'

'He was able tell me exactly where and when he was with
them both, sir.'

'Exactly?' That was unlike Simms. He was never clearer than
vague.

'Turns out it was Boxing Day, two years ago. He was in the Green Dragon and saw them talking to each other. One o'clock, he says. He's certain about it because he had to leave right after and go home for his dinner.'

'That's something.' Another small strand in the web. 'First thing tomorrow we need to go round the banks. I want to know where Henry had that box and what's in it.'

'Yes, sir.'

'Talk to Inspector Reed, too. You heard about the explosion off York Road?'

'I think I felt it, sir,' Ash replied.

'He was there when it happened, talking to Crabtree. Neither of them injured, thank God, but he needs to look into the cause of the blast.'

'Naturally, sir. That's his job.'

'Have a word with him and get the details on where everything stands.'

'Yes, sir.' He gave a small cough. 'I happened to run into Mark Conway last night, sir. The detective constable from D Division,' he explained when Harper looked baffled.

'Yes?' He wondered just how accidental the meeting had really been. Did it even matter?

'He'd be very interested in a promotion and a transfer, sir.'

'I'll get everything rolling this week.'

'I'll let him know.' He nodded at the suit. 'I hope everything goes well for the funeral. I hear there's likely to be a crowd.'

'There certainly will be. That's why it's on a Sunday, so people can go.'

The Famine Church. That's what everyone called it when he was a boy. Back then he'd never understood why. Now he knew about the history, the fact that Mount St Mary's had been built during the years the Irish were starving and leaving their homes, some of them ending up in Leeds.

The incense caught the back of his throat. Mary sat on the pew beside him, clutching his hand tightly. This was her first funeral and she seemed as overawed by it as he was. Annabelle was sitting off to the side with the others who'd deliver the eulogies. She was all in black, a long crinoline gown gathered high at the neck, broad black hat and veil, polished black button boots. The clothes of grief.

It was a large church, full of statues and icons, and it was packed with people. Maguire's family, distant relatives and neighbours. Friends. Admirers: many, many more of those. The coffin lay in front of the altar on a plain bier, ready to be carried out once all the words had been spoken.

Harper didn't know the Catholic service. It was safer to follow everyone's lead, to stand and sit when they did and mutter his responses. He listened to the sermon, the priest droning on and on, then some of the other speakers. Finally Mary turned on the pew and loudly hissed,

'That's me mam.'

Annabelle stood at the lectern, as poised as he'd ever seen her. Her face was calm as she looked around the congregation. She raised her head and without trying, her voice seemed to carry to every nook and cranny in the building.

'I knew Tommy Maguire when we were little. He was younger than me, trailing around after the rest of us, the lad with the dewdrop on his nose and the confused look in his eye. Happen he was in love with me back then. That's what people said, but I don't know if it's true. If he was, at least he had the good sense to grow out of it.' She smiled for a moment, then her face became sombre again. 'He knew what life was like round here. He wasn't one of those who had to read about it, he'd already lived it. And all those books he looked at later on the working class? He could have written them. He'd experienced it himself. You've heard everyone tell you what he did for the labourers, the gas workers, starting the party. If you really want to see the people he helped, just turn your head and look at the person beside you. It's every one of us in here and all those who'll be waiting outside for the hearse.' She let them think for a moment. 'He gave more to Leeds than any of us have managed to do. He helped me. When I began searching around and putting into words the things I'd always known inside, he was there to show me and encourage me. If he looked up to me when we were little, the tables had turned.

'He saw sadness and he saw beauty, sometimes in the same thing. There are plenty in the unions and in the Independent

Labour Party who don't believe that women need a voice. Tommy was never one of those. He knew what the vote could mean to everyone. He believed that this was *our* country, where all of us belong, and that we should all have our say in it.' She paused and her face softened as she smiled. 'And he wrote poems, but I'm sure you know that. Published in the *Labour Leader*. He might have been able to speak out loudly in public, he might have been able to persuade. But inside, his soul cried, and the poems are what came out. For love, against injustice. He was proud of them. He had every right to be, too.' She stood a little straighter and began to read from the piece of paper in her hand.

'Here in the heart of the cloud-wrapt town,
Where strong men thrive upon weak men down,
Where trade prepares its rank soul for hell—
Oh here, along with the damned I dwell!
And maidens are brought from near and far
To sate the lust of the Minotaur!
I prey on your budding womanhood,
And drain the colour of life from her blood;
I scale her skin till 'tis yellow and dry;
And dim the lustre that lighted her eyes;
The marrow out of her bones I draw,
Her breasts I grip with a cancerous claw,
Her husk, in the end, to the dogs I fling—
A bloodless, soulless, sexless thing.'

Annabelle bowed her head, crossed herself and returned to her seat.

Mary behaved perfectly, as if she understood the solemnity of the occasion. At her age he'd have been squirming around, bored. But she seemed entranced by the ceremony, watching quietly even during the long minutes of the mass.

Finally the pallbearers raised the coffin to their shoulders and carried it down the aisle to the hearse, the congregation filing slowly out behind. Harper held his daughter's hand and waited near the church door until Annabelle appeared, gazing at the procession as it started towards York Road.

'You did him justice,' he told her.

'I hope so.' She sounded worried. 'It's the last chance I'll ever have.'

They joined the people following the coffin, moving slowly and quietly, with everyone else. He could see men standing on the pavement, caps in their hands, heads bowed in respect. One or two here, a dozen or more there.

Up ahead, only the sharp sound of hooves on the cobbles and the quiet rumble of the hearse's wheels. Nobody talking, nobody breaking the moment.

Turning on to Beckett Street, the slow, shallow climb toward the cemetery. Suddenly the entire road was lined with men and women. All in their Sunday best, standing still, waiting for the body to pass by.

Hundreds of them, Harper thought. He'd never seen anything like it. What would Maguire have made of it all? Chuckled to himself, probably, pleased as punch but astonished by it all. Too late now, too late for him to see how they all felt.

Yet no one had done anything to save him. He was as bad as everyone else. He was horrified when he saw the way Maguire had lived. But he'd never given it a thought until he looked at the corpse.

Harper was still lost in his thoughts when they reached the cemetery. The coffin was carried slowly to the grave, and the crowd was so thick that they had to stand close to the iron gate leading into the place. Policemen had stopped traffic along the road.

His ears couldn't make out the short service, but Annabelle was listening intently, a single tear rolling slowly down her cheek until she wiped it away. And finally it was all done, the gravediggers piling earth on wood as people milled around in groups, talking, smiling as if the last two hours had never happened.

'I need to get back to the Victoria and make sure everything's ready,' Annabelle said. 'Dan and Ellen were setting it all up when I left.'

The big meal. Fifty or so invited. He'd forgotten all about it.

'Do you need me there?' It was more like begging than a question. There was still work waiting at Millgarth.

'You go on.' She smiled. 'You wouldn't know most of them, anyway.'

On the street a constable was directing all the traffic. He was older, hair white, almost too big for his uniform. He saluted quickly as he saw Harper.

'Right old mess, sir.'

'Yes.' He watched the crowd dispersing. 'A grand turnout, though.'

The bobby clicked his tongue against the roof of his mouth. Peyton, Harper thought suddenly; that was the man's name. 'I know you were there, sir, and with respect, but he was no more than a rabble rouser.'

'There are plenty here who'd disagree with you.'

'I daresay. More'n a thousand, that's what the sergeant reckoned. But I've as much right to my opinion as any of 'em, sir.'

'You do.' But he didn't want to hear it, not today.

Groups of people were walking away. A few were talking animatedly, but most stayed silent. He needed the quiet. That was the way funerals always affected him. They made him reflect, and this one more than most; it wouldn't be too long before he'd be attending Kendall's. Was this what life became, he wondered: seeing the people you liked slowly vanish? Attending a series of funerals?

He strode out, down towards Millgarth. Work. It was a good way to clear the head.

'I don't know,' Reed began. 'I had a feeling Crabtree was about to tell me something when the explosion happened.'

'What do you think he was going to say?' Ash asked. They were sitting in the parlour. Off in the kitchen, Elizabeth was preparing a late Sunday dinner, and the smell of roasting meat filled the air.

He looked at the sergeant and shook his head.

'That's the thing – I really don't know. I'm going to talk to him tomorrow about the blast.' He recalled the man's expression in the boiler shed and the way he'd tapped the dial. 'He looked worried.'

'How would you feel if I came along with you when you talked to him, sir?'

The question took him aback. It was intruding on his work.

'Why?' Reed asked suspiciously.

'I thought we could kill two birds with one stone. Ask him about both things.'

'I'm not sure.'

The sergeant dipped his head. 'Your choice, sir.'

Reed looked at him. There was a rumour running around that Ash was going to be promoted; a bobby he'd seen had mentioned it that morning.

'Let me think about it,' Reed told him.

'Of course, sir.' Ash stood, a big man who seemed to fill the room. At the front door he said goodbye, then, 'I could go and see Mrs Crabtree.'

'You can, but I don't think it'll do you any good.' He shrugged. 'She's not likely to say a word against her husband.'

'Maybe not,' the sergeant agreed. 'but she'll know him better than anyone.'

'Try it, then. You never know.' He liked Ash. The man was a natural copper. Even when he was smiling the wheels still seemed to be turning, as if his mind never stopped. Perhaps it didn't. Perhaps that was what made him so good.

'Yes, sir. I'll drop by and have a word with her in the morning. Do you think the husband will be at work?'

Reed didn't even need to consider his answer. 'I'm certain of it.'

'It looks like a swarm of locusts have been through the place,' Harper said.

Annabelle was gathering up the plates and empty glasses. Ellen was helping, while Mary sat at a table with a pencil and a piece of paper, quietly drawing.

'What did you expect? It was an Irish funeral.' She placed another pile on the bar for Dan to wash and smiled with satisfaction. 'Mind you, we gave him a good farewell. I think he might have enjoyed that. Even his mam wasn't too sad by the end.'

'I'm sorry I missed it.'

She chuckled. 'No, you're not. You'd have felt like a spare part, not knowing what to do with yourself. It was like the Saturday nights when I was her age.' She nodded at Mary. 'Everyone would get together for music and a laugh. Talk about Ireland.' She shook her head at the memory, silent for a moment, gazing at something only she could see. 'I'll miss him, you know. I meant what I said. Every word of it.'

'You have us,' Harper said and Annabelle started to smile, a grin that reached all the way to her eyes.

'I do, and that's all anyone could want. Why don't you take Mary upstairs? See if she's ready for some supper.'

'I had some of the food down here,' a small voice said. She didn't look up from her drawing.

Annabelle rolled her eyes. 'Just make a cuppa, then. I'll be up by the time it's mashed.'

'Da,' Mary asked when they were alone, 'what happens when someone dies? Do they really go to heaven?'

He'd been dreading the question; he'd half-expected it straight after the funeral. And he didn't have an answer for her. The best he could offer was something vague, even when she pinned him with the same direct stare her mother used. God help the men when she grew up, he thought. They won't stand a chance against her.

TWELVE

He couldn't leave Ash to do all the work himself, and the detective constables they had all needed more experience before he'd trust them with anything important. Harper filled out the requests for the sergeant's promotion to inspector and for Conway to move from D Division. It felt strange to sign himself as superintendent. That rank still belonged to someone else. How long before it fitted him?

He had the key to the deposit box. He only needed to visit the banks until he found the right one. That should be easy enough, at least to start. The real work would come later.

It began when he sat down with the manager of Beckett's Bank on Park Row. The building was as hushed and reverent as a church. The man sitting on the other side of the desk was examining the key.

'This is one of ours,' he said as he nodded his head. 'Might

I ask how it ended up with the police, Superintendent Harper?'

'It's part of our enquiries, sir.' Make it official, he thought. 'I'd like to see inside the box that key opens.'

The manager pursed his lips. He had a thin face. His side whiskers were white, neatly trimmed, his hair short and fading from his forehead. Full, dark frock coat, a starched high collar and a back as straight as a ramrod.

'You have to understand that we'd normally only give access to the holder of the box.' His voice was formal.

'He won't be coming back,' Harper said with a dark expression. 'Mr White is dead. You probably saw it in the papers.'

'I did.'

'Then I'm sure you can understand why I need access to that box, sir. Mr White was murdered. He left that key to another man in his will. I have reason to believe there's important evidence in it.'

'By rights the person named in the will should be here, with a copy of the document,' the bank manager said primly.

'I'm afraid he's a little indisposed at the moment.' He saw the man swallow nervously. 'In Armley jail, awaiting trial for receiving stolen goods. Now, Mr—'

'Raymond.'

'Mr Raymond. I'd like to see inside that box.' It wasn't a request any longer. It was a demand.

The man waved an arm and a young man appeared, looking awkward and out of place in formal clothes that were a size too large.

'He'll take you to the deposit area. You have to understand that this is very unusual.'

'Murder often is,' Harper began. Then he added, 'I'm grateful for your help.' Catch more flies with honey than vinegar, he thought. He might need co-operation from the bank again.

The room was underground, airless, hidden behind a heavy steel door. It was sterile, with no smell to it. The young man found the box, number 415, took a key from his waistcoat and stuck it in one of the locks.

'You'll need to put your key in the other one, sir.' His voice wavered, barely broken. Harper did as he was told. In a moment the lad had pulled the box out from the wall with a practised movement and placed it on the table. 'Just let me know when you've finished, sir.'

Then he was alone. His mouth was dry and he felt a ripple of anticipation through his body, the quick beat of his heart. Maybe now he'd find out why Henry had been murdered. Slowly, holding his breath, he raised the metal lid.

Inside there was a heavy, bulging envelope. Harper eased it out and pushed the box away.

The envelope was dusty under his fingertips, as if it had lain there for years. A heavy red wax seal held it closed. Strange, he thought. Such an old-fashioned method, he thought. He pushed his thumbnail underneath, breaking it then gently peeling it back.

Harper worked the flap open and jammed his fingers inside, no idea what he'd find. Papers, a stack of them from the feel, and two smooth pieces of metal, cold and slick.

Very gently, he tipped everything on to the table. A sheaf of notes, closely written in fading ink, tied together with twine. A small silver flask, absolutely plain, nothing engraved on the sides. A silver cigarette case. Nothing on that, either. He turned them both in his hands. Heavy, good quality. But what did it all mean? Henry White had never been one to write things down. He'd watched the man sign a statement and that had been a drawn-out affair.

And this was all intended for Willie Calder. What was it?

He scooped it all up and carried it with him. Plenty of time to examine everything properly at Millgarth.

Reed had looked at himself in the mirror before he left for the fire station on Park Row. The night before he'd polished the brass buttons of his uniform jacket and his cap badge. Now they winked in the morning light. He was proud to be a member of the fire brigade, but after two weeks in civilian clothes it felt strange to see himself like this again.

Elizabeth had long since gone to work; always an early start at the bakeries, before dawn arrived.

The tram journey was so familiar that he felt himself falling straight back into the rhythm of the job. There'd be plenty to do, of course. But he knew the first task: off to the factory where Crabtree worked to discover the cause of the explosion.

He walked into the yard at little after nine. Men must have worked hard all Sunday. The cobbles were swept clean, piles of debris neatly gathered here and there. A couple of courses of bricks and twisted metal were all that remained of the boiler shed.

At the office he introduced himself, sitting with the manager he'd yelled orders at on Saturday. The man didn't even recognize him at first. Things were calm. But silent. No power to run the machines, and it would be a month before that would return. In the meantime the men were idle and unpaid.

'Jack Crabtree,' Reed said.

'I've got him checking all the machinery. We might as well use the time to make sure they'll work properly once we're up and running again. He was lucky when it happened. You, too,' the man added.

'Not everyone was.'

'I know.' His face fell. 'Charlie Clay. He'd only been here three years, too. Nice lad.'

'Crabtree was looking at the dials on the boiler before we went to talk. He called Clay over to keep an eye on things.'

'What?' Suddenly the manager was completely attentive. 'He never told me any of that. Are you sure?'

'He was probably in shock. He looked dazed after the blast.' Reed was willing to give Crabtree the benefit of the doubt, at least in public.

'Maybe so.' The man looked doubtful.

'I need to talk to him about it all.'

'Whenever you want. I think I'll be wanting a word when you're done, too. I've put in an order for the new boiler and they're going to start building the new shed in a few days. If you have any recommendations to make things safer . . .'

'I'll tell you as soon as I can.'

Crabtree was by himself in the vast emptiness of the factory. His tools were laid out on a piece of oilcloth and he had part of a machine disassembled.

'Complicated business,' Reed said.

'Everything is unless you know what you're doing.' Crabtree

stood upright, wiping his hands on a rag. 'What can I do for you?'

'The explosion.'

'What about it? You were there.'

'I know,' Reed told him. 'That's why I have some questions. The way you were tapping those dials and looking worried, for instance. What was the problem?'

'J.D.,' Harper said.

'Sir?' Ash looked at him quizzically. 'Is that supposed to mean something?'

He tossed the packet of papers across the desk.

'Henry White's deposit box. His writing. It's a diary. Something like that, anyway. A confession, maybe. He says he did a lot of work for someone called J.D. And these were in there.' He pointed at the flask and cigarette case. 'What I can't see is why he'd pay good money to keep them hidden away or why he'd leave them to Willie Calder. I've been racking my brains; I've no idea who J.D. is.'

'There must be a few, sir. Common initials.'

'I must be missing something. Read it through and see if anyone comes to mind.' He frowned. 'Have you made any progress on the acid attack?'

'I did come across something curious.' The smile came and disappeared under the heavy moustache in an instant. 'Mrs Crabtree wasn't at home, so I took a wander to the chapel the family attends.' He glanced up.

'Go on.'

'The preacher was there, sweeping out the room they use for meetings. The Crabtrees go every week. They have done since it opened ten years ago. Mrs Crabtree runs something for the wives, going out and doing good deeds, that sort of thing. The father takes the Sunday school.'

'We already knew most of that.'

'Bear with me a moment, sir. When we were chatting it came up that a couple of families have withdrawn their children from the Sunday school in the last few months. One of them even stopped going to the chapel. The preacher went to see them and they wouldn't tell him why.'

'What are you trying to say? How does that tie to the acid?'

'I'm not sure, sir. It just struck me as odd. I thought it might be an idea to have a word with those families later.'

'That's fine. I'll leave it with you.' Any lead at all was worth pursuing, no matter how obscure. 'In the meantime, see if you can make more of Henry's scribblings than I did.'

Ash glanced out of the window. Drizzle was beginning to fall. A fire was burning steadily in the office hearth.

'I'll be glad to, sir.'

Harper sat, watching rain trickle down the window. He'd barely begun in his new job and already he felt cut off from real policing. Kendall had warned him that things would change and there would be limits. He just hadn't expected life to alter so quickly.

The other times he'd done the job it had only been for a day or two, juggling tasks to carry out his own work as well. All he'd had to do as acting superintendent was to keep things bobbing along. Now it was different. A stack of reports to read. How could people generate so much paper, he wondered? At four o'clock he was expected at a meeting with the Chief Constable and all the other division heads.

He was already debating whether he'd done the right thing in accepting the promotion. God help him.

'I always tap the dials,' Crabtree said. 'It's habit. Sometimes they stick. Tapping gives an accurate reading.' But he looked away as he spoke.

'Tell me something,' Reed asked. 'Are you a God-fearing man?'

'I am, sir.' He looked the fireman in the eye. 'But you already know that about me and my family.'

'Tell the truth and shame the devil?' He dredged the phrase from a distant childhood memory, words his mother said.

'That's right.'

Reed stared at Crabtree, his voice low and level. 'Then why are you lying to me?'

For a few seconds the man was quiet. His body was tense, fingers moving slowly over the material of his trousers.

'I was worried about the boiler,' he admitted finally. 'It's acting up a bit. That's why I told young Charlie to keep an eye on things.'

'What was wrong with it?' He was getting to the heart of the matter now. Crabtree had begun; soon he'd have it all. From there, perhaps, he could lead into the acid attack, while the man was still so open and raw.

The pressure in the boiler kept dipping, Crabtree said. Never by much, and it came back quickly enough. But something was wrong and he didn't know what; probably a valve that was sticking. It had been that way most of the shift, and he'd intended to ask permission to shut the boiler down and strip it fully.

'You see,' he said, 'that's why I wanted Charlie watching it, in case the pressure dipped too low.'

'Is that what happened?' Reed asked. 'Did that cause the explosion?'

'I think so.' He closed his eyes and sighed. 'As best as I see things, the pressure must have dropped then come back, but it kept rising because the valve didn't open. Ewart should have seen that. He could have opened the valve by hand, there was a safety handle right there.'

'Then why didn't he?'

Crabtree stared, looking very lost. 'I wish I knew, Inspector. I really do.'

It could have been some sudden surge that took him by surprise. He might not have been watching properly. Any number of things. Whatever the reason, Crabtree insisted that the lad should have been able to open the valve.

'Could it have stuck? Jammed?'

The man shook his head. 'I only had it apart a week ago. It was fine.'

The error had been human. So often the case. A fire started by a cigarette or tobacco from a pipe. Carelessness, someone not paying attention.

'I'll put all that in my report.'

'It won't bring him back, will it?' Crabtree said. His voice was dull.

'No.'

'He was a good lad, too. Serious about his work.'

'It's a bad thing to happen, so soon after your son.'

He saw the man stiffen, sensed the rise of his defences.

'That's different. Completely different.'

Crabtree was hiding something; Reed was positive of that now. But how could he pry out the secrets?

'I know that Arthur's alive,' the inspector said, 'but he's going to have to live with his injuries for the rest of his days. Every time he looks in the mirror—'

Crabtree spat on the ground. 'Do you think I don't know that?'

'And you don't have any idea why it happened?'

The man shook his head. Whatever had been in the air had vanished, broken.

'Thank you,' Reed said and walked away.

'Why don't you just ask Willie Calder who this J.D. is, sir?' Ash placed the papers on the desk. 'I've been through all that and I don't have a clue. I've thought and thought and I can't come up with anyone who fits the bill.'

The man from Henry White's pages was a shadow. Dangerous, with a temper, and violent, from the way he was described. And there was the real problem: if he was that bad, the police should have known about him. But they should have had an eye on so many things. How had Calder managed to go free and unnoticed, for so long?

Harper prided himself on what he knew about the job. But the more he saw, the more he realized that he understood nothing. He barely skimmed the surface. Maybe that was something to bring up at the meeting. How could they learn more about all the criminals in Leeds?

'Perhaps I will.' He stood and stretched his back. Too many hours sitting in a chair; he wasn't used to it. At least he'd get a little fresh air walking to the meeting at the Town Hall. The rain had stopped. Just enough time for a cup of tea in a café first.

As he shrugged into his overcoat, Harper said, 'Come with me, and you can tell me about Detective Constable Conway, since you think he's so good.'

THIRTEEN

'He's hiding something,' Reed said, lighting a cigarette. 'As soon as I brought up the subject of his son, it was like a window closed.' He studied Ash's face. 'Do you know what I mean?'

'All too well, sir,' the sergeant said with a nod. He had tea and a bun in front of him, leftover stock that Elizabeth had brought home that afternoon from the shop. She'd left the pair of them in the kitchen to talk. 'Did you find your answers about the explosion?'

'Yes.' Much good it did him, though.

'Any ideas about what Crabtree's not telling us, sir?'

'No. How about you? Did you talk to his wife?'

'She wasn't there. But I had an interesting conversation or two in the end.' He explained what he'd learned. 'Thank you for the time, sir.'

'I hear you're going to be an inspector yourself soon.'

The sergeant shrugged. 'Maybe. I'm not about to jinx it.'

At the front door they shook hands. Reed watched as Ash vanished into the evening.

'You look dead to the world,' Annabelle said. 'Sit yourself down. Have you eaten yet?'

He was exhausted. The meeting had dragged on until six, then he'd returned to Millgarth to finish the day's work. Now, as he sat in the parlour, the grandfather clock began to strike nine.

Harper felt numb from meetings and dealing with forms and reports. How had Kendall stood it for so long? He stirred as she put a cold slice of meat and potato pie on the table.

'Is Mary asleep?' Harper asked. Even as he spoke, he knew it was a stupid question.

'She wondered where you were.'

'Tell me something good,' he said with a weary sigh.

'I'm speaking on Saturday evening.' She fidgeted with a

notebook, glancing through the pages. 'I've been trying to work out what to say. I thought I had it, then Maguire's funeral made me think again.' Annabelle gave a deep shrug. 'So I'm back to square one. I'll get there.'

'It made me think, too, seeing all those people waiting for his coffin to pass.' He stirred his tea and took a sip. 'He did more good than he could ever know.' Harper reached out and took her hand. 'Maybe you will, too.'

She chuckled and shook her head. 'I'm just a woman with a big gob. The only thing I'm likely to do is make enemies because I speak out.'

He knew all about the insults and the threats she'd received. No worse than many other women who were in favour of the vote, she said. But they weren't his wife . . . Twice he'd gone to visit men who'd been foolish enough to put their addresses on the damning letters they sent. Timid, frightened men when he knocked on their doors. He hadn't needed to say much to send them scurrying.

'People round here look up to you, you know,' he said.

'Give over.' But the words made her blush, her face reddening in the light from the gas mantles. 'They've got more sense than that. You don't know what you're talking about.'

But he did, Harper thought later as they lay in bed. People came to talk to her as if she knew things they didn't. For advice, to be pointed in the right direction. Annabelle gave a small snore and turned over, away from him. He smiled in the darkness.

'Good morning, Superintendent.'

Harper looked around, expecting to see Kendall enter. But there was no one else, only him. The new rank hadn't sunk in yet. It wasn't real, it wasn't attainable.

Yet there it was. Superintendent T. Harper, the black letters fresh on the door of his office.

More work waiting for him. A glance told him it was all routine, nothing urgent among all the papers. He'd made a decision as he sat on the tram: most things could wait until he found Henry White's killer. Only then would he be ready for this new job.

*   *   *

'Well, Willie?'

Calder sat and stared at the envelope on the table. All around them the sounds of the jail echoed.

Harper had brought him a packet of Woodbines. They'd vanished into Calder's pocket with barely a nod. The dapper man they'd arrested was long gone. He was dirty now, as feral the rest of them. He could have been here a few years, not just a few days.

'Well what?'

'Go on. Open it,' Harper said. Reluctantly, the man obeyed, tipping out the papers and the silver. His eyes widened at the flask and the cigarette case. He picked them up, stroked and caressed them before taking out his spectacles and inspecting them closely.

'Beautiful work,' he said admiringly. 'So smooth.'

'Where are they from?'

'No idea.' Calder's voice was dreamy, lost in the objects, turning them over and over before finally setting them down and glancing at the papers. 'What's all this, anyway?'

'Your legacy,' Harper told him. 'Everything Henry left you.'

'It's not going to do me much good in here.'

'Read those. If you can identify J.D., and you're right, I might have a word with the judge.' He sniffed the air; old sweat, vomit, desperation. 'Less time in here for you.' He saw hope start to flicker in the man's eyes. After a few days in Armley, an offer like that would be a big temptation. 'I'll come back in the morning. See if you have any answers for me.' He slid the silver into his pocket, noticing the way Calder's eyes followed the items. 'Who knows, Willie, if you help me enough perhaps I'll let you keep these when you get out.'

White had left the papers for a reason. He'd expected Calder to understand them. Wait and see, he told himself. It was only one day. Wait and see. At least he'd done something worthwhile today. Now he could go back to his desk with a clear conscience.

'Begging your pardon, sir,' Sergeant Tollman said as he knocked on the office door, 'but there's a telephone call for you.'

Harper hated the instrument. He knew how useful it could be, but it never felt right to him. More than that, his hearing made

it awkward to follow a voice on the crackling, faint line. And it
never brought good news.

'Who is it?' Harper asked. He glanced at the clock. Almost
six. A little while longer and he'd go home.

'The governor at Armley jail, sir. Says it's urgent.'

He felt fear, cold, clammy, creeping up his spine.

'Hello?' He shouted into the instrument, the receiver pressed
hard against his good ear.

'Superintendent? You were out here today to visit one of the
prisoners.'

'That's right. Calder. What's happened?'

There was only one reason Governor Hobson would be doing
this. He gripped the telephone so hard his knuckles turned white
and felt the fear rise in his belly.

A small hesitation. 'Someone's murdered him, Mr Harper. One
of the guards found him in his cell an hour ago.'

Too many thoughts in his head. A roar, a tangle of them.

'How?'

'He was stabbed.' He could hear the tremor in Hobson's voice.

'I'll be there as soon as I can.'

The hackney jounced and rattled along the cobbles on the
way to Armley. He stared out at the endless streets that stretched
into the distance. An ocean of them, more than he could ever
count.

How could it have happened? Cell doors were locked. Calder
should have been safe enough. He knew the jail was like any
other place. It was violent, it had a pecking order. But Willie
hadn't been in long enough to make enemies. Something else
was going on.

There'd be an inquiry once the investigation was done. The
governor would be blamed, of course.

Too late for poor Willie, though.

Hobson was terrified, his face pale and empty. His hands were
shaking and he seemed to shrink into his suit as he led the way
down the corridor. Behind their doors, the prisoners shouted,
baying like they could scent death. The air was so thick with
tension he felt he could slice it.

The guards stood, grim-faced and alert, holding on to their

cudgels. One was posted outside a thick metal door, pushing it open as the governor approached.

Calder lay on his back, sightless eyes gazing up to the ceiling. His mouth was pulled back in a rictus grin; none of the peace of death for him. When Harper touched his skin there was still a little warmth and give in it. Blood pooled on the bunk under the body, soaked into the ticking of the mattress. A single wound, above and from the front.

'Right. Tell me what you know,' he said as he looked around the cell.

'I came to check on him, sir.' The guard stood to attention as he spoke. 'We keep them locked away most of the time.'

'How long ago was all this?' He looked on the table, knelt on the floor to examine under the bunk.

'About an hour and a half, sir.' He hesitated. 'The door wasn't locked. I found the prisoner like this and rang the alarm.'

'Who's in this wing? What kind of prisoners?'

'It's mostly men on remand along this corridor,' the governor replied. 'Every cell door should have been locked.'

Harper stood, eyes moving around the room. No papers. The only places they could be were under the body or beneath the mattress.

'Give me a hand to roll him,' he ordered the guard. Plenty of blood, but no notes. Not folded away in the dead man's pockets either. His mind was racing as he asked questions. Had Willie been killed for some scribbling on scraps of paper? Who would even know he had them?

'Who could have arranged for this door to be unlocked?' Harper said.

'The only one was the guard on duty,' Hobson replied. 'His shift ended at three. I've sent someone to fetch him.'

'Right. I want to question the other prisoners along this corridor and I want every cell in the wing searched. Some papers are missing.'

A procession of men came in and out of the room he'd commandeered. Every single one of them had been deaf, dumb, blind while the killing happened. Of course. No one was going to grass.

Hobson knocked on the door. Another man stood behind him: young, with a thick head of dark hair and heavy whiskers, an intent expression on a thin face.

'The guard wasn't at his lodgings,' the governor said quietly. 'The landlady said he'd packed a bag and left.' He looked like someone whose world had collapsed.

'I took a rummage through his room, sir.' The young man took over. 'Nothing to say where he might be going. Not much of anything. I've sent a message to the railway station with a description. They'll keep an eye out for him if he hasn't already left.'

Impressive, he thought. Someone who didn't need to be prompted into action.

'Very good, Mr . . .'

'Conway, sir. Detective Constable Conway, D Division. The jail is part of our manor.' He gave a smile.

Conway? It took him a second; the man Ash had recommended for the sergeant's job. Definitely a good choice.

'Let me bring you up to speed.' He told Conway everything he knew. The man listened carefully, asking a few thoughtful questions.

'What's so important about these papers, sir?'

'I don't know. I was hoping Willie could tell me. I told him I'd come back in the morning after he'd read everything.'

It hit him. The whole thing was an echo of Henry White. Harper had given him a day, too. And both men stabbed to death before they could tell him what he needed to know.

'. . . after they put the body in the mortuary.'

'Pardon?' Thinking, or his ear was tired. Whatever the cause, he'd missed what Conway said.

'I'll search the cell thoroughly once the body's gone, sir.'

The young man's manner reminded him of the way he'd once been. Full of energy, eager, with something to prove. Only ten minutes together and he was already certain the lad had a good future at Millgarth.

'You get on with it. Report on my desk in the morning. Find out everything about this guard.'

'Yes, sir.'

'Still want to work for me, Conway?'

The man grinned. 'I think it would be good, sir.'

'So do I. I'll be glad to have you.'

He knew he'd gone home and slept, but he scarcely recalled it. By seven he was back in his office, gazing out of the window at the city awakening.

Conway had been as good as his word. The report was waiting. The man must have worked all hours to complete it. But there was nothing hopeful inside.

The guard's name was Claude Talbot. He'd only worked at the jail for a few months, kept himself to himself, no real friends at work. Lodged at the far end of Armley, and his landlady barely seemed to recall him. Only two weeks in the house; she didn't know where he'd lived before that. He'd returned home from his shift, packed a bag and left. No word, simply vanished.

A flurry of questions came to mind. Had anyone come to the jail to see Talbot or visited him before work? Had anyone sent him a note? Harper scrawled in the margins of the pages and wondered if they'd find any answers.

'I have a job for you,' he told Ash when the sergeant arrived.

'Yes, sir.' He unfolded the newspaper. Calder's murder was the headline, of course. A killing in jail was meat and drink to journalists. They'd cobbled together a story. Two facts, bolstered by plenty of fantasy and speculation. Harper shook his head in disgust.

'Talk to Calder's wife. She's locked up in the women's wing. By now she's probably frantic. Give her some assurance. I already told the governor, I want her well guarded all the time. See if she can give you any reason for someone taking a knife to her husband.'

'I will.'

'I'll be up there later myself. Your friend Conway's working on it, too.'

Ash beamed. 'He's a good lad, isn't he, sir?'

'Seems very competent.'

Alone, the superintendent took a fresh sheet of paper and wrote the names of everyone involved in the case, seeing how they connected. Maybe he'd find something in there . . .

FOURTEEN

Three hours later he still had his head down, concentrating on the work. The fist knocking on the door dragged his head up, then made him stand quickly. Kendall, gaunt as death and with a face that was almost white. Harper sprang forward and helped him into a chair. Dear God, he thought, could a few days have done so much?

'Sorry, Tom,' he said breathlessly, fanning himself with his top hat. 'I came into town and I suddenly had a bit of a turn.'

'You just sit there,' Harper told him. 'I'll fetch a glass of water.'

By the time he returned, he'd given orders to summon a doctor.

'Thank you.' Kendall gave a weak smile. 'I just ran out of puff.'

He took a sip of water and began to cough, bending forward and gasping for breath, holding up one hand, pretending he was fine as he clutched Harper's arm with the other.

'Talk to me, Tom,' he said when he could speak again. 'Tell me what's going on here.'

One eye on the door, Harper brought him up to date on the cases, finishing with the murder of Willie Calder.

'You must have seen it in the paper.'

Kendall nodded. 'Doesn't mean I believe a single word.' He tried to laugh then sucked in some air and sat back, sweat on his forehead. 'This guard. Does he have a record?'

'No.' It was one of the first things he'd checked this morning.

'Find out where he worked before.'

Harper stood back as Tollman escorted the doctor into the office. The physician reached into his leather bag, taking out a magnifying glass and a stethoscope. The examination took less than a minute.

'He needs to be in hospital now.' It was a blunt statement. Kendall looked up helplessly. He knew the truth just as well as the doctor and he was too tired to argue.

'I want a hackney to take him to the infirmary.' He stood by the front desk, counting tasks off on his fingers. 'Send a constable to see Mrs Kendall and take her to him. And someone to inform the Chief Constable.'

'Right away, sir,' Tollman said. 'Should I have someone accompany him to the hospital?'

'I'll do it.' The man had watched over him when he was a green new detective. This was the least he could do in return.

It was like lifting an invalid into the cab, weightless, nothing more than skin and bone. They sat and stared out of the window as the horse trotted along the Headrow, weaving in and out of carts.

He could feel his heart thudding, but as he glanced across, the older man seemed content. Almost serene.

'We'll have you looked after in no time.'

'Don't you worry about me, Tom,' Kendall said softly. He stayed quiet for almost a minute. 'That guard at the prison. If you look back far enough I bet you'll find he crossed paths with whoever paid him.'

'Yes.' More digging, more questions and shoe leather. But that was how the job worked.

Ten minutes after they reached the infirmary Kendall had been examined and was on his way to a bed on the ward. He submitted without argument: a sure sign he was ill. Harper waited until the man was comfortable, then went outside and hailed a cab to go to Armley.

Reed finished his report on the explosion, blotting the ink carefully. He was back in the rhythm of work, proud to button up the uniform in the morning and see the admiring stares on the tram into town.

Two copies: one for the fire brigade records, the other for the owner of the factory. What he did with it was up to him; Reed had given his assessment and recommendations. His judgement: Jack Crabtree had no blame for the blast. It had either been a pure accident or due to negligence by Charlie Clay, the lad left in charge; it was impossible to know which.

He sat back, thinking. Maybe, if the boiler hadn't blown up, Crabtree would have revealed more. For a moment he'd seemed on the verge. Afterwards, when Reed returned, that moment had passed. He'd tried; he'd failed. With a sigh he pushed the file to one side and took the next one from the pile. A suspicious blaze in Beeston.

It was the first time he'd seen Mrs Calder since he arrested the couple at the house in Headingley. The short time in jail had stripped away her civilized surface. All the planes of her face were sharp as flint, her eyes hard, hair greasy. The blue dress, the prison uniform, was smudged with dirt, the long apron a grubby off-white.

She'd been crying, her eyes red and damp. Ash sat with her, talking quietly. She nodded.

Harper remained in the corridor, watching through the glass in the door. Better to leave it to the sergeant. He'd established a rapport; there was no sense barging in and ruining that.

He walked quietly away, back to the governor's office. Hobson had willingly abandoned it to the murder investigation. Conway sat at a desk, poring over a prisoner's statement.

'Any leads?'

'Not that you'd notice, sir.' He took out a packet of Woodbines and lit one, watching the stream of smoke rise towards the ceiling. 'Our search came up with four homemade knives, even a still hidden away at the back of the laundry room. But not Calder's papers. They seem to have vanished.' He frowned and ran his tongue around the inside of his mouth. 'How would anyone know he even had them? You only brought them yesterday afternoon. Did you tell anyone?'

'No.'

'It seems that Talbot knew. Someone gave him order to kill and to take them.'

Harper had asked himself the same question.

'He must have seen Willie with them. Maybe Calder boasted they'd make him rich or get him out of jail.'

Conway frowned. 'Talbot must have contacted someone. I've talked to the others who were on shift with him. According to them, he disappeared for a quarter of an hour.'

Long enough to send a message. To whom, though? Conway was doing a good job. The lad could think on his feet. He'd make an excellent sergeant. And with Ash as inspector he'd have the best men in the city working for him.

'Keep on it. Where's the body?'

'They took him to Hunslet this morning, sir.'

Down to King's Kingdom for the post-mortem. He looked around. There was nothing useful he could do at the prison. Ash and Conway seemed to have it all in hand; they were thorough.

'I'll leave you to it. Report to Millgarth this afternoon.'

Another hackney ride, bouncing and bucking, smelling the thick industrial stink of Leeds. Plenty of muck, in the air and in the river. But that meant lots of brass, at least for a few men.

Dr King stopped in mid-cut to stare at him. His apron was bloody, grey hair wild, and he had a cigar clamped between his lips.

'You're a superintendent now, eh?'

'I'm not quite sure I believe it myself,' Harper told him.

'I remember when you were a constable and here for the first time.' He moved the cigar to the other corner of his mouth. 'Shouldn't you have someone else attending this?'

'I was there when it all began. I want to see it through.'

'Laudable, laudable.' He wiped his hands on some grubby linen and ran his fingers inside the high collar. 'And here he is.'

Naked, beyond help, Willie Calder lay on the table. The stab wound on his chest was livid and red. His torso had been opened from throat to groin, the flesh clamped back.

'I only saw one wound last night.'

'That's all there is,' King said. 'It doesn't take more than that. There's nothing unusual about him from my examination. If you're hoping for clues, you'll go away empty-handed.'

'Nothing hidden away on his body?' It was unlikely; still, he had to ask.

King stared at him sharply. 'On his body? Don't be bloody ridiculous, laddie. Take a look at him. Of course there's not. He didn't have anything in his pockets. Satisfied?'

'Yes,' Harper said reluctantly and the doctor shook his head.

'Now, if you've finished with your damn fool questions, I want to complete this and then carry on with the rest of my work.'

*   *   *

Late in the afternoon Tollman marched a bobby into his office to be disciplined. He'd been discovered in uniform in the back room of the Yorkshire Grey with a jug of beer and a prostitute. Robert MacDonald. His second offence: the year before he'd been found in a box at the People's Theatre with a different whore.

'What do you have to say for yourself?' the superintendent asked.

MacDonald stood sharp, at attention, looking straight ahead. 'I'm sorry, sir.'

'No, you're not,' Harper told him. 'You might be sorry you were caught, but that's all I can see.'

The man's eyes widened. The superintendent waited, but MacDonald had the sense to say nothing.

'Well? Anything else?'

'No, sir.'

'Then you're fined three days' wages. And the next time it happens you'll be sacked from the police.'

'Yes, sir.' He could see the fury on the man's face, the way he gritted his teeth before answering. 'Thank you, sir. It won't happen again.'

It would; he knew that. Another month, another year, MacDonald would be standing there again and he'd tell the man to turn in his uniform.

'Dismissed,' he said wearily.

By six his eyes felt gritty. He needed Ash and Conway here, to know what was going on at Armley. Waiting . . . it always seemed to be the worst part. Not knowing, impotent.

Finally, close to half past, the pair of them arrived. Conway took his time, glancing around the office for the first time then hanging up his heavy overcoat and bowler hat.

'What have you found out?'

'Mrs Calder was very helpful with a list of her husband's clients,' Ash said. 'People he bought from and the ones he sold the goods to.'

'That's a start. What about his murder?'

Ash sighed. 'She has no idea, sir. But she did say there were parts of his life he kept very secret from her. And she'd never heard of J.D.' He tapped his head. 'Willie kept everything up here, nothing written down.'

Damn it, he thought. 'That doesn't help us, does it?'

'I'm sorry, sir.'

He was being unreasonable; he knew it. But what he needed were answers, not brick walls.

'Mr Conway. What about you?'

'I've been hunting the guard, sir. If he's left Leeds through the railway station, no one's spotted him. The other guards at the jail don't know much about his life outside work.' The man smiled. 'But I might have something.'

'Go on.'

'I went to the place he worked before. An ironmonger in Farnley. Turns out he was let go for theft.'

Harper raised an eyebrow. 'They hired him as a guard at the prison after that?'

'He didn't mention it when he applied, sir, and no one checked.'

Dear God, Harper thought. Not that Leeds City Police were much better; it appeared they'd take almost anyone, too.

'How does that help us?'

'The ironmonger told me where Talbot worked before that.' His eyes twinkled. 'Turns out he had a job with a silversmith.'

'What?' The hair rose on the back of his neck. 'Where?'

Conway's expression darkened. 'That's where we hit a wall, sir. It was an old chap. He died. That's why Talbot was looking for another job.' Harper opened his mouth to speak, but the man continued. 'I've checked, sir. It's the truth; the silversmith died and the business closed. Nothing suspicious about the way he went.'

If Talbot was stealing silver from his employer, he might have known Calder and Henry White. *If*. He sighed.

'Right, gentlemen. Well done.' He nodded at Ash. 'Get that list copied and out to every division. I want all those men brought in for questioning.'

'Yes, sir.'

Harper turned to Conway. 'See if you can track down any relatives of that silversmith. Did he talk about the business, any suspicions about Talbot? You know how to do it.'

'I will, sir.'

'Start tomorrow,' he ordered. Nothing was going to bring Calder back, and Henry White was in the ground, food for the worms. A few more hours wouldn't make any difference. He slid two letters from his drawer and pushed them across his desk. 'From now on it's Inspector Ash and Sergeant Conway. Congratulations, gentlemen.'

It was a pleasure to see them both beam so widely and shake hands. Harper recalled the way he'd been when he became a sergeant, then an inspector. Overjoyed but wary. Scarcely able to believe it at first, like each new rank was a suit of clothes he still had to grow into.

It felt exactly the same now. Awkward and uncomfortable.

'Go home,' he told them. 'Get some rest.'

He watched them leave together, grinning and happy. They both deserved it. Now he had a visit to make before he climbed the stairs at the Victoria.

FIFTEEN

I n the hospital, Mrs Kendall sat beside the bed. The only sound was the quick clack of her knitting needles as she worked, her hands moving rapidly.

He tapped lightly on the door and she paused, looking up, then smiling.

'Hello, Tom. It's good of you to come down.'

Kendall was sleeping. All the agitation had fallen away from his face; he looked younger, carefree. But his breathing was so slight that Harper had to watch to be certain the chest rose and fell.

'How is he?'

'Not so well.' She reached out and stroked the back of her husband's hand. 'The doctor gave him something to help him rest. They won't come out and say it, but I don't think it'll be long now.' She gave a wan smile. 'I think it was the work that was keeping him going.'

'Is there anything I can do?'

She shook her head. 'Just come and see him when he's awake. Tell him what's going on at the station. That'll raise his spirits.'

'What about you?'

'We're prepared. We've known about this for months.'

It wasn't the answer he expected. Not even one that told him much. But it was all she was going to offer. He wished her goodnight and walked back down the corridor, out into the evening.

'Penny for them.'

'What?' Reed blinked, realizing he'd been staring at nothing.

'You were miles away,' Elizabeth said. She had the account book for the bakeries open in front of her, copying numbers from a small pile of receipts.

'Just thinking.' He took a sip of tea. Stone cold. 'About the acid attack.'

She put down the pen and blotted the page. 'I went to see Annie again today.'

'How is she?'

'Mending. Well, her body is, at least,' Elizabeth added after a moment. 'Do you remember how she used to be?' He shook his head; he'd never really known the girl. 'Always liked to laugh, ready to smile. Now it's hard to get a word out of her. Do you know what she told me?'

'What?'

'She said she felt like a monster. That's such a horrible thing for a girl to say. God, Billy, she's only thirteen. I just wanted to hug her and never let her go. She's coming back to work next week.'

'What? Serving people?' Reed asked, surprised.

'In the back, out of sight.'

'Do you think she's ready?'

'She says she is. The girls will look after her. And it'll be better than just sitting at home and brooding.'

'I feel I let her down. I haven't found out who did it.'

'You did your best.' Her face softened. 'That's all anyone can ask.'

But failure rankled. It always had, it always would.

'I haven't given up, you know,' he said impulsively.

Elizabeth looked at him quizzically. 'But you're back on the job, Billy love. Where are you going to find the time? And didn't you say Ash is working on it?'

'He can't do everything on his own.'

She hesitated before gently asking, 'Do you think it'll make a difference to Annie?'

He didn't understand. 'What do you mean?'

'Even if you find out who did it, it's not going to change the rest of her life, will it? And if it ends up in court she'll have to be there, in front of everyone.'

He didn't understand. 'You don't want it solved? But the Crabtree boy—'

'Is disfigured, too.' She looked at him with affection. 'I know. He's going to have to learn how to deal with life, the same as her. Knowing who did it and why isn't going to put things back the way they were.'

'It was a crime, the man who did it has to pay for that.'

'Yes,' she agreed solemnly. 'He does. But I wonder about the price of it all.' She shook her head. 'Maybe I'm wrong.' It was her way of making peace, ending a discussion on a hopeful note.

'We'll see.'

But now he could feel the grim determination rising again. He'd find out who threw that acid. No one respected failure.

Harper adjusted his tie as he stared in the mirror. He was wearing his best suit, the beautiful grey one Annabelle had given him for their first Christmas together. Four years on and it was a little snug around the waist, but Moishe Cohen's wonderful stitching and the quality of the cloth still made it perfect.

He heard the rustle of her dress as she came up behind him and ruffled his hair, grinning.

'I was very glad to see you weren't neglecting your duties at home last night, Superintendent.'

'Simply serving the public, ma'am.'

'You'd better not be serving all the public that enthusiastically,' she warned. But her eyes sparkled.

'Da?' A small hand tugged at his trouser leg. Mary was dressed, her hair in ringlets, gazing up at him.

'What is it, sweetheart?'

'Why do you wear that?' She mimicked tying a tie. He looked at Annabelle. She shrugged, looking amused as she waited for his answer.

'That's how men dress,' he told her. 'You and your mam, you wear dresses, don't you?' The girl nodded. 'Men wear suits and shirts and ties.'

'But *why*, Da?'

'Because that's the way it's always been.' It was the only answer he could give her; he was already late. For all he knew, it was correct. He kissed the top of Mary's head, then Annabelle's lips, and left for work.

A hint of blue off to the east, but a chill breeze was whipping down from the north, enough to make him glad of his heavy overcoat. Spring hadn't arrived yet. Walking down from the tram stop on Vicar Lane, he gave a newsboy a penny ha'penny for a copy of the Post. But as soon as he saw the headline, he stopped in the middle of the pavement.

POLICE STUMPED ON JAIL MURDER

It was true, but he didn't want it all over the front page of the newspaper. Harper crumpled it into his fist and marched to Millgarth.

Ash and Conway were in the office, standing by the fireplace and warming themselves.

'In my office,' Harper said.

Once the pair of them were seated, he held up the paper. He could feel the fury roaring through his veins.

'Well?'

'It wasn't me, sir,' Ash said, and then Harper could see the hurt in his eyes. Stupid. He knew better; Ash would never betray the force. Harper turned to stare at Conway.

'I haven't spoken to anyone about it, sir,' he said quietly. 'And I'd never talk to reporters.'

'Someone has. Go and see Governor Hobson at Armley. I want to know who spoke and I want them punished. Understood?'

'Report back here at five,' he told them.

The sergeant left, but Inspector Ash hung back.

'This acid-throwing case, sir.'

With the murder of Willie Calder it had slipped to the back of his mind.

'What about it?'

'It deserves some time, too, sir.'

He was right. Two children hurt, damage that they'd carry for the rest of their lives. It was rare for Ash to request anything.

Harper looked into the dark eyes. 'Fine. Spend the morning on Calder, this afternoon on the acid.'

'Thank you, sir.'

'I want you here at noon to bring me up to date.'

'Yes, sir.' A contented smile under the moustache. 'Gladly.'

He did an hour's work, treading water in the sea of paper, then pulled on his overcoat and began walking along the Headrow.

Kendall was sitting up in his bed, alert, almost back to his old self.

'Tom.' He cocked his head. 'Shouldn't you be in your office, Superintendent?'

'I'll call this my charity work,' Harper said with a grin. 'You're looking better.'

'It passed.' He breathed out slowly. 'Took long enough. Thank you for what you did. I've never felt like that before. At least they've said I can go home later today.'

'I'm glad.' The day before he'd wondered if Kendall would make it out of the infirmary alive, but now . . . The transformation had been so huge, so fast. The kind of thing to make him hope the man might defy all the doctors' expectations.

'How are your cases?'

Of course Kendall would think about that. He brought the *Post* from his pocket and unfolded it on the bed.

'Nowhere.'

He waited as the man read.

'What are you doing about it?' Kendall asked. His voice was grave.

'I sent someone up to Armley to find out who talked. I know it wasn't Ash, and I'm sure it wasn't the new man we have.'

'What makes you certain?'

'Ash recommended him.' A nod; it was enough.

Kendall's bony fingers tapped the newspaper. 'I can see why

you ducked out of the office. Have the reporters been hounding you?'

'Not yet.' He hadn't even thought about that. They'd come like wolves, he was sure.

'They will. You might as well get used to it.'

'I can ignore them.'

Kendall shook his head. 'Do you want some advice, Tom?'

'Please.' So much to bloody learn.

'Give them a few minutes. Talk, but don't say anything – and make sure it's nothing that can be twisted.'

Harper laughed. It seemed so ridiculous.

'I know it has nothing to do with policing, but it's all part of your job now,' Kendall told him. 'You need to get used to the politics.'

Once again, he wondered at the wisdom of taking the promotion. The only thing he gained was rank; it seemed he'd lost everything else.

'You might even like it in time,' Kendall told him. 'Just make sure you spend more time solving crimes than I did.' He gave a rueful smile. 'That's my only regret.'

'Don't you worry about that.' He fidgeted with his hat, moving it round in his hands. 'And I should get back to work.'

'Thank you for coming, Tom. Even more for the other day.'

A quick handshake, and he was gone.

'I might have something, sir,' Ash said.

'Tell me about it over some dinner.'

Now they were in the George on Lower Briggate, feeling the building shake every few minutes as trains rattled by on the viaduct.

He'd returned to Millgarth to find reporters for the *Post* and the *Mercury* waiting. He did what Kendall advised and surrendered a few minutes to them. A few anodyne statements, a pair of bland answers, and they left, satisfied.

'What have you found?' he asked Ash after the waiter brought his liver and onions.

'I've been talking to a few of those men Mrs Calder named, sir.' Ash cut into his meat pie and gravy pooled on the plate. 'Asked them about anyone named J.D.'

'Well?' Harper wondered hopefully.

'Nothing. One of them did know Henry White. And Talbot, the guard. By name. He even says he saw them together a few times.'

That was a big step forward. 'Do you believe him?'

Ash nodded. 'I was very careful with my questions, sir. The only way he could have answered was if he really did know.'

'Then that's another piece of the puzzle.' Slowly, very slowly, things were beginning to build.

'Still doesn't help us find the killer, does it, sir?'

'Not yet.' He exhaled slowly, frustrated. 'How can someone called J.D. be involved in this and we have no idea who he is? How can he stay that deep in the shadows?'

'Maybe Sergeant Conway can find out at Armley.'

'Let's hope so.'

He felt more hopeful. A pale sun had come out, there was early spring warmth on his face, and he was beginning to believe that, bit by bit, they could uncover the murderer.

Harper pushed open the door of the station and stopped suddenly. The place was silent. At first he thought it must be his hearing. But where was Tollman? No one behind the desk.

The telephone began to ring, the bell loud and shrill. No one rushed to answer it. Eventually it fell silent.

He stood, scarcely daring to breathe.

Careful not to make a sound, Harper moved around the counter, grabbing the truncheon the sergeant kept there. He looped the strap over his wrist and fitted his fingers around the hard wood.

Harper edged down the corridor, straining to listen. His palms were slick with sweat. He could feel the clammy dampness on his back. Something was wrong. Dangerously wrong.

He eased a door open with his fingertips, watching it glide away from him. Nothing. His heart beat a tattoo in his chest. A second door. Nobody there. Next, the detectives' room. He waited, his mouth dry, trying to swallow, hand resting on the knob. A twist, a sharp turn and he pushed it wide open.

Just enough time to twist himself off to the side, out of the way. The shotgun blast was so loud it made his bad ear ring.

Plaster fell. No wounds he could feel. Nothing screamed with pain as he scrambled to his feet and charged into the room.

The man had the gun broken open, fumbling as he tried to put in a fresh cartridge. Harper brought his truncheon down hard. The shotgun fell as the man screamed and clutched his hands. Before he could do anything Harper hit him again, a swift crack on the skull. He watched as the man crumpled to the floor.

It seemed that he'd hardly done a thing, barely moved but as he turned the man over and clicked the handcuffs closed on his wrists, Harper was panting as if he'd run a mile, hands shaking. He knew the man's face: Constable MacDonald, the bobby he'd disciplined the day before, reeking of gin.

Where were the men? What had MacDonald done to them?

The noise of the shot still filled his ears as he hurried through the station. Tollman and another officer were locked in a cell downstairs. A bruise blossomed over the sergeant's eye. He held his handkerchief to a cut on his forehead.

'Heard the shot, sir.' His voice was hoarse, creaking. 'I thought he'd got you.'

'No such luck. It'll take more than that.' Harper grinned. 'Are you all right?'

'He took me by surprise.' It was more apology than explanation. 'Walked in and pulled his gun.'

The constable helped him to his feet as Harper turned the key and opened the door. The sergeant looked old and unsteady.

'Don't worry, he won't be giving you any more trouble.' He was still breathing hard, scared to think about what had happened. 'Get him down here,' he told the constable. 'Then I want a doctor in to look at Mr Tollman and the prisoner. In that order.' He thought for a moment. 'And once you've done that, make us all a cup of tea.'

'Yes, sir.' He dashed off.

Tollman sat on the bunk in the cell, too worn to move.

'Need a hand?'

'If you don't mind, sir.'

Harper held him by the arm, steadying him as he climbed the stairs and returned to the front desk. He could hear the bobby trying to move the man in handcuffs.

'Just drag him,' he yelled. Then, to Tollman,

'MacDonald. Who'd have credited it?'

'I never expected that from him,' Tollman admitted. 'He wasn't a good copper, but . . .'

Anger, drink. A grievance. Revenge on those who'd caused him pain. It had happened before, although that was usually bobbies caught out on their beats and given a kicking. Never at a police station. And never a man with a gun.

'Times are changing,' Tollman said with regret. 'And not for the better.'

All he could do was nod his head in agreement.

'Do you want to go home?' Harper asked.

'I'll be fine, sir.' He managed a grin. 'Might be more than you can say for MacDonald by the time he reaches court.'

He inspected the damage in the passage. The shot had taken chunks of plaster from the wall. He knew exactly how lucky he'd been. Even a hair slower, he'd be on the floor now, his life bleeding away.

Harper shivered. Too close. Far too close. Christ. He swept tiny pieces of debris from his hair and clothes. His best suit, as well. At least it wasn't ruined; that was about the only good thing from the business. Annabelle would never have forgiven him.

SIXTEEN

He wrote his report and sent it to the chief constable. Workmen would arrive in the morning to repair the wall and the door to the detectives' room. As good as new, at least on the surface. Dive below that and nothing could ever be the same again. Everyone who walked into Millgarth would be a suspect. No copper would ever feel completely free or safe in the station.

The reporters had been back, of course. He'd left Tollman to deal with them. But one person he hadn't been able to keep out was Annabelle. She stormed through the door, eyes blazing with anger and fear, stopping short when she saw him.

'Someone came into the Victoria and told me. I took a hackney straight down.' She held him at arms' length, eyeing him up and down. 'Are you hurt?'

'No.' He wasn't going to say more than that. She didn't need to know exactly how lucky he'd been. 'Where's Mary?'

'I left her with Ellen.' She took a breath. 'I didn't want to bring her in case . . .' She hugged him close and he stroked her back, feeling the fine wool of her jacket, smelling her faint perfume. A little of the hearing had returned in his bad ear; it was no worse than before, as far as he could judge. That alone felt like a miracle. 'For God's sake, Tom. I was that worried about you.'

'Not a scratch,' he whispered. In more than fifteen years on the force, this was the closest he'd come to death. And he'd still managed to walk away without a graze.

'I thought being a superintendent would make you safer,' Annabelle said and he began to laugh. It was so ridiculous. She was right; behind a desk he should have been in no danger. Instead, it had come to him. Only restlessness and sheer luck had saved him. He shook his head, amazed by the good fortune of it all.

'Would Ellen mind looking after Mary for a few hours, do you think?' he asked suddenly.

'I daresay she'd enjoy it.' Annabelle eyed him suspiciously. 'Why?'

'I'll meet you in front of the Grand Pygmalion at six and take you out.'

Her eyes narrowed.

'What are you up to, Tom Harper?'

'I'm alive,' he told her. 'I'm unhurt. I want to take my wife out to celebrate that.'

There was plenty to do first. The chief constable had telephoned; so had the mayor. The other stations had sent messengers, some on foot, some by bicycle, to check everything was truly well.

MacDonald was in a cell, shackled hand and foot. He'd come round with no problem after the doctor had seen him. Suffering from a little concussion and still drunk. But he'd be sober enough when he appeared in court. He wasn't likely to be a free man for many years.

Harper shuddered as the blast echoed through his mind. The

split-second he realized he was looking at a gun and dived away to the side.

'Bit of a to-do, sir?' Ash asked as he walked in. 'And you didn't invite me?'

'Just a visitor who decided to redecorate the station.'

Ash surveyed the damage. 'He hasn't done a very good job. I preferred it the way it was.'

'He's behind bars if you want to tell him.'

'I'm sure there are plenty already queueing up to do that.'

'I daresay.' He hadn't asked; he didn't want to know. As long as MacDonald could walk into court and the injuries didn't show, that was all he cared. The man deserved whatever he got. 'You spent the afternoon on the acid case?'

'Yes, sir.' He settled himself more comfortably on the chair. 'I had an interesting little natter with Mrs Crabtree.'

'Does she know who did it?'

'No. It's painful to see. She's torn apart.'

He could only imagine what it must be like. To have your child disfigured that way would be . . . he didn't possess the words to describe it.

'What, then?'

'It was more what she didn't say, really.' He paused, gathering his thoughts. 'I had the sense she was hinting at something but she daren't come out and say it.'

'Daren't?' he asked in surprise.

'To do with her husband.'

'What? She thinks he did it?' That was ridiculous.

Ash shook his head. 'That he caused it.' He paused and corrected himself. 'Or something he did caused it, anyway.'

Even if she came out and accused him, it would hold no weight; no court could force her to testify against him.

'Did she give you any idea what it is he's supposed to have done?' the superintendent asked. His interest was piqued.

'She began talking about the families that have left the church.'

'How do you mean? She wanted you to talk to them?'

'I think so, sir. I tried one of them but nobody was home. I'll see them both tomorrow.'

'Very good.'

He turned to Conway; the pair of them had arrived together. 'Tell me what you've learned at Armley.'

'Not much about Willie Calder, sir. I decided to look a bit harder at the guard.'

'I thought we already knew about his part,' Harper said.

'It seems he has a bit more of a past than we thought, sir. He was a bit of a lad when he was young. Did some thieving for a gang in Hunslet before he found a proper job. That's how he first met Henry White. He'd keep a little back for himself, go up to the Bank and flog it to Henry.' He paused and ran his tongue over his lips. 'There's a rumour he killed someone, too. About ten years ago.'

'Gossip or something more?' Harper asked. Talk was cheap and murder was rare.

'I couldn't find anything to back it up. He was probably just boasting to make himself sound big. You know how it is.'

'Yes.' If he had a conviction for everyone who was supposed to have committed murder there'd be no criminals left in Leeds. He saw Conway look nervously at Ash.

'Excuse me, sir, but are you all right?'

'Me?' he asked. 'I'm fine. Why?'

'It's just that your hands are shaking, sir.'

He looked down. The sergeant was right. It was slight; he hadn't even noticed. Christ, but how? He couldn't even feel it. He pressed his palms down on the desk.

'It seems I am,' he said, surprised. 'Perhaps we'd better call it a night, gentlemen. Back to it tomorrow.'

Alone, he stared, trying to will it to stop, but his body wouldn't obey. Shock, he decided. It would pass.

He was ten minutes late. She was waiting impatiently in front of Monteith's, the huge department store on Boar Lane. The Grand Pygmalion, people called it, four floors of everything a family could desire.

He'd hurried along the streets, weaving in and out of the crowds on their way home. Now she was looking at him with one eyebrow raised.

'What time do you call this?'

'Something came up as I was leaving. I'm sorry.' He'd spent

too long in the office, trying to keep his hands still. In the end he'd had to give up.

Annabelle was surrounded with bags, five that he saw.

'How could you buy so much?' he asked. 'You only had an hour and a half.'

'An hour and forty minutes,' she said. 'And never underestimate the things a woman can do, Tom Harper. You ought to know better than that by now.'

She had money, plenty of it. Her first husband had provided well for her and the Victoria brought in a pretty penny. The money from selling the bakeries was sitting in the bank. There was no reason for her not to splurge when the fancy took her. Annabelle picked up two of the bags.

'Count yourself lucky I don't make you take them all,' she said with a grin and a wink. 'Where are we going to celebrate, then?'

A glass of brandy helped, as they sat waiting in the chop house. She watched him, saying nothing until he'd finished and replaced it on the table.

'It's not the best way, you know.'

'What?' He thought he'd hidden it well.

'I've got eyes, Tom.' She kept her voice at a low hiss, loud enough for him to hear, but no one else. 'Look at you. You've got a palsy like an old man. And don't tell me it's nothing,' she warned before he could speak. 'There's not a speck of colour in your cheeks, either.'

He was ready to object, his pride stung. But he held his tongue. She was right, of course; it was pointless trying to keep anything from her.

'Yes.'

'I remember,' she began, then stopped for a few moments. 'Well, it was something that happened a long time ago. I thought it hadn't touched me, then the next day I couldn't stop crying. Same thing as you. It was shock.'

He listened to her, then asked, 'What was it that happened to you?'

'It doesn't matter,' she told him and looked away. 'It was years back. History.'

They ate and chattered about this and that. Very slowly, he felt the tension ebbing. When he glanced down as he ate his pudding, the shaking had stopped. He held up a hand.

'Steady,' he told her proudly.

'That's good.' She put her hand over his. 'Might take a little longer inside, though.'

He'd expected to catch a hackney home from the stand on Briggate, but she steered him further up the street. It was evening, but still busy, men and women shopping after work, some out for the evening.

Outside number seventy-six, a barker was shouting, trying to drum up business.

'Roll up, roll up, ladies and gentlemen! See two thousand, seven hundred and sixty pictures a minute pass before your naked eye! Real moving pictures at five scenes for a shilling!'

He'd heard about it; everybody had. The place had opened the month before, with crowds down to Duncan Street. Annabelle and Mary had been twice. He'd just never found the time, always caught up in work.

The sign in the window, sitting in front of the curtain, was hand-written: Issott's Kinetoscope Parlour. Inside, they sat on a bench, crowded up against ripe, sweating bodies. Harper remembered what the shop had been a few months before, a pork butcher. But all the thoughts vanished as the machine behind them started to whir.

'You remember that chap a few years ago?' she asked in the cab on the way home. 'Le Prince?'

He nodded. He recalled the disappearance and the fact that the man had made the first moving pictures, here in Leeds.

'Who'd have thought what would happen from all that, eh? Weren't those something, Tom?'

He didn't trust himself to speak. The films had just been short, but it didn't matter. He'd been right there, in the barber's shop, the razor so close he could still feel it on his cheeks, then in the public bar, ducking the blows from the brawl.

It had taken his breath away. It was . . . better than life. And for a few minutes he'd forgotten about fear. Nothing else had existed apart from those films.

'Now do you see why I was talking about them?' she asked as the cab moved along North Street with the clop of hooves on the cobbles.

'Yes.' He smiled. 'Next time I should go with you.'

'You see? I knew you'd learn. There's hope for you yet, Tom Harper.'

Reed ate supper with the family, not really hearing all the talk and gossip going on around him. Once the meal was done, the girls helping Elizabeth clear everything away, he went up to the bedroom and changed into an old, heavy suit and tied the laces on a pair of worn boots. No collar or tie.

'I'll be back later,' he shouted at the front door, hurrying along the street before she could say anything. She'd want to know what he was doing and he wasn't entirely certain himself. Spend time in a few pubs. Talk, listen. There was a secret about the Crabtrees.

The family was chapel; they'd never set foot in a public house. But rumours passed around, and a pub was always a good place to hear them.

An hour later he leaned against the bar in the Black Horse on Mabgate. He was no more than half a mile from home but it felt like a different world. All the workers off from their shift at the Hope foundry across the street, the smell of hot metal on their skin.

Reed was talking to a man with a powerful thirst, downing pints of beer like they were water.

'I've got a little lass meself,' the man said. 'Twelve year old. Working in the mill. I tell you, any man who tried anything with her, he'd not live to tell the tale.'

Reed wasn't even sure how the conversation had reached this point, but he let it carry him.

'Is that what you've heard, about men doing that?'

'About them as are supposed to believe in Jesus an' that.' The man stared at him, eyes not focusing even though his speech was clear enough. 'It's not right.'

'Anyone in particular?' Reed asked. He watched the man drain his glass. 'Another?'

'Aye, go on, then. Not heard no names, just people talking, you know.' He shrugged. 'No smoke without fire, though, is there. And they're all funny, these Holy Joes. Wouldn't put it past them.'

No evidence. No names. He tried other pubs, a few minutes in the City of Mabgate, up to the Fountain Head and the Cemetery Tavern on Beckett Street. But he didn't hear anything else. After two hours he'd had enough; time for home. Still, he had some food for thought. Something for tomorrow. With luck, he could give Ash what he needed to crack the case. That wouldn't be a failure at all.

SEVENTEEN

Superintendent Harper felt his heart thudding as he approached Millgarth. It was stupid, he told himself. He'd come here thousands of times and nothing had ever happened.

Now his palms were slick and his skin felt clammy. It was as if the pleasure of the films last night had never happened. At the door he hesitated, forcing himself to push down on the handle and enter. Tollman was behind the desk, large as life and twice as ugly. The gash and bruises stood out on his face.

'Good morning, sir.'

Harper exhaled slowly, letting himself return to normal, his pulse and his breathing slowing. There was still the reminder outside the detectives' room, the shattered plaster, the broken wood. Another day or so and that would all be gone and a new door hung. Only the memory would remain. At least he hadn't started shaking again. In a strange way, that had terrified him more than facing a shotgun.

He saw the papers piled on his desk and his mood turned grey. He knew he had to deal with them, at least the urgent ones. Meanwhile, it promised to be a sunny day outside, the sky a sweet, pale blue, not a cloud to be seen.

He was hard at work when Ash appeared with two cups of tea.

'Thought you might be ready for one, sir.'

He was, mouth as dry as if it was full of dust. But none of

the palpitations and fear he'd experienced as he approached the station. Lost in the routine, he'd managed to forget them.

'We need results on these murders.' He sipped, letting the liquid swirl around his tongue. 'There are two people dead, remember. It doesn't matter that the world won't miss them too much.'

'Yes, sir.'

'We need to find this guard, Talbot. And we need to discover who the hell this J.D. is that White mentions in his writing. Any thoughts?'

Ash shook his head. 'I wish I did, sir.'

Harper sat, thinking, trying to see a way through this. But the more he looked, the murkier it became.

'Go back and look at Henry White again,' he suggested. 'See if you can dig more out from that angle. I'll set Conway on looking for Talbot. We've got links to White and Calder, but there's something more; there has to be.'

'I'll tell him, sir. He had to give evidence in a case from D division this morning. And I'll see if I can find that family in the acid case later.'

Alone, Harper hurried through the papers. Most only needed a signature or initials. Two requests for reports that would take more of his time. But by eleven he'd finished, sitting back with a sigh of relief.

Time to go out and be a real copper again.

'You're not serious, asking me that.'

Cal Clough sat with a full pint of bitter on the table in front of him. The superintendent had brought it over and set it down before placing himself across from the man and saying, 'How many times did you sell silver to Willie Calder?'

It was a blunt opening. But it could work.

'Cal, we both know you'll steal anything that isn't nailed down,' Harper said. 'It's hardly a secret. I'm not going to nick you for it, I just want an answer.'

Clough eyed him warily. He saw a small, feral man, whip-scrawny, his face all sharp angles and suspicion. There was a world of doubt in his eyes.

'You mean it? No charges?'

'None. I promise.'

Cal scratched the back of his neck and adjusted his cap. Little gestures, buying time as he made his decision.

'Four or five times,' he said. 'No more than that.'

'Why so few?'

'Willie only bought silver. And it had to be summat good. He'd just send you away otherwise. If he bought, he paid a decent price.'

'You know he's dead, don't you?'

Clough gave him a withering look. 'Of course I bloody do. God rest him. I read the papers, don't I?'

'I want his killer.'

'Good luck to you, then. But I can't help you with that.'

'You don't know what I need yet, Cal.'

'I can guess.' He picked up the beer and drank the top inch, smacking his lips at the taste. 'You want names.'

'I want someone called J.D.' The initials hadn't been mentioned in any of the newspapers; it was the one secret the police had.

'Eh?'

'J.D.,' he repeated. 'Who do you know with those initials?'

'No one. Well, there was Joshua Dalton, but he died two years ago.'

Could Dawson have been the man? Harper thought back over the diary, the notes, whatever they were meant to be. No dates on them, but they seemed more recent. And Dalton . . .

'He never stole silver, did he?'

'Only if it was there,' Clough said. 'He was a cash man, really.'

He remembered now. Dawson would break into a house and prowl silently, stealing anything he could find, especially cash, even from the bedrooms while the owners slept. No, he wasn't the J.D. that White had written about.

The superintendent placed the price of another pint on the table.

'If it comes to you, let me know. And ask around, Cal. I want this man. There might be a bob or two in it for someone.'

Another avenue that ended up at a brick wall. Every way they turned it was the same. But J.D. existed. Someone had murdered Henry White. And Harper found it hard to believe that Talbot the guard had killed Willie Calder off his own bat. Someone was behind it all, pulling the strings. J.D. It had to be.

As soon as he walked into Millgarth, he felt it. The crackle in the air. Tollman was talking to a constable but jerked his head up and sent the bobby on his way.

'There's a body, sir,' he said.

'Who? Where?'

'Over in Holbeck. The cut that runs behind Marshall's Mill. That new sergeant is there.'

'Conway?'

'That's the one.'

Harper calculated for a moment. He should stay in the office, be there to deal with any emergency. But a body . . . that tempted the detective in him. He wanted to see it.

'Is there anything important waiting?'

Tollman pursed his lips. 'Not that I know, sir.' A slow grin spread across his face. 'Going over there?'

The superintendent winked. 'Just for a little while. Hold the fort.'

It was a chance to stretch his legs. Down by the railway station, through the arches, all rebuilt after the fire a few years before. Marshall's Mill, Temple Mill and all the others just beyond, the air heavy with the damp smell of wool and flax. Chimneys sending smoke pouring into the air. Leeds. Industry. Business.

They were gathered on a patch of scrub ground, the tall brick bulk of the mill behind them. Four men in uniform, Conway next to them, talking to John Calder. That made sense; Holbeck was Calder's patch.

Two more bobbies were at the bottom of the bank, the water over their boots, trying to haul out the body.

'Who is it?' Harper asked.

'Talbot,' Conway replied, his face grim.

The superintendent stared at the corpse. He'd been at Armley. He'd probably seen the guard, but he didn't remember him. The man down there didn't ring any bells.

'This was in his pocket, sir,' Calder said. He held up a letter with Talbot's name and address.

'No other papers?' He held his breath, hoping against hope
that the man had been carrying Calder's diary, the papers so
important that they needed to be locked away in a bank deposit
box.

'Nothing.'

'Right, get him out and take him over to King's Kingdom.'
He looked at Sergeant Calder. 'A word, if I might?'

They walked away, staring across at the strange Italian chimneys of Tower Works. Even this far away, the clatter of their
pin-making machinery was loud.

'Yes, sir?'

'I know this is your patch.'

'It is, sir, and I know it well.'

The man was establishing his rights and putting up his defences.

'You do, and you have an excellent record. But please
remember, this is more than a random murder. Claude Talbot is
the man who killed your brother.'

'All the more reason to go after whoever killed him, sir.' Calder
stood a little straighter. 'With all due respect, sir—'

'Which always means with no respect at all.' Harper took the
barb from his words with a smile. He knew how it worked; he'd
done it often enough himself. 'I need your knowledge on this.
You're very good at your job. But I'm going to bring Inspector
Ash in to run things, and you and Sergeant Conway will work
under him. They've been involved from the start.'

'Gladly, sir,' he agreed after a moment.

It was a very fair compromise. This way Calder remained
involved, his pride intact.

The superintendent turned as he heard the shout; they'd
managed to drag the corpse up from the bank. Harper watched
the constables dig through the man's clothes, searching for
anything else. A cheap clay pipe, tobacco in a pouch. A few
coppers, two silver coins. A pocket watch in the waistcoat. A
handkerchief. Conway was right: no more paper.

'Turn him over,' Harper ordered. The wound was there, at the
back of his head. Deep, rounded. A blow like that would have
killed him instantly. His skull was shattered, an ooze of brains
glistening in the light.

No bruises on the face. Probably killed right there and tossed down the bank. Harper looked around. The spot was well hidden, behind a stone building, out of sight of the mill. He turned his head. There was another building to the west, faces crowding at the windows.

'Look at that,' he said to Conway.

The sergeant picked up the idea quickly. 'I'll go and ask if they saw anything.'

'They probably didn't, especially if it happened at night. But it's worth a try. Who found him, anyway?'

'Two lads skiving off school.' He grinned. 'So scared they ran home and told their mams.'

Calder was staring down at the corpse. 'Are you sure he killed my brother, sir?'

'As much as I can be. Why?'

'I just wanted to know.' He couldn't take his eyes off Talbot.

Harper clapped a hand on the man's shoulder. 'Now we have to find who killed him. Are you with us?'

'Yes, sir.' There was bitterness in his voice. 'It's my case, too. Besides, when we find the killer, I can shake his hand.'

There was nothing more he could do here. Conway was bright, Calder was good. Once Ash arrived and imposed his order on everything the investigation would move smoothly. Before he left, though, he squatted and opened the dead man's coat, feeling inside the cheap, shiny lining. It was a common hiding place; worth trying for the moment it would take him.

There. A soft, pliable lump. Harper pulled out his pocket knife and slashed the material. He reached in and pulled out a small wad of papers. The same ones he'd taken from Henry White's deposit box; he recognized the writing. Not all of them, the tied packet wasn't thick enough for that. But it was a start. He'd look at them properly in the office.

The fire brigade had been called out to a warehouse a hundred yards downriver from Leeds Bridge. Not too much damage done, nobody hurt, the engine and men sent back to Park Row.

Reed stood in the small building that had caught the force of the fire. Charred wood, steaming puddles on the floor. It must have started over in the corner, he decided, where the bricks were burned and buckled. But it didn't feel like arson; nothing seemed deliberate. He pointed.

'What do you keep over there?' he asked.

The man beside him, the red-faced owner, said, 'Paraffin.'

'And there?' He indicated a section of the wall which had completely gone.

'Paper, card,' the man answered. 'Why?'

God almighty. Next to each other like that? He might as well have put in an order for a fire. Reed explained, not sure if the owner was really listening or if it went in one ear and out of the other. The man only seemed to care about his insurance claim and how long before he was back in business.

There was no rush to return to the fire station. Reed walked through the market and down to Millgarth. A greeting from Tollman, then squeezing through the corridor where two workmen were repairing the wall, smearing it thickly with fresh, damp plaster.

He'd heard all about it. Everyone in Leeds had. Harper the hero, one of the newspapers had called him. Yes, it took courage to face down a man with a shotgun, and Tom had never lacked that. It was one or two of his other qualities that left something to be desired. The ones that were never mentioned.

He rapped on the office door. The superintendent looked up from his papers, mouth broadening to a smile.

'Come on in, Billy.' He sniffed the air. Reed knew the smoke and dampness clung to his uniform. 'Straight from a job?'

'Yes. Nothing that big, though. Sir.'

'Give over. You know better than that,' Harper told him. 'How long have we known each other? There's no one else around, is there?'

Reed took out his cigarettes and lit one. 'I was thinking about the acid attack again.'

'I thought you'd handed that back to Ash.'

'I couldn't let it go,' he admitted, without saying why. Earlier, the hose trained on the blaze, he'd come to understand something. He was a fireman now. That was where he succeeded or failed. Much as he liked the idea, he couldn't play the copper any longer. He needed to pass on what he'd learned and be done with it.

'Did you find something?'

'I had a nose around a couple of pubs. Ran into someone who was talking about some filthy business.'

'What sort?' He watched the superintendent cock his head, angling it so he'd be able to hear everything clearly.

'Church folk and young girls.' He shrugged. 'No names, no pack drill. But it's like the man who told me said: you don't get smoke without fire.'

'You know better than that when it comes to rumours, Billy.' All too often they had no substance at all.

'Maybe,' Reed agreed. 'It's still worth a look. It would explain a lot, like those families who took their children out of Crabtree's Sunday school class and left the church.'

Harper nodded. 'I'll tell Ash. He's been thinking along the same lines. This gives him a little more information. Good work.'

Reed smiled. 'From what I've read, you've done some good work of your own.'

'Don't believe a word of it. I was lucky. I still get the terrors when I think about it.' He held up his hands. 'These started shaking and I had to wait until they stopped. I thought I was over it and it happened again last night. Lucky I was at home.'

'I see that in the fire brigade, too.'

Harper stared at him eagerly. 'What's the solution? How do you stop it?'

'There isn't one, Tom. It's like life: you just take a deep breath and get on with it.'

EIGHTEEN

It was early afternoon when Ash returned, with Conway at his side. No sign of Sergeant Calder.

'We left him asking around in Hunslet, sir. He knows the area, after all. The three of us went to see Dr King.'

'What did he have to say?'

'What you'd expect. A single blow killed Talbot, nothing else needed. No sign of a fight, no grazing on his knuckles. Sounds like he was with someone he trusted and he turned his back on them.'

Harper took the papers from his desk drawer.

'He'd hidden these away in his coat lining. I'd left them with Willie Calder. The only thing is, these aren't all of them.'

'What about the rest?' Conway asked.

'It seems as if Talbot only kept the ones that refer to J.D. He probably threw the others away.'

'J.D. could have killed Talbot,' Ash said.

'I'm quite certain he did,' Harper continued. 'But he didn't find the papers because they were hidden in Talbot's coat lining.' It gave a shape to the killing, a reason. He stared at the officers. 'Find J.D., gentlemen.'

The room was hot, flames leapt in the fireplace. Harper felt the sweat trickling down his spine. He stood over by the window, anywhere that might be a little cooler.

Kendall's chair was close to the hearth, but he still had a heavy rug over his lap. He sat hunched over, seeming even smaller than he had in the hospital. It was as if the life was slowly leaking out of him, like air from a balloon. All so quick, too; hardly a moment had passed since he was the superintendent and Harper just the inspector.

'You've got a real mystery, Tom,' Kendall said after hearing about Talbot's death and the papers in the coat lining. He nodded eagerly, eyes alive for the first time since the visit began. 'I'd agree with you, though. J.D. sounds like the real suspect.'

'But we can't find anyone with those initials. Do they mean anything to you?'

He could see the man thinking, working through the files in his mind, all the memories of criminals. Years of them.

'Three,' Kendall said finally. 'But they're all dead now.' He gave a small, wan smile. 'Not a lot of help, is it?'

'I'm afraid not.'

The servant arrived with a tray, teapot and cups. Mrs Kendall bustled in behind, taking over and pouring. He understood. She wanted to keep an eye on her husband; she knew how fast he was slipping away. Every minute had meaning.

'Too many bodies, Tom,' he said once they were alone again. 'You've got three of them now. Stand back and look at the bigger picture. That's what you need to do with your rank. Let Ash and – what's the new fellow's name?'

'Conway.'

'Let them do the leg work. You promoted them, so trust them and leave them to get on with it. You're the one who needs to be able to connect all the pieces.'

Sound advice. But could he keep himself removed enough from the case to take it?

'Have you asked about this J.D. at the other divisions?' Kendall asked.

'At the meeting. Nobody knows the initials. But at least we've decided we need to share information and make our records central.'

'About time, too. It's more than I ever managed,' Kendall admitted with a sigh. 'New brooms, eh?' He smiled.

'It doesn't help us catch him.'

'Not with this one. It might with others. One more thing, Tom.'

'What's that?'

'Tollman dropped in. He told me what you did when that madman took over Millgarth.'

Harper hadn't intended to mention it. The story in the newspapers had been enough. All he wanted was to forget, to put it all behind him, to lose the fear. No more hands shaking when he least expected it.

'Don't believe all he says.'

'I don't think Tollman exaggerated. You did more than I could have.'

'I did what had to be done. Nothing more than that,' he said firmly.

The conversation continued for a few minutes. He could see the man growing weary and made his excuses. In the hall, as he shrugged into his coat, Mrs Kendall said, 'Thank you for coming. It means a lot to him, you know. One or two have visited. Not many, though.'

He wasn't surprised. Illness scared people; they were afraid they'd catch something.

'It's always good to see him. He seems happier out of the infirmary.'

'He is,' she agreed. 'But it won't be much longer now.'

'He might hold on.'

She stopped him with a hand on his arm. 'We both know the truth and we might as well admit it. Denying it isn't going to help at all. Poor Bob, he's like a spring winding down now he's not working any more.'

'I'm sorry.' It was all he could think to say.

'Don't be,' she told him. 'He loved what he did. And we've had a good life together. But the thing about lives, Mr Harper, is that they end eventually. All of them. And maybe that's not bad.' She sighed and smiled. 'Maybe you'll see it yourself when you're older. Many years from now,' she added.

'I'll come and see him again.'

'Please do. He'd like that.'

He was still awake when Annabelle came back from speaking at the suffragist meeting. Downstairs the pub was busy, a Saturday night crowd out to celebrate and forget work, bills, everything, for a few hours.

He didn't hear the hackney on the cobbles outside, or her footsteps on the stairs. The first he knew was when she burst into the parlour, face flushed with excitement and pleasure.

'You should have seen them, Tom.' Annabelle dumped her papers and books on the table. Harper rose from the chair and hugged her. 'They were on their feet, cheering. I really think we're getting somewhere.'

'I'm glad.' She'd put so much into the movement. Her belief, her time as a speaker and secretary of the Leeds branch. A publican, a businesswoman who'd grown up poor but made a success of her life: someone like that was a proper inspiration, a powerful voice for suffragism.

'No problem getting Mary to bed?'

He laughed. Every time it was the same question, as if he'd never done it before.

'Not a peep out of her. Come on, tell me all about it.'

He listened as she went through it all, until her words began to fade as tiredness took over from elation.

'What about you?' she asked.

She'd already left by the time he arrived home. Ellen had given Mary her supper then brought her down to him.

'I visited Kendall,' he answered quietly. 'He's not long for this world.'

'Maguire, Kendall. And it's only March.' She shook her head. 'It's not a good start to the year, is it?'

Sunday. The weeks seemed to slip by too quickly, gone before he even realized it. Spring had arrived, even in the middle of the city. The smell of new life, buds on the trees, and the sense of warmth in the air pierced the smoke and the soot.

Today all the machines were quiet. No pall of smoke pouring from the chimneys and the factories as Harper strode along North Street, past Cohen and Son, Tailors, where Moses and his family lived above the shop, beyond the tangle of streets that made up the Leylands, where most of Leeds's Jews made their homes and their livings, more of them arriving every year.

He'd spent half the night awake with Annabelle's gentle breathing as the backdrop to his thoughts. In his mind he saw the faces of those who were dying and those already gone.

And he considered the job.

For the last week he'd tried to be Kendall, to do things the way Kendall would. He'd tucked Tom Harper in around the edges. And he'd discovered he couldn't work that way. It felt *wrong*. He was a working copper. He'd been promoted because he was good at his job. He solved crimes. If he spent his time behind a desk, he wasn't doing the thing he managed best.

He had to be a superintendent on his own terms. He needed to be out there, to be part of the investigations. He'd still take care of the forms, the reports and the meetings, but that would be one part of the work, not all of it. Leeds Police was going to have a very active superintendent at A Division. And if the watch committee didn't like it, they could demote him.

Decision made, he walked into Millgarth with a smile on his face. The corridor smelt of fresh plaster. The wall was startlingly white where it had been repaired. The door to the detectives' room was new, not even varnished yet. Another month and they'd be as battered and worn as the rest of the police station. The story of MacDonald and his gun would pass from news to legend. It would slide into history. Slowly forgotten and better that way.

*   *   *

An hour of paperwork, keeping his head above water, and he'd had enough. The city was Sabbath quiet until the church bells began ringing. St John's first, then the Parish Church, and finally Holy Trinity over on Boar Lane.

Harper put down his pen, blotted his signature on the form, and slid into his coat, tapping his hat down on his head before leaving his office.

It wasn't that far to Copper Street, no more than a few minutes' walk up the cobbles of the Bank. He stopped outside Henry White's old house. Upstairs, the curtains were drawn, and even his tin ear could make out the sound of voices inside, a mother and her children. Someone new was making a life there.

Round the corner, on Brass Street, he knocked on the door of number thirty-seven. Mrs Thorp answered, her face tightening as she recognized him.

'What do you want?' she asked.

'You didn't waste any time renting out Henry's house.'

'Why would I?' she said. 'The will went through without any problem. It's not making me any money if it's empty.' The woman eyed him. 'Did you bring me back them keys?'

He smiled to himself. She wasn't the type ever to forget a debt or a slight. He reached into his pocket, pulled them out and dropped them into her waiting hand.

'You ever find what they was for?'

'Yes,' he told her. She waited, but he wasn't about to say; it didn't concern her. 'Did you find anything else when you were clearing out Henry's house?'

She shrugged. 'Not much. Sold it all to the rag and bone man.' She snorted. 'Not that he gave me more than a few pennies. Told me I should pay him to drag it away. Anything else?'

'No, that's all.' He raised his hat. 'Good day to you.'

As he walked in to the station he could feel it; a dampening of the mood. Subdued, muted. He looked at Tollman.

'Bad news, I'm afraid, sir.' He took a breath. 'Mr Kendall died this morning. A heart attack. I just got the message from Chapeltown.'

'I see. Thank you.' He walked through and settled behind his desk. Kendall's desk until so recently. The office still smelled of the shag tobacco he smoked. The scent had become embedded in the place.

Five minutes later he was on his feet again, walking out and hailing a hackney.

It was too soon for the house to have the look of mourning. The body would barely be cold yet.

The servant let him in, bobbing a quick curtsey. Her eyes were rimmed and red from crying.

Olivia Kendall sat quietly in the parlour. A fire was set in the grate, but not lit; there was none of the overwhelming heat of yesterday.

'I'm sorry,' he told her. He never knew what to say. Words always seemed contrived and false.

'Don't be.' She gestured for him to sit. 'It was quick. That's the blessing, as if God didn't want him to suffer.'

Was she religious, he wondered? Kendall had never mentioned it.

'It was over in a few seconds,' she continued. 'This morning. He was sitting up in bed. Kitty had brought us tea. He put his down on the table and turned to me. Then it happened.' A smile that was a mix of sadness and relief. 'As fast as that. No pain, the doctor said . . .'

Better than the torment cancer would put him through. Quick, over in a moment. If there was any good way to die, that had to be it. At home, in his own bed.

'I'm glad.' But it sounded wrong, he thought; inadequate, callous.

'So am I,' she said firmly. 'You never want to see someone suffer. Not when you've loved them for years, Mr Harper.'

'The police will give him a good send-off—'

She was shaking her head. 'Family and friends only. That's what he said. I know he'd want you there. I'll put a notice in the paper, but that's all.' She hesitated for a moment. 'Would you let the chief constable know?'

'Of course.' It was the least he could do. But the man would insist on a memorial service later, that was certain. Kendall had been a decorated senior officer.

Gently, he turned down the chance to see the corpse. He'd

rather remember the man who'd taught him to be a detective, someone vital who he'd served under for so long. Outside, walking down the street, he breathed deep, drawing the air into his lungs, feeling alive and grateful.

Reed leaned back in his chair, listening to Ash.

'Superintendent Harper passed on what you'd heard in the pubs. I thought it might be useful to hear more.'

There was no deference in the man's voice now. Why should there be? Ash was an inspector; they were equals. And he'd earned the promotion, no doubt about that.

'I told him everything I knew,' Reed said. 'It's just gossip.'

'There's often a reason for it.' He saw Ash's mouth twitch into a smile under his thick moustache. 'It ties in with some of the things I've heard, too. Was there any detail? Any names?'

'Nothing like that.' Reed shrugged. 'Just talk. The man had been drinking. I thought it was worth passing on; there might be something in it. How does it fit in with what you've learned?'

He asked a few questions as Ash explained.

'You're right, it all seems to go together very neatly,' Reed agreed.

'It's getting people to talk about it that's the problem.' Ash turned the battered bowler hat on his lap. 'Of course, you'd know that. Any idea how to approach it?'

'Well—' Reed began. Then the bell began to clang, and the fire station became a welter of noise and action. The clerk dashed in and shouted, 'Up on Woodhouse Lane, sir, by the church,' while men fitted the horses into their traces on the engine.

'I need to go,' Reed said.

'Of course.'

Conway paced around the superintendent's office. He'd only stayed seated for a minute, then he was up on his feet and walking around, as if keeping still constrained him too much.

'You remember I said that Talbot had worked for a silversmith when he was young?'

'Yes, I do,' Harper answered. Following the sergeant's movements was making him dizzy.

'I managed to track down the silversmith's relatives and asked if they knew anything. The son didn't, but he still had his father's ledgers and notes.'

'Oh?' It was strange, the things people kept. Somewhere, in a trunk, he still had the cap his father wore to work every day. He hadn't looked at it in years, but it seemed like the essence of the man. A keepsake. Daft, and he knew it, but . . .

'Turned out he dismissed Talbot for thieving. Threatened him with the police if he didn't return what he'd stolen. Looks as if Talbot couldn't hold a job well.'

The superintendent stroked his chin. 'It's interesting, but I don't see that it has much bearing on this.'

'He was nicking silver. He could have known Willie Calder then, sir,' Conway said.

Maybe he had. But everyone who knew the truth was dead. And it was history, and didn't have any bearing on the killing that he could see.

'Good work,' he said. The man had followed the trail. He was eager. 'See what you can find that's more recent.'

The young man blushed. 'Yes, sir.' He hesitated. 'I'm sorry about Mr Kendall. I didn't know him, but . . .'

'We'll miss him. All the force will.'

NINETEEN

'Tom,' she began, arms around him, gently stroking his hair.

As soon as he'd come through the door he held her. He needed the warmth, the life of another person. Harper had taken his time, staying at Millgarth until dusk had fallen, then walking home.

He'd cut through the Leylands, wandering along Noble Street where he'd grown up. At one time he'd known who lived in every house. Now they were filled with families from Russia and other countries he couldn't even name. The ones who'd been here before had moved or died. In their place were people looking for the chance to live, for their children to grow. Times changed.

He didn't need to explain to Annabelle. That was why he loved her. Simply being here, with her and Mary, made his life easier. Harper pulled away from his wife and cracked the bedroom door open to watch his daughter sleeping, standing long enough to have the sense of her breathing and know she was safe.

In the kitchen, Annabelle pulled a plate from the oven. 'I kept it warm for you.'

He ate without even noticing the food. It was something to put in his mouth and chew.

'How's Mrs Kendall?' she asked when he'd finished.

'Relieved, I think,' he answered after a moment.

'It's better than pain,' she said.

'Yes.' He remembered the man coming into Millgarth, terrified as he tried to breathe. Or old and fragile in his own parlour. Yes, he thought, perhaps this was for the best.

Everything had happened so suddenly, as if everything he'd known of Kendall was a house of cards that tumbled. It was like one of those films they'd seen the other night, moving from health through illness to death in a few blinks of the eye.

'You know, the problem isn't the people we care about dying,' Annabelle said. She took hold of his hand, squeezing it gently as she looked into his eyes.

'Isn't it?' he asked in surprise.

'No.' She shook her head. 'It's the rest of us, everyone left behind. The dead have gone, they don't know anything. We're here with the holes in our lives. I've been thinking about it since Maguire died.'

He realized she was right. They were the ones who remained to count up the memories and feel the sorrow.

A funeral wreath hung on the door of the station. At the front desk, Tollman had found a framed photograph of Kendall in his superintendent's uniform and placed it on the counter.

'The service will be next week sir,' the sergeant said. 'Small do. Family. Burying him at St George's Fields.'

Harper nodded and walked through to his office. Ash sat at his desk, nib scratching on the paper as he wrote up a report.

'Tell me you've found something.'

'I think I have, sir.' For a second he could feel his spirits rising, then the inspector continued, 'It's not about Henry White or Willie Calder, though.'

'Go on.'

'The acid, sir. I really believe we're getting close. Last night I visited one of those families that left the Baptist church.' Harper waited. 'They have a little girl, same age as our Martha was when we took her in.' His mouth creased into a smile. 'When I asked why they didn't go to services or send the lass to Sunday school any more, they went quiet.'

'What do you mean? They didn't want to say?'

'Exactly, sir. I pushed them a bit but they didn't want to talk. On top of what Mr Reed learned, it's making me wonder.'

'There were two families, weren't there?' He seemed to recall that.

'That's right. I'm off to see the other one tonight.' Ash raised an eyebrow. 'I left a message for Mr Reed. I thought he might fancy coming along.'

'I bet he would.' Maybe they'd be able to solve *this* bloody case, at least.

The day dragged. A long meeting with the chief constable about the way MacDonald and his shotgun could hold a police station hostage. For the better part of an hour Harper made suggestions and the chief turned down every single one of them. In the end they'd achieved nothing and he left, fuming inside at the waste of time.

Then the divisional meeting, all the superintendents together. Kendall's funeral wasn't an official affair, but he'd guessed correctly; there would be a memorial service with every available officer in attendance. That had to be planned, people delegated to take care of all the details.

By the time he stood on the Town Hall steps and looked up at the pale spring sky, it was almost four o'clock. He hadn't eaten since breakfast.

A roast beef sandwich and a cup of hot sweet tea from the cart on Butts Court, off behind the Green Dragon. Then back to the grind, the mountain of paper that would be waiting. New rules, regulations, committees. He sighed at the thought.

Conway was in the detectives' room with Sergeant Calder

from Hunslet, deep in a discussion that tailed off as he entered.

'Something new on Talbot?' Harper asked.

'I was telling Mark that I got a whisper earlier, sir.' Calder breathed and beer fumes filled the room. 'I was down at the Garden Gate public house and one of the lads I often use for information said something. It seems Talbot charged people to take things in to the prisoners at Armley. No one searched him because he was a guard.' Harper nodded and the man continued. 'The way I heard it, he got a bit greedy. Started wanting too much for his services, and some people weren't happy.'

'So he could have been killed for that?' Harper considered it. Plausible, beyond a doubt. But inside he didn't believe a word. The story felt too neat, the timing wrong, just after the murder in the jail. It was too pat. 'Who told you?' he asked.

'My man's reliable, sir,' Calder said. 'I've been hunting for someone to back it up. No luck so far.'

'I'm not so sure about it, but keep trying.' The superintendent nodded and turned to Conway. 'What about you?'

The sergeant shrugged. 'I feel like I've spent the day pounding my head against brick walls, sir. I'm sorry.'

'Sometimes it's like that.' He knew the feeling, knew it well. 'Too often.' He turned away, asking, 'Sergeant Calder, can I have a word, please?'

'Sir?' the man asked once they were alone.

'Do you think that rumour about Talbot is true?'

'Honestly, sir?' the sergeant asked. 'It sounded good at first, but not turning anything else up . . .' He let the sentence drift away.

'I understand that you didn't know about your brother's illegal business.'

Calder straightened his back and stood a little taller. 'I told you I didn't, sir,' he replied firmly. 'I'd have turned him in.'

'Calm down,' Harper said. 'No one's accusing you. But Willie was your brother. I need to know if there's anyone you can think of who might want to kill him.'

'Sir, as far as I knew, he was a senior clerk. Nothing more. He had a job, he went to work every day.' The sergeant kept his eyes straight ahead as he stood to attention, but his voice had softened. 'I saw him a few times a year, sir, but that's all. We've never been a close family, if you know what I mean. There's me, two sisters, and Willie. Was, anyway,' he corrected himself.

'What about your wife? Did she know her sister-in-law well?'

'She's dead, sir. I'm a widower.'

'I'm sorry.' He ought to learn about the men and avoid stupid mistakes, he thought.

'It was quite a while ago, sir.' He hesitated for a moment. 'I've been racking my brain about Willie. I'm a copper, I should be able to spot a wrong 'un by now. But I never noticed a thing.'

'He's family. You wouldn't expect it.'

'Maybe so,' Calder agreed with a sigh. 'Like I say, I didn't see him too often. But there was nothing flashy about his house. Nothing obvious.'

'I saw it,' Harper agreed. 'Keep thinking. I need whatever help you can give. Right now we've found bugger all.'

'I just never knew my brother well, sir. I'm sorry.'

'Thank you.'

It didn't matter which way they moved, it swiftly came to nothing. There had to be an answer somewhere. A path that would lead them neatly from Talbot to Willie Calder and then to Henry White. He knew the connection was there. All they had to do was find it and follow it.

Afternoon began to fade into evening, the sky reddening off to the west. Sometimes it was hard to tell with the pall of smoke hanging over Leeds. But the relentless tick of the clock on the wall marked the hours.

Finally, Harper gave up. It had been a frustrating day, but so many were like that, always had been. Most crimes were solved quickly, in less than a day. But so many were simple affairs, built on passion or anger, or committed by people so stupid they were easy to catch.

It was the ones like this that caught in the craw.

He scarcely noticed the tram journey, couldn't recall whose faces he greeted in the bar. Harper was simply glad to open the door and be in his own parlour. Before he could remove his coat, Mary had dashed across to wrap her arms around his leg, and he hoisted her up into his arms.

This was what made it all worthwhile. His daughter, his wife. This was why he could accept all the failures and mistakes at work.

'What have you been doing today?' he asked as he carried her through to the kitchen, past the political books and the draft of a speech on the table.

'I hope you're hungry,' Annabelle called. 'I made more of the cottage pie than I thought.'

He smiled.

'Are you ready?' Ash asked. They stood at the end of a street in Burmantofts, decent through terraces with front gardens the size of postage stamps. Most had plants neatly growing, everything carefully weeded, tended with pride.

Reed took the last couple of puffs on his cigarette and ground it out under his boot. He was wearing a coat over his fire brigade uniform. In his belly he could feel the bubbling, the way it had always been, all the way back to the army when he was preparing for action. The anticipation.

Side by side, they strolled down the street and knocked on the door of number forty-one. The sky had darkened, night was close. He could hear the voices and laughter suddenly stop inside.

'Mr Cecil Lester?' The man nodded, looking from one face to the other. 'I'm Inspector Ash with Leeds City Police. This is Inspector Reed. Would you mind if we came in for a quick word? It won't take long.'

'All right. Just give me a minute.' It was both question and statement. The man closed the door on the latch. A few words, then hurried footsteps.

Ash took off running.

They'd been had. Christ, Reed thought. The oldest trick in the world and they'd fallen for it. Both of them. They should have known better. Lester had darted out of the back door, through the yard and into the ginnel. And here he was, standing on the front step like a bloody spare part.

He brought his fist down on the wood. 'Mrs Lester,' he shouted. 'Police.'

*   *   *

She was a timid woman, perched on the edge of her chair and constantly turning her head towards the back door, as if her husband might return at any moment.

The children were upstairs; he could hear them. The soft murmur of voices, footsteps moving around and trying to be quiet.

'How old are they?' Reed raised his eyes towards the ceiling.

'Ten, eight, seven, six.' The words came out as a mumbled rush.

'We have four,' he told her. 'All working now, except the youngest. He's staying in school a year or two longer.' Reed smiled. 'He's the one with the brains.'

A quick tap on the door and Ash entered, shaking his head, his face grim. He took a seat to the side, ready to listen.

'Why did your husband run off, Mrs Lester?' Reed asked.

'I've no idea,' she replied. But it was a lie; they all knew the truth. She kept her eyes down, not looking at them.

'Has he done something bad?'

The silence hung, bleak and heavy.

'Does it have something to do with your daughter?' Ash asked, his voice so soft it seemed as if they might have imagined it. The woman took a deep breath and nodded.

Reed sat. The other man seemed to strike an immediate connection with her; better to let him work and hear some answers.

It came out slowly, hesitantly. The family had moved to Leeds from Barnsley. They'd always been chapelgoers and started attending services as soon as they settled in the house. The little ones began going to the Sunday school. Jack Crabtree taught the class. Everyone knew the Crabtrees, they took part in all the church events. People liked them. People trusted them.

At first they didn't believe the things Sarah said. She was only eight, after all. Girls imagined things at that age. She could have had the devil in her. Her father took his belt to her to drive out the evil. But Mrs Lester noticed the change, the way the girl became quiet, crying often. That was impossible to ignore. So was the blood on her drawers.

Sarah wouldn't say. After all the disbelief and the punishment, who could blame her? Slowly, though, her mother wormed it out of her. After the Sunday school class was done, Jack Crabtree was pleasing himself with Sarah and another girl.

'When did you tell your husband?' Ash asked.

'After I'd talked to the mother of the other lass.' She raised her head defiantly. 'They needed to know, they had the right. She talked to her husband and they went to the pastor. After that, they left the chapel. I had a word with my Cecil. He went down there, and the pastor turned him away. Said Jack Crabtree would never be like that and our Sarah was making it up. We never went back after that.'

Reed could have cut the atmosphere in the room with a knife.

'Where did your husband buy the acid, Mrs Lester?' Ash shifted slightly on his seat, voice still low and calm.

'At the chemist, I suppose.' She blinked. 'I didn't know until it had all happened.'

'How did you find out?'

'I heard about it and asked him.' She shook her head. 'He's never been any good at lying to me.'

'Why did he go after the boy?' Reed asked the question almost before realizing he'd spoken.

'He said that Jack Crabtree had made our Sarah suffer so he was going to do the same to his family. That lass in the shop, he really didn't mean to hurt her,' she added, regret filling her voice. 'Honest, he didn't.'

'You know that young Arthur Crabtree didn't have anything to do with it. He was innocent.' Ash's voice was little more than a whisper.

The tears flowed down her cheeks. 'I didn't know he was going to do it or I'd have stopped him. I know it's not the lad's fault. But the sins of the fathers, that's what my Cecil thought.'

'Mrs Lester, do you know where your husband's gone?'

She shook her head again. 'I've been expecting you lot since I found out. I never asked him what he'd do.'

'We'll find him,' Reed told her. 'He has to pay for what he's done. You understand that, don't you?'

'I do.' With those words all the heart drained out of her. 'Every night I think about that lad and that lass. None of it's their fault. It's Jack Crabtree. He's evil, that's all it is. And he made my Cecil evil with him.'

She was empty. Everything she'd been keeping inside had flowed away and she had nothing more to give them. Reed believed her. She truly had no idea where her husband had gone. The man probably didn't have a plan. He'd show up, sooner rather than later. The beat bobby would keep an eye on the house and on his work.

Outside, it was full dark. Somehow the night felt empty.

'Good God, that's a bleak story,' Reed said as he lit a cigarette.

'Always the children who suffer, isn't it?' Ash asked. He pulled out his pocket watch. 'About time to go over to Crabtree's house and arrest him, if you want to come along.'

'Arrest him? You'll never get the evidence.'

'Maybe I won't. But happen he might want to admit it all after a little questioning.'

Reed stared at him, remembering the girl that Ash and his wife had adopted a few years before. She'd been sold to some men. Who knew all the things that had happened to her? Ash would batter the truth out of Crabtree, but make sure nothing showed. Or perhaps he wouldn't need to. He was big enough; perhaps threats would be ample.

At one time, Reed would have relished helping. He knew all the tricks to use, exactly how rough to be. But now he realized that he didn't have the stomach for it any longer. His life had changed. He'd help with the arrest, then walk away.

'We'd better go before it's too late.'

Ash gave a dark smile. 'We'll have Cecil Lester before you know it, too. He doesn't seem like the type who'll go on the run well.'

'Crabtree's admitted it?' Harper asked.

'He has, sir.' Ash's knuckles were red and swollen; he rubbed them lightly. 'I had it all written out and he signed it. It wasn't just Sarah Lester and the other girl. There were quite a few more over the years, apparently.'

And who would ever know all their names, the superintendent wondered? The innocent, the ones who couldn't defend themselves. Arthur Crabtree, Annie from the bakery, they'd carry the scars on their faces as long as they lived. But the Lester girl and the others, they'd have their wounds, too. Ones they could never talk about, ones that didn't show on the skin.

'What about the man who threw the acid? Lester.'

'He bolted last night when we went to his house. I daresay he'll show up today or tomorrow, sir.'

'Carry on,' he said finally. 'Once this is done and dusted we can concentrate on the Henry White business.'

TWENTY

'Ash said you were with him when he arrested Crabtree.'

They were in Reed's office at Park Row fire station. The day was oddly warm, the window open wide, drawing in all the noise from the street, the rattle of hooves and iron wheels, the fragments of conversation that flickered past in a second.

'His wife knew what he'd been doing, Tom.' He sighed. 'You could see it in her face. Ash said the woman had been dropping hints.'

It had been as straightforward as Reed expected. Crabtree had talked to both of them before. He let them in to the house, led the way through to the scullery. As Ash spoke, Crabtree reached out and took his wife's hand, squeezing it tight. With each sentence his face grew more pale.

Reed stood close to the back door, in case this man tried to escape, too. But once the handcuffs were on, he went reluctantly, with no real resistance. As they left, the fire inspector glanced back to see Mrs Crabtree still sitting at the table, silent tears coursing down her cheeks.

'That was it. Ash took him to Millgarth and I went home.'

'He admitted everything last night.'

'I'm sure he did.' He wasn't going to ask more. He didn't want to know. 'Have you found Lester yet?'

Harper shook his head. Every bobby in Leeds had the man's description. He wouldn't be free much longer.

'We'll find him. I'm not worried about that. What did Elizabeth say when you told her you'd solved the case?'

'It wasn't me who solved it,' Reed reminded him. 'But she's glad it's over.'

'How's the girl?'

'Annie? She's started working again. In the back room where no one can see her. Keeps a scarf tied round her head and jumps a mile if you talk to her.'

'What do you think? Will she ever get back to normal?'

'I don't know.' Reed leaned back in his chair and lit a cigarette. What could normal be like for her now? 'Whatever happens, it's been a bad business, Tom. Christ knows how many kids Jack Crabtree hurt.'

'He won't be doing that again.' Harper stood, extending his hand. Reed shook it without hesitation. 'Look after yourself, Billy. Don't take any stupid risks.'

'Everyone home safe. That's what we always say here.' The smile faded from his face. 'Sad news about Kendall.'

'It was. There'll be a proper memorial service. I'll see you there.'

Commercial Street was full of people. They spilled off the pavement as he passed the Irish Linen shop on the corner of Lands Lane. A man pulled a woman back sharply, just before a cart would have knocked her down.

Leeds felt like a city that was too full, Harper thought. Everywhere was crowded, straining at the seams. Along Briggate and Boar Lane it was almost impossible to move for the crowds. The trams hurried past, an endless series of them bringing people into town and carrying them home again. And over it all, the thick industrial aroma. The stench of business and empire.

Sergeant Conway was waiting at Millgarth, pacing restlessly around the detectives' room and smoking a cigarette.

'Where do you have to go today?' Harper asked.

'I'm still digging into Willie Calder, sir. There has to be something there.'

Somewhere, the superintendent thought. So far, though, they hadn't been able to ferret it out.

'Let's go, then.' Harper smiled. He wanted to work with the new man, to get a proper sense of him. So far he seemed impressive, someone not too hidebound by routine and the rule book.

Time would tell. He followed as the sergeant strode across St Peter's Square, past the mission, and stopped to take his bearings.

'I'm sorry, sir, I don't know the streets too well around here yet.'

'You'll learn. Where are we going?'

'I got a lead on someone called Four-Finger Harold.'

Harper chuckled. 'Harold? Is he still around? He tried to pick a pocket in Fidelity Court just after I'd started on the beat. They had him tied up like a chicken when I arrived.'

'I was told he knew Calder very well.'

'I suppose it's possible. I'll tell you this: he's one of the most incompetent criminals in town, though. Can't do anything right.'

Conway sighed. 'Maybe he was pulling my leg, then. Being new and that.'

'We'll see.' He changed the subject. 'You've known Ash a long time?'

'Fred and I started on the force together. Same batch of recruits. We always got along like a house on fire. He's an interesting lad.'

'He is,' Harper agreed. 'What about you? Are you married?'

'Six years.' Conway grinned with pride. 'Two children, a third on the way. I hear you have one, sir.'

'That's right. A daughter.' They came to the narrow opening of a court, dark and miserable, the ground just dirt beaten down by generations of feet. It all stank of piss and vomit.

There were no numbers on the houses. Angry shouts came from one of the buildings, rattling the loose glass in the window.

'Third one along,' Conway said. 'The room at the back.'

They'd both seen too many places like this. Homes for the desperate. Places beyond hope. The house was full of dirt, mould, sweat, every bad thing under heaven. Harper clamped a handkerchief over his mouth. At the edge of his hearing he caught a low sound. Something familiar that he couldn't quite place.

The sergeant knocked. No answer.

'Try the doorknob,' Harper told him. It turned easily and he pushed it open.

The buzzing of flies erupted like a storm. They were all over the body, turning it into a seething black lump. As Conway waved his hand, they rose, only to settle again a few seconds later.

'Looks like he's been dead a little while, sir.'

'A day at least,' the superintendent guessed. Smelt like it, too, but the weather had been warm. 'Let's get him over to Dr King. He can tell us what happened. I'll go back to the station and arrange it. You take a look around.'

Even with the stench in the court, it seemed like blessed relief to be outside, to draw air into his lungs. He breathed deep, walking quickly, issuing orders once he reached Millgarth. Soon enough some poor men would have to move the corpse. Better them than him; he'd wait until it had been cleaned and cut open. And meanwhile he'd let Conway do the searching on his own. He gave a quick, small smile. Maybe rank did bring a few privileges.

But what had happened to Four-Finger Harold?

'It doesn't take much to see the cause of death, Superintendent,' King said. 'Knife in the heart. Like those bodies you brought me a little while ago.'

'Henry White and Willie Calder,' Harper told him. The doctor waved his arms. Flies had laid their eggs deep inside Harold's corpse and even in the chill of the mortuary they were starting to hatch.

'Yes.' He brushed another insect off the corpse. 'I need to get this one out of here before these things end up everywhere. Give me a hand.' He opened a door and Sergeant Conway pushed the table into a thick-walled room. 'With luck, that should kill them,' King said with relief.

'How long has he been dead?' Conway asked.

'A day, more or less. With this weather it's impossible to be certain. Does that help you at all?'

'It does. Did you see anything else?'

'It didn't look as if there'd been a fight,' the doctor answered after a little thought. 'No sign of resistance, no grazes on his knuckles.' He balled his hand into a fist to illustrate. 'That's all I can tell you without cutting him open. That, and he must have lived in squalor.'

'He did, sir,' Conway said.

'Pity the poor man, then.'

'Who gave you the tip about Four-Finger Harold?'

'I heard it through someone I know in Armley, sir.'

'I think you'd better track him down. Having that name pop out of the blue then finding him dead seems like too much of a coincidence. I don't even see where he fits into things.'

'Don't you worry, I plan on finding out, sir.' Conway had a glint in his eye. 'And I'll make sure I get the proper story this time.'

They parted outside Millgarth. Harper watched the man walk away. For once he didn't feel any envy.

The plaster was still drying on the wall, with the fresh, acrid smell that caught in his throat. The wood of the door was still too new, too bright. But already the memories were becoming dulled, Harper thought as he entered. No more shudders of fear as he entered the building, and he couldn't pinpoint exactly when they'd stopped. His hands didn't shake.

Life rolled along. The incident had quickly become part of the past, much like Kendall's death or Maguire's. He could picture every second of it, but now he felt like an observer, as if it had happened to someone else.

Stupid, he decided. What did it matter, anyway? There was work to do.

'Elizabeth will be pleased,' Annabelle said. 'Once word gets out that you've arrested someone, it should all be back the way it was.'

They were sitting in the bar of the Victoria. People kept interrupting to say hello, to wish her well and discuss something or other. Harper was used to it. This was her domain. Ellen was upstairs with Mary while they enjoyed a rare evening down here.

By the second glass of gin, her face was flushed and she sounded happy.

'It'll never be right for the girl, though,' he said. 'Or the lad.'

'I know.' She breathed deeply. 'I didn't mean it that way. But the shops—' She stopped as an older man he didn't recognize came and bowed. This was how it always was during their times down in the pub. People liked her, they enjoyed her company, to share a few words. It made him proud to see it all, to watch them paying court to her in her little empire.

'Elizabeth is going to take care of the lass; she already told me that,' she went on.

'I saw Billy Reed this morning. The girl's back at work. Just not where people can stare.'

'Happen it'll help. Maybe there's something the suffragists can do for her.' She took a small pad and pencil from the pocket in her dress and made a note.

'You used to remember everything,' he said with a smile.

'Too much on my mind these days,' Annabelle told him, but he noticed that she turned away from him as she spoke. 'This way I make sure I don't forget. Just because I clump around like an elephant doesn't mean I have the memory of one.'

The good weather had faded overnight. It was still close, warm for so early in the year, but the sky was grey and heavy, a misting rain falling. A day to wear a mackintosh, Harper thought, feeling the dampness on his face as he walked down George Street from the tram.

Ash was waiting, staring down at the yard and the mounted patrolmen, wearing their capes and ready to leave.

'I'm sorry I didn't report back last night, sir. It was late when I finished.' There was a spare, sober quality to his voice that made Harper stop.

'What is it?'

'A rumour I heard. I spent half the day trying to see if there was anything to it.'

'Well? Spit it out.'

'That Cecil Lester had killed himself.'

'Has he?'

The inspector shook his head. 'Not that I managed to find. Couldn't even discover where it all began. But you'll see why I was busy, sir.'

'Of course.' If they'd found Lester's body, the case would be closed. They hadn't even had a confirmed sighting of him since he'd run. The man had gone to ground.

'I've got someone watching the house,' Ash continued. 'But I don't think he'll go home. People know what he's done, there won't be many doors open to him.'

'Have you announced it?'

'No, sir. It wouldn't be right for that lass of his, the one Crabtree . . .' He let the words fade away.

'Where are you with the Henry White murder?'

'No further along, sir.' Harper could hear his frustration. 'Mark Conway told me about old Harold. Too odd not be connected, isn't it?'

'Same method of death. But I don't know how it fits. Someone's three steps ahead of us.' The superintendent corrected himself. 'He knows where to turn and who's involved while we're still running around and playing blind man's bluff. Or Harold could be in there to throw us off the scent.'

'True enough.' Ash snorted. 'Any suggestions, sir? I'm damned if I know what to do.'

'Not really. But now we have another murder, I'll be out working today, too.'

He gave orders, such as they were. Conway would go back to the man who'd told him about Harold and follow the crumbs of information from there. Ash would look at Henry White once again, to see what they'd missed. There might be some tiny scrap they'd passed by before. And Harper intended to do his own digging into Willie Calder's life. Between them, surely they'd be able to tug some of the pieces together.

TWENTY-ONE

E mmeline Calder was supervising as men packed up all the items in the house. She'd been released from Armley Jail; with her husband killed, no one had a mind to pursue the case against her.

Her face still wore the grey prison pallor, and her hair was gathered in a tight bun at the back of her head. There was no sign of the servant girl; she'd have been dismissed, for the same reason the woman was leaving this place. A life she could no longer afford.

'Did Willie have much put by?' the superintendent asked.

She shook her head. Her eyes glittered with resentment and her mouth was a thin, sharp line. 'If he did, he never told me about it,' she said.

The woman seemed to move from room to room like a ghost. He followed. 'Where will you go?'

'His brother's rented me a place in Holbeck.' She stopped and turned suddenly. 'You know him, he's one of yours.'

Detective Sergeant John Calder.

Her new home would be nothing like this. No more grandeur. She'd be starting all over again, selling much of what she owned to survive. But that was what happened. Mrs Calder would have her life of genteel poverty, a life that would shrink with each year. At least she had family keeping an eye on her. That was more than many.

'Who do you think killed your husband?'

'I don't know,' she answered quietly. 'I've thought and thought. He was fair. Only bought silver and he paid a good price for it.'

'He broke the law doing it,' Harper reminded her. The police had given the house another thorough search, but they hadn't found more than the few items they'd used to arrest him. Calder had been a very careful man.

'At least you have plenty to sell.' Every table had been filled with trinkets, each room had good furniture.

'That's right.' She stared at him, face blank. 'I can sell off my past piece by piece, to keep myself alive a little longer. What do you want?'

'I'm trying to find out why your husband was murdered. Who this J.D. man was that Henry White mentioned in the writing he left for Willie.'

'If you ever find out, come and tell me. Maybe it'll make me feel better when I'm asking for something on tick at the corner shop.'

'You could help me.'

'Your man asked before, remember? When I was in a cell. I didn't know anything then and I don't know any more now. Willie's dead, that's all there is to it. And I have to live.' She plucked at her left hand then tossed her wedding ring down on the table. 'That'll be off to the pawnbroker this week. It's not as if it's doing me any good.'

She was bitter. She was broken, he decided as he walked up towards the Otley Road. But he believed her. Willie had probably kept a lot hidden, even from her. Certainly from his brother.

As he caught the tram a thought came. On impulse he alighted at Raglan Road. The street veered off at an angle beside Woodhouse Moor. The small police sub-station stood on the corner of Clarendon Road, hardly big enough for the tall man inside.

'Hello, George,' Harper said.

The man grinned, a broad smile cracking his long face. 'Hello Insp—, I mean, Superintendent, sir. What brings you all the way out here?'

George Forshaw had already served a quarter of a century on the force by the time Harper joined. He was still a constable, still content, and he'd forgotten more about policing than most men ever learned. But these days Woodhouse was more his speed, working the day shift then strolling up the road to his home in Hyde Park.

'Bartholomew Bush.'

The name had come unbidden. He didn't even know when he'd last thought of the man. But he was someone who might have a few answers.

'He's still alive, sir. Saw him Monday morning. Not as active these days. But who is?' Forshaw added ruefully.

'Still in the neighbourhood?'

'Oh yes. The only way he'll shift from here is in a wooden box. The same house, sir, if you remember it, and he's usually at home.'

'Has he been up to much lately?'

The constable chewed on his lower lip. 'Nothing I've heard. I doubt he could manage it these days, but he'd never admit he's past it.'

At one time Barty Bush had been a very successful thief. He planned his crimes meticulously, laying all the goods off to fences before he went home after a burglary. Even when the police knew he'd done a job, it was rare they could prove it.

Now the years had caught up with him, Harper saw as Bush opened his front door. Heavy white eyebrows, forests of hair erupting from his nostrils and ears. Almost bald on the top of his head, wispy side whiskers creeping down to his jaw. With his back bent, he appeared every inch an old man. It was hard to imagine the daring crook he'd once been.

Bush peered, then fumbled a pair of spectacles from the dressing gown he wore over the shirt and tie.

'Harker,' he said, but a flicker of doubt crossed his face. 'No, that's not it.' He snapped his fingers. 'Harper! Harper! Sergeant, isn't it?'

'It's Detective Superintendent now, Mr Bush. You're not up to date. Do you mind if I come in?'

Tea in the scullery. He noticed that the old man's hands shook as he moved the teapot to the kettle. A few minutes of small, polite conversation before Harper moved to the nub of the matter.

'What do you know about Willie Calder?'

Bush turned his head abruptly. 'I know he's dead, young man. I'm not addled. I read the newspapers. Why?'

'Did you ever do business with him?'

'I might have.' Bush's mouth curled into a smile. 'He was a funny one, was Willie, even when he was starting out.'

'Funny how?'

'Very . . .' He groped for the right word. 'Exact. He'd only buy silver, and it had to be *good* silver. No rubbish. Not like most fences.'

'Did he work with anyone back in the beginning?' Harper asked. 'Do the initials J.D. mean anything?'

'No,' the man answered after a minute. 'Doesn't ring a bell. My memory's cloudy but I don't remember any J.D.'

'What about *anyone* who worked with Willie Calder?' He was beginning to feel desperate. Their thin, slow progress kept grinding to a halt. Coming to see Barty Bush showed how low he'd sunk. The man looked as though he hadn't committed a crime in years. But nonetheless, Harper was here and hoping the man might offer him a glimmer of hope.

'There was someone,' Bush said softly. He seemed to be looking back through the years, straining to pick out the face. 'Like I say, he was always an odd one, was Willie. Kept his job.' He chuckled. 'Claimed he wanted to be secure if he ever decided to go straight.' He began to cough, pulling out a handkerchief. Finally the bout stopped; he was red-faced and gasping for breath. The superintendent poured him a mug of water from the jug.

'Do you need something?' Harper asked, looking around the room.

'Just my youth back.' He smiled, and very slowly he calmed. 'Willie Calder. He knew his silver, right enough.' He ran a tongue over his lips. 'It must have been a good twenty years ago. Back when I was still busy. Out most nights and making sure I avoided you lot.' A quick, wicked grin and Harper saw a flash of a younger man. 'There was talk then that Willie had a partner.'

'Not his wife?'

'A man,' he insisted. 'I don't think I ever paid it much mind. I sold him bits and bobs, but that was all. I never did much with silver.' He shrugged. 'I'm sorry. That's all I can tell you.'

'Is there anyone who might know the name?'

Bush shook his head and smiled. 'You'd need someone as crocked as me. Someone who's been around a while.'

'Thank you, anyway.'

He was at the door when Bush called out, 'Mickey Dyer.'

'Who?' Harper didn't know the name.

'That's who you should to talk to. He knew Willie quite well in the old days. I hear that he's still alive.'

'Where?' He almost shouted the word.

'You ask. Someone will know him, mark my words.'

Sergeant Tollman smiled when he heard the name.

'Old Mickey. I can't remember the last time I saw him. We used to have him in here four and five times a year, passing through on his way to appear in the dock. Before your time, sir,' he added. 'That's why you won't know him.'

'Where would I find him?'

'He used to have a room on Marsh Lane. There's a good chance he still does.' The sergeant shook his head. 'Mickey Dyer. Well, well, well. He never had much luck.'

He understood when he found the man. Still on Marsh Lane,

right enough, in a room that was no more than seven feet by six. Just enough space for a bed, a table and chair, with a basin for washing. The plaster on the walls bulged soft and brown with damp.

Dyer perched on the chair. He had piercing eyes, alert and wary, a full head of wild grey hair, and a face that looked younger than his years. His right leg was missing below the knee, and when he moved, he hobbled around quickly with the help of a crutch.

'Will Calder?' the words came out as a rasping bark. 'Isn't he dead?'

'He is.' Harper tossed two pennies on to the coarse blanket. 'I heard you used to know him.'

The man snorted. 'Knew all sorts once upon a time.' He tapped his stump. 'Man trap as I was trying to get into a place in Bramhope,' he explained simply. 'Went bad and they had to take the leg off. That was me done as a thief.' A wan smile. 'Don't let anyone tell you that you'll get rich begging. All you end up with is a place like this.'

The superintendent added another penny to the pile. Dyer never glanced at it, but he knew it was there.

'Who used to work with Calder?'

'He had a partner called Toby . . .' The man frowned as he searched his memory. 'No, don't remember his surname. Willie would take in the silver and this Toby, he knew the best places to sell it.'

'What happened to him?'

'Toby? He's been in his grave for donkeys' years now.'

Suddenly the superintendent was very attentive. 'How did he die?'

'Been so long I don't recall.' Harper threw down another coin but Dyer simply frowned. 'That won't help me remember. I think it was natural. But I've seen so many; after a while you lose track.' His hand snaked out and scooped up the money.

'Do you remember how long ago it was?'

'No,' Dyer admitted with a chuckle. 'The years all blend together, don't they?'

*   *   *

'Toby,' Tollman said, stroking his chin. 'Toby . . .' His face brightened. 'You just wait here a second, sir.'

It was closer to ten minutes when he returned, brushing dust from the dark blue of his uniform.

'Took me a little while. Tobias Joshua Emsley,' he announced. 'Fencing stolen property. Last arrested him in 1876, sir. No wonder you didn't know him.'

It was before Harper had even been old enough to join the force. He'd still been rolling barrels around Brunswick Brewery and wondering what to do with his life.

'Anything in the record about him dying?'

'Not here, but I can send someone to the Town Hall to look for a death certificate.'

'Do that.' It wasn't really a lead. It had all the substance of gauze. But it was what he had. He turned away and walked to his office as the telephone began to ring.

'Sir,' Tollman shouted. But it sounded like the ghost of a voice, no strength to it.

'What?'

The sergeant's face was white.

'That was D Division, sir. Someone's shot Sergeant Conway in Armley. He's dead.'

TWENTY-TWO

I t was bedlam. Uniformed police and detectives everywhere. The hackney couldn't even get close. Harper paid off the cabbie and walked along Town Street, feeling the shadow of Armley Jail looming over his shoulder.

God only knew how Ash had heard, but he was already there, trying to force some sense on to things. He had a grim expression, barking out orders. As Harper approached, a young copper took hold of his arm and tried to stop him.

'I'm Superintendent bloody Harper,' he snarled and pushed forward. The body lay on the pavement. Someone had found a sheet to cover him.

He elbowed his way through the police line.

'Tell me what you know,' he said. Ash turned, his eyes filled with shock and disbelief.

'From what I've been able to find out, sir, Sergeant Conway was coming along the pavement here.' He indicated with his hand. 'According to two of the witnesses, a man came out over there—' he pointed to a ginnel between two rows of houses, '—fell in behind Mark, raised a gun and shot him in the back of the head. Then he ran off before anyone could stop him.'

So calculated. So deliberate. So brutal.

'Do we have a description?'

'Nothing that's going to help. Dark hair, cap. The ones who saw it can hardly believe it happened. Not in Leeds.'

He knew what they meant. There had never been anything like this here. A copper gunned down in the middle of the day. It wasn't murder, it was assassination. He looked at all the uniforms milling around, confused, doing nothing. A cap, dark hair – like the man seen with Henry White before he died.

'Get this lot busy,' he said. 'I want men talking to everyone in the area. And I mean *everyone*. I want any possible sighting of the killer investigated.'

'Yes, sir. We got quite a few of the lads from D Division here. After all, they worked with Mark before he transferred to us.'

'Thank them. Use them.'

They were going to need every scrap of help. He'd have men working around the clock on this, and they'd be happy to do it. Conway was one of their own. They all knew that any man on the force could be under that sheet. They'd find that murderer.

'Inspector?'

'Sir?' Ash turned.

'I'm sorry. I know you were friends.'

'Thank you. I need to go and see his wife.'

He remembered Conway saying that they were expecting another child.

'Tell her we'll make sure they're looked after.'

Ash nodded. 'I'll get everything organized here first.'

Harper felt a hand on his shoulder. Superintendent Leeman, the commander of D Division.

'Christ, Tom.' His voice was empty. 'I thought it couldn't be true.'

'Shot him in cold blood.'

Leeman had been a policeman for almost thirty years. He'd seen almost every bad thing happen. But not a single one of them could have imagined this. It crossed the line.

'We'll work together,' Harper said.

'Yes.' The man gave a curt nod, his eyes still on the corpse. 'Anything you need, just let me know.' After a moment, he added, 'Conway was a good copper. Very good. I was sorry when he wanted to transfer. But it was a promotion, who could blame him?'

They both turned. Down the road voices were yelling at each other. Two bobbies were dragging a man who was shouting the odds.

'Bowman! Temple!' Leeman called. 'Who is he?'

'A drunk, sir.' One of the coppers tried to salute. 'He was telling everyone that all coppers should be shot.'

'Take him to the station. I'll talk to him later.'

'Yes, sir.'

'And Bowman,' Leeman told him, 'don't be gentle with the bugger.'

Leeman's men knew the area. They started the canvassing, going from door to door. The coroner's wagon arrived and took away Conway's body. It had barely gone before a pair of women appeared from the houses with buckets and brushes to scrub the blood off the pavement.

'You find whoever did that, you let me at them for five minutes,' one of them said. All Harper could do was nod. Every way he turned, he was surrounded by policemen. Those who'd finished their shift had arrived to help. They wanted the murderer.

Nobody killed a copper and got away with it.

An hour and bits and pieces of information kept trickling in. There was more from people who'd seen the killer, so they had a clearer picture. Thick jacket, boots, muffler knotted around his neck, cap pulled down over his forehead. Broad, with dark hair.

It was a start. But it was still too general. Was it the man with Henry? Who knew?

People had fled, shouting and screaming, as the shooter ran

from the killing with the revolver in his hand. A pair of detectives were trying to follow his trail.

Harper raised his head as the sound of a carriage drew close. The chief constable stepped out, head bowed, hat in his hand.

'What do we have, Superintendent Harper?'

'It's every bit as bad as you think, sir.'

'What can I do?'

'Just get stuck in, sir. We need all the help we can get.' The chief had been a working copper in his day; he knew the drill. It would hearten the men to have him working with them. It would show he cared.

The man did it, too, knocking on doors alongside a pair of uniforms, asking questions and noting down the answers.

Harper summoned Ash. 'I want some of them going over what Conway was doing up here. He must have been on to something.'

'I already have a detective sergeant following that thread, sir.'

'Very good. You're in charge here for now. I'm going down to see Dr King. I don't imagine he'll have much for us but I need to know.'

'Right enough, sir. I hear there are more heading over here from C Division, too.'

'The only problem is that the murderer's long gone by now.' He stared out over the valley, at the chimneys and the city, the air filled with the haze of smoke. 'Down there somewhere.'

'Don't you worry, sir. We'll find him,' Ash promised.

King was already working on the body, everything else set aside. He was thorough, talking as he cut, removed, and weighed. But all he could do in the end was confirm what they already knew: Conway had been killed by a shot to the back of his head, fired at close range. He'd never stood a chance.

'For what it's worth,' the doctor said quietly, 'it would have been instant. Conway wouldn't even have known.'

That was no solace for a life lost. And that consolation wouldn't help his widow.

On to Millgarth. The men who were there clamoured around for news. Half of them had volunteered to go up to Armley and help.

But what could they do? The area was already brimming with coppers.

'Go home,' he told them. 'Get some rest. We'll be needing more of you tomorrow.'

He scribbled a note and passed it to Sergeant Tollman for someone to deliver to Annabelle. He had no idea when he'd be home again.

A hackney back to Armley.

Some housewives had set up a table on the pavement. A shop-keeper had donated meat and bread and two of the women were making sandwiches.

He took one, washing it down with the tea someone poured for him.

Ash seemed to have aged ten years in the last few hours. His face looked haggard and torn, as if duty was the only thing keeping him going.

'News?'

'We're still trying to find out who Conway came to see up here.' He took a slow breath. 'He didn't put it in his notebook. The word's out so I'm hoping someone will come forward.'

'What about the killer? How far have we got following him?'

'Sightings down past the mill to the canal, but that's as far as it goes.'

'Nothing down there?' Harper asked in disbelief.

'The boats that were passing have all gone, sir. And there aren't many these days, anyway.'

They were getting nowhere. It was a mess. One look at Ash's eyes showed he knew it, too. Harper patted him on the shoulder. 'You're doing everything you can.'

'Not enough, though, is it, sir?'

'We can't turn the clock back and stop Conway coming up here,' Harper told him. 'And we'll get whoever did it, I don't care how long it takes. Is the chief still here?'

'Left a few minutes ago. But he did his bit.'

They both knew they needed to examine every possibility. Why had someone shot the sergeant?

'Could this have been an old grudge, do you think? Conway used to work up here.'

'I don't know, sir. I've been looking. So far there's nothing to say either way.'

If it wasn't, then it all went back to Willie Calder, then to Henry White, and whoever had scared him enough to serve six months rather than give up names. That was where it all began.

'Sir,' Ash said, dragging him out of his thoughts. Harper turned his head and saw a constable with a downy brown moustache. The man had approached on his deaf side; he'd never heard him.

'What is it?'

'This gentleman would like a word, Superintendent.' He pointed at a fellow standing a few yards away.

'Can I help you?'

'Tolliver.' The man strode towards them, a salesman's bright smile on his face, hand out, ready to shake. Forty, perhaps, the hair of his thick side whiskers turning grey, bowler hat tapped down firm on his head. Not rich, but not poor, either. His suit had seen better days, but it had been cared for. Polished shoes with scuffed toes, cracked leather and worn heels. As long as he had something to offer. They didn't have time for visitors.

'Do you know something about the murder, Mr Tolliver?'

'I know where your sergeant was going.'

For a second, all he could do was stare stupidly at the man. Then: 'Well, where?'

'He was on his way to see Gravedigger John.' Tolliver looked around proudly. Harper glanced at Ash. A quick shrug of the shoulders; neither of them had ever heard the name.

'Who?' the superintendent asked.

'Gravedigger John.' He repeated, then paused for a moment. 'He hides stuff for people. Stuff they've stolen. Buries it in the churchyards. That's how he got his name.'

Ash was already moving away, dispatching someone.

'How do you know Sergeant Conway was looking for him?'

'He stopped at my shop to ask where he might be, of course.' He said it as if it was the most obvious thing in the world, and nodded towards a place farther along the other side of the road and Harper saw the sign: Tolliver & Sons, Second Hand Furniture. We Buy And Sell.

'Did you know Mr Conway?'

The man hesitated before he replied. 'I'd tell him things sometimes.'

Good, the man was an informer. That helped.

'I think you'd better talk to me about it, Mr Tolliver. I want everything you know.'

The man rambled, flattered to be the centre of attention and milking it for all he could. But at heart he didn't have much to say. Conway hadn't told him where he'd been or why he was looking for Gravedigger John. Still, it all helped, and the man didn't refuse the shilling Harper offered when he was done.

'A couple of the local lads have gone to bring this John,' Ash said when he returned. 'Seems he's quite well known around here.'

'Now we have somewhere to begin.'

Armley only had a police sub-station, too small for all the men on the investigation. Instead they'd taken over the empty second floor of a grocer's shop, a room that stretched back a good thirty feet from the street. Not perfect, but it was on the spot and it had gas lighting. From the window, Harper could look down and see where Conway had been shot.

Gravedigger John didn't come willingly. A pair of grim-faced bobbies dragged him up the stairs, holding his arms tight to keep him upright. The man was rank, with uncombed, greasy hair and a beard that hung all the way to his belly. Ragged clothes and filthy hands, his nails torn. He stank of spirits, so drunk his eyes couldn't focus. Useless.

'Sober him up,' Harper ordered. 'I want him back here and coherent in ten minutes.'

John's hair was dripping and he shivered from the cold water when he returned. But at least there was something besides alcohol in his gaze.

'Henry White,' the superintendent began, shouting out the name when the man said nothing.

'Dead.' John mumbled and looked down at the ground.

'I know that,' Harper yelled. 'Tell me what you had to do with him.'

'I used to look after things for him.' The man mumbled so low he could barely catch the words. He took hold of John's chin and dragged his head up.

'What things?' he said slowly, clearly. 'Where did you keep them?'

The liquor was powerful on his breath. 'Things he stole.'

'When did you see him last?' He could feel the pulse pounding in his neck, his fingers tight on the other man's jaw. 'When?'

'Before he went into jail the last time.' John's eyes were open wide now, the whites large around the pupils. He was becoming more sober by the second. Scared. Petrified.

'Did he leave something with you?' A nod. 'What?'

'A sack. I buried it.'

'Where is it now?'

'Still there. He never came back for it.'

Harper felt a surge of hope. He tried to steady his breathing, to calm himself down a little.

'Where did it come from?'

'Burglary, of course.'

'Where?' He stared into the man's eyes.

'He didn't say.'

'Who was he going to sell to?'

John looked uneasy, shifting from one foot to the other. 'Said someone wanted to buy it, but they didn't want to pay him enough.'

'Who?'

'He didn't tell me. Just J.D. this, J.D. that.'

'J.D.?' Harper asked, feeling a sharp jolt right through his body. 'Are you sure about that?'

'Yes,' John answered, then looked at him. 'Why?'

He had it. The connection.

'Who's J.D.?'

'I don't know.' He could feel John starting to panic and draw in on himself. 'Never heard it before he said it.' His eyes moved around, searching for help. 'Honest.'

Harper believed him. The gravedigger was so terrified he'd have given them the world if he had it.

'You're going with Inspector Ash and a pair of constables, and you're going to dig up that sack.' John started to open his mouth, but the superintendent didn't give him the chance to speak. 'Whatever it is, I don't want to hear it. You'll do as I tell you and then you'll make sure you don't go far. Understand?' He waited. No nod. No answer. He took the man by his lapels. 'I said, do you understand?'

'Yes,' John answered grudgingly.

TWENTY-THREE

What did it all mean? He had a definite link between this J.D. and Henry White. And the initials were in the papers Willie Calder had put in his deposit box. That linked the three of them together. But what did it prove? Where did it take them?

Gravedigger John didn't have the wit to lie, and he couldn't have made up the name J.D. So White was hiding the silver from J.D. after agreeing to sell it to him. Holding out for a better price.

A short while after that, Henry White had gone to jail rather than name any names after he'd been arrested carrying stolen silver. That part didn't make sense, and the superintendent couldn't immediately see his way through the haze; but somewhere behind it all there had to be a pattern.

Conway must have learned that John knew something.

Harper scribbled notes of passing thoughts and ideas as he tried to make sense of it all. Where had Conway found his information? How had his killer found out? Had someone already been following him? Why? What did they suspect? Was it J.D.? Questions, more questions, and no bloody answers.

Ash's boots banged on the steps, followed by the jangle of metal as he tossed the sack to the floor. Some of the hessian had disintegrated, and dark earth clung to the material.

'He buries things deep, I'll give him that,' the inspector said with admiration. 'No wonder it was still there.'

But Harper was already on his knees, fingers working on the knot that kept the bag closed. Finally he tipped everything out on the floorboards.

Five pieces, none of them particularly large.

He brushed the dirt away. The silver was tarnished, but the

craftsmanship glowed. There was quality here. Someone had spent a lot of money on these items.

The superintendent bit his lip, trying to recall. No, he was absolutely certain; no one had ever reported these items stolen.

But why not?

'Good God,' he said as he turned each one in his hands. A snuff box on tiny, dainty legs. A small, two-handled cup. Other items he couldn't identify. He dug down in the sack, scrabbling around and hoping for something more. But it was empty. 'What do you make of that?'

'I don't know,' Ash said. 'We need to get it all identified and valued, don't we, sir? Maybe we'll have a better idea after that.'

He wasn't about to entrust the silver to a constable and the inspector was needed to co-ordinate everything here. He'd take it himself.

'We know that Conway had talked to Tolliver. Find out where he was before that,' Harper said. 'It could be the key.'

'I'll keep looking.'

It felt ridiculous to be carrying expensive stolen silver in a brown paper package tied with string. But it was all he could find, watching as a helpful grocer wrapped it for him. The hackney jolted and bounced over through Leeds, dropping him off on Commercial Street.

People milled around. He squeezed through the press of folk on the pavement and into Noble's, the silversmith. The man was an expert; he'd helped the police before.

'This is beautiful work,' Noble said as he examined each piece. He had a loupe carefully screwed into one eye, holding the silver in the light as he stared. 'Simple and perfect. Very good indeed. I'll need to clean it up, but it's definitely the real thing and it's worth plenty of money.'

'How much?' the superintendent asked.

'A very conservative estimate?' Noble considered the sum for a moment. 'I'd say two hundred pounds. Probably more than that.'

A small fortune, Harper thought. 'I need to know what you can tell me about it all. We've found it but I don't recall anything like this going missing.'

'I know.' Noble removed the magnifier and gave a satisfied smile. 'Believe me, I'd have heard about silver of this quality being stolen. Off the top of my head, I don't know where these are from. I'm happy to try and find out.'

'I'd appreciate that.'

'Leave it with me.' He calculated quickly. 'Come back this time tomorrow and I'll see what I can do. I'll clean these up properly, too.'

To Millgarth again, keeping an eye on everything and making sure everyone had the latest word. Then it was over to the Town Hall to brief the chief constable. It felt as if he was constantly on the move. And back to Armley by half past eight.

Lights illuminated the room. Someone had brought tables and chairs, and coppers worked, their shoulders hunched. Ash strode around like a schoolmaster, stopping to answer questions or ask them. A fever seemed to burn in the place. Everything was urgent. Everything was *now*.

'Any progress?' Harper asked.

'Not that you'd notice, sir. There are still some men out asking questions.' Ash brought a half-hunter from his waistcoat pocket and flicked the lid open. 'They should be done by ten.'

'Nothing from the search?'

'We had to stop when it grew too dark. We'll start again in the morning.'

'Go home,' Harper told him. 'I know Conway was your friend, but you won't be much good here if you're dog tired.'

'In a little while, sir.'

'Make sure you do,' he said. How often had Kendall given him the same order? And how often had he obeyed?

'I went to see Mark's wife.'

'How is she coping?' But even as he spoke, he knew it was a stupid question. For god's sake, her husband had just been murdered, her world had fallen apart. He should really have gone himself, he was the senior officer. But his mind had been on the investigation, not the widow and family. Now the guilt began to gnaw at him.

'As well as you'd expect, sir.'

'I'll visit her in the morning. Is there anything I can do?'

'Just make sure the force takes care of them.'
'I will.'

He was home by midnight, the cab drawing up outside the Victoria. The pub was dark, the streets empty, with only the eerie, bobbing glow of the gaslights along Roundhay Road. Harper glanced in at his daughter, caught in the innocence of sleep, then settled into his own bed.

'Have you caught him?' Annabelle asked, her voice completely awake.

'We don't even know who did it. Got a description, that's all.'

'I was downstairs in the pub earlier. It was all they were talking about.'

No surprise, he thought. It was the first time a policeman had ever been shot in Leeds. It was the kind of event people would remember. The centre of conversation for weeks.

She snuggled against him, quickly drifting off to sleep again. Harper's thoughts eddied and swirled as he lay. He didn't know when he finally rested, but he was awake before five, washing and dressing quickly, catching the first tram into town.

Papers were waiting on his desk, but they were nothing that related to the killing; they could wait. There was no new gossip among the beat bobbies; nothing had happened overnight. He took a hackney to Armley.

Ash was already there, giving commands to a full complement of men. Some were assigned to the investigation; others had finished their shift and arrived to volunteer their time. It was something they could do, the way they could help.

The inspector's suit was brushed, he'd combed his hair and shaved. But the dark rings stood out under his eyes and his voice sounded exhausted.

'I told you to go home last night,' Harper said.

'I did, sir.' Ash shook his head slowly. 'Couldn't slow my mind down enough to sleep. In the end I gave up and came back. My Nancy's gone over to the Conways to do what she can.'

'Do we have anything new?'

'One possible. The men were in the public houses last night. Someone swore they saw Sergeant Conway coming out of a building a mile up Town Street earlier yesterday.'

'Who lives there?' Harper asked urgently. 'Get them in here.'

'That's the problem, sir: it's empty. Hasn't been anybody living in the place for a couple of years.'

'Wrong address?' he asked. 'What about the places either side?'

'We've tried all around. No one remembers seeing Conway or anyone else.'

'What about the man who told you?'

'I went round to his house first thing, sir, dragged him out of bed. He swears it's true, he saw it with his own eyes. And Mark Conway had arrested him before. He knew him.'

Two steps forward, one step back. It wasn't the dance he wanted.

'Keep trying.' The superintendent looked around at all the willing faces with pride. 'No shortage of people.'

'Hardly surprising, is it, with a murdered copper. He's family. I've had to send half a dozen home because I've nothing for them to do. They'll get some sleep and come back later.'

'We need progress.' He heard the echo of Kendall in his words, all those times the man had said that exact thing to him. He saw Ash push his lips together and set his jaw, the way he'd done so often himself. 'I'm sorry. I know you're doing everything you can.'

'I've been thinking sir. Mark was killed with a gun. A revolver. There aren't many who could have them, sir. As far as I can tell, anyway. We ought to look into gun owners. Just in the background, in case we can't get anywhere else with the investigation.'

The superintendent nodded. 'You'd do well to go through items taken in burglaries.' He paused, trying to remember. 'I think there was one last year when a pistol was taken. But I'm sure we found it and arrested the man.'

Ash's face fell. 'Yes,' he agreed. 'Sorry, sir.'

'Never apologize for having ideas,' Harper told him. 'We need to try everything.'

'What we need is success.'

'No one could be doing a better job for Sergeant Conway than you.'

Ash gave a quick nod and returned to work.

Outside, a young reporter was waiting in his cap and heavy

coat, clutching a notebook and pencil. He looked weary; God only knew how long he'd been standing there.

'Superintendent!' he called. The poor lad had hope in his eyes. Harper thought. And people needed to know what was going on. The killing of a policeman would have shocked them all. Maybe they'd be willing help the coppers for once.

'Come on. I'll give you twenty minutes over a cup of tea.'

It was closer to half an hour in the end, the newspaperman scribbling away between questions.

Harper was open in his answers; at least, he sounded that way. It was an act, the senior officer's trick Kendall had suggested to him. Sleight of hand, as much as any magician working the music halls. He kept back many details, quite deliberately, things only the killer and the police would know.

All too often bobbies would blab to the papers for the price of a drink. But for once they'd all been tight-lipped, too stunned, too horrified to talk. That body on the cobbles could be them.

By the time the superintendent finished, the man was grinning. He knew he had a good article, and the competition wouldn't even come close today.

'We're doing everything we can,' Harper finished. 'We're going to find whoever killed Sergeant Conway, we'll put him in court and we'll see him hang.' He paused to let the reporter's pencil catch up. 'But we also need all the assistance that members of the public can give us.'

Of course it was a brazen appeal. But it was true. Anything, everything would help. It was better to have leads to chase down, even if they came to nothing. Right now, they were scrambling, hunting for scraps, although he was never going to admit that.

The reporter lapped up the words like cream, full of gratitude as he left. Now he just had to hope the article did some good. It would be on the front page this evening, read all over town.

He counted out his coins for the waitress, but she wouldn't take them. 'I heard you. You're one of them trying to find that bobby's killer, aren't you?' When he nodded, she continued, 'Your money's no good here, luv. None of you.'

He thanked her and left it on the table anyway. People would never stop surprising him with their kindness.

Another hackney back into the city centre. Time to find out about the items that had been buried.

Noble the silversmith took him through to the workroom behind the shop. The silver was there, glittering, hypnotic in its beauty. The superintendent bent and looked close, admiring it.

'What can you tell me about it?' he asked.

'It's the most remarkable thing. Every piece of silver carries a hallmark to say who created it. An identification of the maker.' Noble paused, waiting until Harper nodded his understanding. 'The hallmark here is BB. It took me a while to find out who that was.' He gave a smile of anticipation.

'Well?'

'These were done by a Leeds man, late seventeenth century.' Noble paused and frowned. 'There's a problem, though, a big one. We only have one piece that we know is by him. A spoon. Nothing like these. There's no record of these at all.'

'But . . .' Harper began, and realized he didn't know what to ask. 'Are they genuine?'

'Oh yes, I'm positive of that. But I've no idea where they came from. These are a great discovery, but out of the blue. As far as anyone knows, these don't even exist.'

'I see.' God, this grew more and more tangled. But perhaps there was someone who could help.

The tram took him out along Woodhouse Lane, past the Moor, all the way up Otley Road to the bustle of suburban shops around North Lane. He walked down until he stood outside Willie Calder's old house, on the cusp between Headingley and Kirkstall. Very respectable, three-storey villas.

Through the window he could see the place was empty. No curtains, and he could imagine the way his footsteps on the bare boards would echo around. The place had held secrets, he knew that in his bones. But they'd all gone now. It was just wood and plaster and brick, and soon enough it would be filled with other memories.

The woman had a new home in Holbeck, she'd told him that. He needed to see her. Soon. He thought about Willie Calder, and his mind moved to Henry White, remembering the way the man looked as he was released from Armley, walking out of the gate with a dazed expression, as if he couldn't quite believe it was real. The superintendent could hear his own words as he pressed Henry, giving him a day to come up with the names. It would have been kinder to insist on getting them there and then. Who knew how many more might have been alive if Harper had done that?

Only charlatans could tell the future, though, and no one could change the past. It had happened. Henry was dead, Willie Calder, Talbot the jail guard. Now Sergeant Conway. All gone. It felt like a tale spiralling up and up.

He'd catch up with Mrs Calder very soon. For now, though, he had too much to do. On the Otley Road he hailed a cab to go back to Armley.

The curtains were closed although it was broad daylight. He stood by the step and knocked gently on the door. A woman aged somewhere around sixty answered. Iron-grey hair, gathered back in a bun, a shapeless black gown and kind, quizzical eyes.

'I'm Superintendent Harper,' he said. 'I was the sergeant's commanding officer.'

A slow, silent nod of the head and she moved aside. The door to the parlour was open. The young woman inside tried to rise to her feet but he waved her back down. She was large, probably ready to give birth in just a few weeks.

'I'm very sorry about your husband,' he told her. 'If I could change it, believe me, I would.'

She was small, pale, all the life washed out of her by her husband's death. 'Thank you.'

'I want to tell you that we'll find the man who did this. Mark was a very good policeman. He'd only worked for me for a short time, but I was proud to know him.'

'Fred Ash said he should join you.' She looked at him, empty of tears.

'No one could have guessed what would happen,' he told her. 'No one. But the force will look after you. All of you. I'll make sure of it.'

A few minutes of conversation and he left. What could he say? Her husband was gone, the only things ahead a hero's funeral for him and a lonely life for her. He walked over to the room above the grocer's shop they were using for the murder enquiry.

Coppers bustled in and out. Watching, it almost seemed like a factory to him.

'Anything worthwhile to tell me?' he asked Ash.

'Not much, sir.' His eyes were bloodshot and feverish. Too long awake, too many hours focused on this. 'Someone came forward with a better description of the killer. Saw him as he was running off.' He handed over a printed sheet.

'Very good,' he said, although it added little to what they knew. Dark hair. Close to five feet ten. Wearing a bowler hat and a dark overcoat. Broad-shouldered, fast runner. 'Maybe it'll make someone think. There'll be a piece in the *Evening Post* today, too.'

Ash stretched. 'It's funny, sir. I can almost see him. Then I turn to bring him into focus and he vanishes again.' He yawned.

'Go home and get some rest. You're exhausted.'

'Sir—'

'It's an order.' He tempered it with a smile. 'You need good eight hours of sleep and a proper hot meal.'

'Yes, sir.'

'I'll look after things here.'

TWENTY-FOUR

The men all worked with a will, no one shirking. He went around, thanking each one of them; many had given up their free time, and they all deserved far more than he could give them. But his words brought smiles. One or two had memories of working with Conway and he stopped to listen.

These were good men, solid men. Even if they might not all always be honest men, for now their hearts were in the right place.

The superintendent was still there as night began to fall. Some bobbies had gone home. Others drifted in to replace them; the room was as full and lively as it had been that morning. The *Evening Post* had done him proud, interview on the front page with a big headline. He was reading it when a constable approached, helmet under his arm, a pale, bristling moustache, and stood at attention.

'Superintendent Leeman's compliments, sir, and could you go over to D Division in Wortley?'

'Did he say why?'

'Don't know, sir. That's the message I was asked to deliver, sir.' The man was formal, eyes straight ahead, uniform perfect. In time he'd make a natural sergeant.

As soon as he walked into the station at Wortley he heard the choir of drunks. It was still early and not even a Saturday night; they must have had something to celebrate. It felt disorientating to hear some joy after the bleakness of the last few weeks. There was more sorrow ahead – Kendall's small funeral was in the morning, a memorial later, then a big service for Conway. Death wouldn't leave him alone this year.

Leeman was in his office, smoking a pipe as he read over a paper, the nib poised in his hand. He relaxed as he saw Harper.

'I'm sorry to drag you away, Tom. I wouldn't bother if it wasn't important.' He shouted for one of the bobbies and gave an order. 'Something you should hear.'

'What?'

'She'll be here in a minute. We arrested her with those drunks and she's three sheets to the wind herself.'

Her hat was tipped at a strange, unnatural angle on her head, hair spilling out of its pins. The woman leered when she saw Harper.

'Brought me a fresh one, have you, luv?' She stumbled, holding on to the desk for support. Her dress was old, faded and worn, shiny in patches. Her gaze kept shifting away.

'Shut up, Addie,' Leeman told her. 'Tell this gentleman what you told me earlier.'

'About what?' She slurred her words, confused.

'About Talbot.'

'Oh.' She composed herself, standing like a schoolgirl and swaying slightly.

'Used to have a good time with him.' She chuckled to herself then jerked her head up, turning serious. 'He told me once that he knew someone important.'

Harper shot a glance at Leeman. 'Important?'

'That's what he said,' the woman mumbled, turning her head to look at him.

'Who? Did he say?'

'Don't know. Didn't ask.' Her mouth curled into a smile. 'But he told me it was a man who'd killed people.'

'What?' Suddenly he was digging his nails hard into his palms. 'Did he give you a name? Anything?'

'Just that no one could touch him.'

Leeman nodded to the constable by the door. 'Give her a drink and turf her out,' he said, then turned to Harper. 'That's all she knows. I thought you'd want to hear it for yourself.'

'Yes.' But what it all meant, he didn't know. Someone important? A killer? Who? 'Thank you.'

'Hard to believe, isn't it?'

'You seem to know her,' Harper said. 'Is she telling the truth?'

'I've had her in here about once a month for years. Has a few drinks and gets loud. That's as bad as she gets.' He sighed and shrugged. 'Most likely we'll find her frozen to death in a gutter one night. Anyway, yes, I believe her.'

'Whoever Talbot was talking about might have been the one who killed him.'

'Or the people he fleeced over taking things into prison for their relatives.'

'I don't think so, do you? I could see them beating him for that, but not killing.'

'Maybe you're right. But anything that helps us catch Conway's murderer . . .'

'Is very welcome,' Harper agreed with a grateful smile. They shook hands. 'I appreciate it.'

Now he had to try and fit *that* into the puzzle.

Ash was back in Armley, looking a little better than he had before, as if he'd managed to find a few hours' rest.

'I've got something interesting to tell you,' Harper said.

'What does "important" mean, though, sir?' the inspector asked when he'd finished. 'A councillor?'

Harper shook his head. 'It couldn't be. There's not a man on the council who'd dirty his hands by killing anyone himself.' They might be venal, but none of them had the courage for something like that.

'They could pay someone to do it.'

'Maybe.' But the way the woman Addie had spoken, it sounded like someone who'd done the act with his own hands. 'It's something else for the pile, at least.'

'I've got one, too.' Ash reached into the desk drawer and brought out a Webley revolver. 'This was handed in half an hour ago.'

Harper handled it carefully, breaking open the chamber. Still four bullets inside. 'Where was it found?'

Ash picked out the spot on the map. 'Right there, sir. Some little lad came across it and took it home.' He shuddered.

Four bullets left, and Conway had only been shot once. Christ . . .

'Did he fire it?'

'No.' Ash shook his head. 'Just as well, too. I think it must have been too heavy for him. He tried to take it out to play with his friends tonight and his mam saw it. She made him bring it down here.'

'Thank God for that.' There could have been a boy or two dead by now.

Harper picked it up again, feeling the iron weight of the weapon. This was it. This had to be the gun that had killed Sergeant Conway.

'Have you sent men to go over that waste ground?'

'Someone to guard it for now. We'll look properly once it's light.'

Annabelle adjusted his tie, standing back to look at her work before giving a nod of approval. Mary stood, awestruck by her father's clothes. She'd never seen him dressed like this before. But this morning was Kendall's funeral, and Harper owed the man the courtesy of appearing in a detective's formal uniform. The wing collar bit into his neck, the frock coat and striped trousers felt too tight. His top hat rested on the table.

'You look a picture.'

'I don't feel it.'

'Da, why are you wearing those clothes?'

'Because it's an important occasion.' It was the simplest answer.

'Are you sure you don't want me to go with you?' Annabelle asked.

'You barely knew him,' Harper replied. And she had three hundred leaflets to deliver. The council election was a month away and she was campaigning for the Independent Labour Party candidate. She'd been out tramping the streets around Sheepscar yesterday, too, knocking on doors and talking to the women, and she'd be back doing that tomorrow and all the days after until people voted, with Mary at her side. Their daughter would grow up with politics in her blood.

A kiss from each of them and he was gone, out into the morning. Only two minutes before a cab came by and he was looking out at Chapeltown Road. It was all houses now, as far as the eye could see. Leeds was growing so quickly that it seemed to be devouring the empty land. Soon there would be no more villages scattered around, they'd all be consumed by the city.

He stood with Sergeant Tollman in St Martin's Church, the only other policeman at the service. Kendall's children were there on either side of their mother. Grown, adults, the sons the image of the father.

He'd never seen most of the congregation before. Relatives and friends, about twenty of them, following the coffin out to the graveyard as the last notes of the organ drifted away.

The gravediggers began shovelling sod on to the coffin and he made his quick farewells. Mrs Kendall would understand, she'd been a copper's wife for years.

'I wasn't sure if you'd be able to come, with that poor man shot.' She gave a teary nod. 'But thank you. You were always his favourite at Millgarth, you know.'

Olivia Kendall was all in black, her plain, modest gown and hat out of fashion. But who cared about little things like that now? Sorrow and pain filled her eyes and her face was pale with loss. She could no longer hide the things she'd pushed down while her husband was dying. She didn't need the mask any more. So many years together and now she was alone. She reached into a large handbag and brought out a small box.

'He wanted you to have this, Tom. He talked about it.'

Surprised, he reached out and took it, not sure what to say.

'There's a note inside,' she continued and swallowed. 'He wrote it. He was very prepared, you see. That was his way, no loose ends.' She pressed her hand over his. 'Just don't forget him.'

'Don't worry,' he told her. 'I never could.'

At home, changing into ordinary clothes, he placed the box on the mantelpiece, out of Mary's reach. It felt strange to be here during the day, the rooms so empty and quiet, as if they'd been abandoned.

'How was it, sir?' Ash asked.

'Quiet. Everything the way he wanted,' Harper answered. 'Have you searched where that lad found the revolver?'

'Had the men out first thing.' His face showed nothing. 'They haven't come up with anything else yet, sir.'

He hadn't expected much. But deep inside he'd hoped for something to help them.

'Any good tips from the newspaper article?'

'Just rubbish, sir. Sorry. I was thinking about what you said yesterday, sir, that Talbot knew someone important.'

'Go on.' The superintendent settled in a chair.

'We've been thinking of important as someone with status. But what if it's not? It could be someone who has the power to get things done.'

Harper pursed his lips. 'Isn't that the same thing?'

'No.' The inspector leaned forward, big hands clasping his knees. 'I mean the type of man who can arrange things. They're all over town.'

Now he understood. Fixers. Hard men with brains who could organize anything for a pound or two. Men who inspired fear in their neighbourhoods, who thought themselves untouchable.

'It's possible.' He wasn't sure he bought the idea, but it was something when they had nothing. 'Ask the local coppers. They'll know who those characters are around here. Bring them in and make them sweat.'

'Yes, sir.' There was satisfaction in the inspector's voice.

'Show them the gun and see how they react. Do we have anything else to pursue?'

'I'm sorry, sir. It's like an empty larder.'

'Do what you can.'

TWENTY-FIVE

He didn't want to do it. But he'd run out of options. With a murdered copper there was a clamour for results. Quick results. And so far he hadn't been able to give the people of Leeds one damned thing.

It wasn't far to the jail, no more than a few minutes' walk. Inside, as the heavy wooden gate banged behind him, the world felt a little colder, the chill creeping into his bones.

Governor Hobson was happy to oblige. After Willie Calder's murder here, Harper expected nothing less. He still had to wait, though, a long half-hour in the small, airless room where the walls seemed to press in on him, and a scarred table and two wooden chairs the only furniture. He was here to sup with the devil himself and he didn't have a long spoon.

Finally the man arrived, escorted by a pair of warders. They seated him and stood back a pace.

'I need to talk to the prisoner alone,' the superintendent told them.

'Orders, sir,' the senior guard replied. 'We have to stay. He's a very violent man.'

Harper knew that well enough. After years of trying, he'd finally managed to arrest Tosh Walker six years before. He was guilty of many things, but they'd put him away for prostituting young girls, abusing them. He'd remain behind bars for a long time yet.

Even in his jail uniform, Walker was an important man. He still possessed a small empire outside. Bit by tiny bit, it had crumbled a little over the years. But his wife and his brother kept the core of his businesses strong, waiting for when he might eventually be released.

Walker looked healthy, as if he'd prospered behind bars. No doubt he had. A few small scars on his face. More on his hands, Harper noticed when the man raised his manacled wrists. The price of skirmishes and victory.

'Well, well. Inspector Harper.' He gave a deliberate pause. 'I'm sorry, Superintendent now, isn't it? I should feel honoured.' His eyes were hard, glinting. 'Married as well, and with a pretty little girl, I hear.' He let his tongue linger over the words.

It was a goad, but Harper wasn't going to let himself show anything. He wouldn't give Tosh Walker that satisfaction. Just a blank face.

'I'm here to make you an offer, Tosh. The best one you've had since you were sentenced.'

'Oh aye? What's that, then?' He'd caught the man's attention.

'I could go after that wife of yours. Your brother, too. From what people are saying, they're always together anyway. Day and night, I hear.' He watched as the man's expression hardened. 'I don't mean a quick raid and hope for the best. I'll be back there every day, every month, taking all your businesses apart until there's nothing left. When you come out of here you'll be able to go and join them in the workhouse.'

Force: that was what Walker understood. To him, anything else was fatal weakness.

'What are you after?' he said finally. His voice was quieter. Hardly defeated, but thoughtful.

'Names.'

'What sort of names?'

'I'm after the one that connects Henry White, Willie Calder, and Claude Talbot.'

Walker threw back his head and laughed. 'That desperate, are you?'

'Well?'

The man raised his hands and made the chains jangle. 'Look at me. I'm in here. They're so scared they need to have me like this. And you really think I know what's going on outside?'

'Take them off,' Harper ordered.

'Sir . . .' the guard began, but the superintendent repeated the command.

'I'll take responsibility.'

Warily, they obeyed. Watching Walker closely as he rubbed his wrists.

'Don't try and kid me, Tosh. You know exactly what's happening,' Harper said. 'You have a finger in more pies than you can count, in here and outside the walls. If you don't help me, you're not going to have a single bloody thing left. That's a promise.' He let his words hang in the air. 'Now, do you want to start again?'

'What do I get if I help you?'

'I told you. Things stay as they are.'

Walker looked around the room. 'I want to be out of here sooner.'

'No.'

'Then I'm not going to help you.'

'Fine. Suit yourself.' Harper stood quickly. The guard moved forward to replace Walker's manacles. 'I've told you what I'll do, Tosh. You'd better remember, I'm a man of my word.'

It had been a gamble. He'd lost. Maybe Walker had the information he needed; maybe not. But threats were all he had to pry it out of him. And they hadn't been enough.

He strode down the corridor to wait at the locked gate. The voice made him turn, echoing loud off the tiled walls. One of the guards, shouting for him to return. Slowly, he walked back to the room. Walker was still seated, a defiant expression on his face.

'What do you want, Tosh?' If he was going to gamble, he might as well stake everything. 'I hope it's worth my while.'

The man took a slow breath. 'If I help you, do you promise you won't go after them?'

'Them?'

'My wife. My brother.'

'I already said.' He stared at the prisoner and for the first time began to believe he held the upper hand. 'It depends on what you tell me.'

'J.D.' Walker said and looked up. 'Does that mean anything?'

He could feel the skin prickling on his arms. 'Who is he?'

A shrug. 'That's all I know.'

'Not enough,' Harper told him. 'Nowhere near enough.' He nodded. 'Take him back to his cell.'

No more words, no more yelling. This time he left with no one calling him back. No deals made and only a fragment of information.

J.D., he thought. Bloody J.D.

Ash had gone; no one knew where. There was nothing fresh, everyone working. This was the boring, everyday part of being a copper. Following every lead, keeping track of each detail. If they didn't find the culprit in two days it always came to this, solid, plodding police work. Sometimes there was a stroke of luck, but he'd given up on that. The only way to end this would be with a hard, back-breaking slog.

Liver and onions at the café in the market. He needed the food to keep him going. But something was missing. He ate, he read the newspaper. Yet without Maguire here to come over to his table and talk for a minute or two, everything seemed adrift, upside down.

This was where they'd meet. It needed Maguire's voice, his good humour, to seem complete. Even before he'd finished the meal he gave up and left.

He was still young. These ghosts shouldn't be haunting him yet.

Over and over he scribbled the initials on the blotter. J.D. Who was he? Why couldn't they even get a smell of him? Over and over until he'd scratched his way right through the paper.

'How can anyone stay that well hidden?' Annabelle asked.

'I've been asking myself that.' They were snuggling close in the bed. His arm was around her shoulders, her head against his chest. 'I still haven't found an answer.'

She shifted position a little, her hand across his stomach. He stroked the sleeve of her cotton nightgown.

'How did things go today?' He needed a change of topic, something to divert his mind for a few minutes. 'Looking hopeful for that Labour candidate?'

'Not really,' she replied, and he could hear her frustration. 'It doesn't help that the man who's standing is worse than useless. He doesn't have a clue.'

'Don't do anything for him, then.'

'I've got to. Party loyalty.'

He knew Annabelle would have been the perfect candidate; round here no one could have beaten her. But she'd never have that chance. Women couldn't vote and they couldn't hold office. The school board was as far as their opportunity extended.

Instead, she did what she could. Supporting the Independent Labour Party, working to help women get the vote: she threw herself into the causes. Just not always happily.

'You can change a few minds round here,' Harper told her. 'They know you. They trust you.'

'Happen they do,' she said. 'But it's not me they'll be voting for, is it?' A long sigh. 'Strange about that thing Kendall left you, isn't it?'

He'd opened the box as he ate. Inside there was a small piece of pottery. It was old, that was obvious, with crude red and black decorations. Harper examined it, holding his breath and feeling that even a firm touch could break it. Then he passed it to her and unfolded the note in the box. It was Kendall's writing, but not the firm strokes he remembered. They trailed off here and there, the words half-formed.

Tom,

We're each of us just here for a short time. Sounds silly, doesn't it, but I've come to learn just how short. But man's been here longer than we know. Maybe we'll never understand how long. Nathan Bodington who runs Yorkshire College loves curiosities and mysteries. He gave me this. The British Museum sent it to him, they'd dug it up on Cyprus. Evidently it was made around seven hundred years before Our Lord was born. I hope you'll think about that, it's more than two thousand five hundred years old. That's a wonder, isn't it? Remember it when you hold the piece. It's as fragile as life, but strong enough to last, long after we're all dust and forgotten. There's a lesson in this. Be yourself, be a good, strong man.

Kendall.

Almost quarter to four. Annabelle was shaking him awake.

'Someone's hammering at the door, Tom.'

Groggy, he threw on a dressing gown, stumbled down the stairs and through the bar. A red-faced young copper was waiting, still trying to catch his breath. The lad must have run all the way from Millgarth.

'Inspector Ash needs you out at Armley, sir.'

'Why? What's happened?'

'Sorry sir,' he gasped, 'I don't know. They just told me to come and tell you. The night sergeant's whistling up a hackney. It should be here soon.'

'Good work, Constable. Thank you.'

Just time to wash and dress and worry about what was so important. Another body? Please God, no. But Ash wouldn't send for him unless it was urgent. Why was the inspector there in the middle of the night, anyway?

Questions tumbled one after the other as he stood on the corner, hearing the clop of hooves and rolling iron wheels as the cab approached.

Even at this hour there was traffic on the roads. The early carts, overloaded and moving slowly. There was already a hard tang in the air, and the day shifts at the factories hadn't even begun yet. He wiped a smudge of soot off his shirt cuff.

Harper ran up the stairs and into the room.

'Where's the inspector?'

Two more minutes on foot, a constable guiding him along the streets.

The house stood at the end of a terrace, a copper guarding the open front door. A small group of neighbours had gathered a few yards away, talking and gossiping and inspecting him as he arrived.

A lodging house. It had the right, sour smell and the warren of doors. A woman with a hatchet face stood, arms folded. Harper could hear movement upstairs and followed the noise. Ash stood by the bed, staring down.

It looked as if the man had fallen asleep on the floor, nightshirt ridden up to his knees, one arm under his head like a pillow. Absolutely peaceful in death. No one he recognized. It couldn't be J.D. Not this man.

'Who is it?'

'Cecil Lester, sir.'

The acid thrower. With everything else going on, the man had slipped out of his mind. And here he was, dead, gone. A story ended.

'What happened?'

'Seems he's been lodging here for a few days,' Ash began. 'The landlady downstairs heard a noise about midnight and came up to look. Knocked on the door and got no answer, so she used her key. Found him like this and went running for a bobby.'

Harper was staring at the body. No sign of injury. No weapons in the room unless there was something hidden under the corpse.

'The lad on the beat must be a bright one,' the inspector continued. 'Lester had been calling himself Cecil Saville. The copper took a gander through his belongings, found something with the name Cecil Lester and put two and two together. He came and told me.'

'Natural causes?' He squatted, feeling around on the floor. Nothing.

'Looks that way, sir. But I thought you'd want to see him, sir.'

'I'm glad you called me.' This was one case done, at least. No chase, no arrest, but final nonetheless. As final as it could be. Harper stood and stretched. 'His poor bloody family, eh?' This was finished but there was still a murderer out there. 'What else have we found?'

'So Tosh Walker doesn't know either, sir?'

'No,' Harper said. 'For once I think he was telling me the truth.'

'Maybe.' Ash swallowed the dregs of tea from his cup. 'You never know with him, do you?'

'No.' Walker always had something, a twist, an angle.

'What about the agreement you made with him, sir? Are you going to honour that?'

Harper smiled. 'Not a bloody chance. I'm going to destroy him.'

'Just let me know how I can help, sir.' Martha, the girl Ash and his wife adopted, had been abused by Walker and his friends. 'After we've cleared up this business, of course.'

* * *

The superintendent left the men to it. They were all busy with their tasks; he was simply excess baggage, the senior officer peering over their shoulders and making them feel uncomfortable.

It was still early. As he walked down the hill a morning chorus of horns echoed down the valley from the factories to start the early shift. Smoke was already beginning to pour from the chimneys. But it was quiet by the canal. The towpath was empty, the water still. A quarter of a mile away a train passed on its way out to Bradford, the deep, rhythmic chug like a call across the landscape.

Another one dead. He couldn't feel any sympathy for Lester, only for the ones he'd abandoned. The man had thought running was better than justice. But justice of a kind had caught him in the end.

There was a haze over the city, a pall, trapping the spring warmth close to the ground. People on the pavement were sweaty and short-tempered. The constables would earn their pay today, he thought, breaking up fights and stopping women from killing their menfolk.

At Millgarth he opened the window in the office, but there was no real breeze to stir the air. In his shirtsleeves he started going through the waiting pile of papers. After an hour he put down the nib, stood up and looked out. The parade square behind the station, the stables for the police horses. A few yards to the south, the open market. Men crying their wares, all the displays and attractions. His mind was wandering.

Yesterday he hadn't had time to look for Willie Calder's wife in Holbeck. Today he'd find her. Maybe she'd be able to tell him something about this mysterious haul of unknown silver with its rare Leeds hallmark. She was the only one left who might know.

He had to talk to three different beat men before he found the information he needed. A widow woman, just moved into the area? A sentence of directions and he was standing outside the front door, hearing the shouting and the roaring from inside. Harper raised his hand to knock, then lowered it again, straining his good ear to listen.

TWENTY-SIX

The voices came from upstairs, going at it hammer and tongs. He recognized Mrs Calder's voice, screeching, yelling like a banshee, but he could only make out a few of the words. A man was shouting, too. He seemed almost familiar, but Harper couldn't place him.

Finally, they quietened into an uneasy truce and he brought his fist down on the wood. A sudden silence, then a scramble and a few seconds later the woman opened the door. It looked as if she'd dressed hastily, her clothes askew, her hair uneven and falling out of its comb. Her face was flushed, cheeks bright pink, the fire still burning in her eyes.

'It's a bad time,' she said as her greeting. She held the door almost closed, and she kept glancing over her shoulder.

'Then I'm sorry to disturb you.' He tipped his hat. 'I have a few more questions.'

'You need to come back in an hour or two.' She pushed the door to and he heard the key turn.

Harper had noticed the man's shadow, coming down the stairs and tiptoeing through to the scullery. He strode to the end of the block, turned and waited. A minute later a man scuttled by. Now he knew him.

Detective Sergeant John Calder.

How long had that been going on, he wondered?

At Millgarth he took Tollman aside.

'Can you get me the file on Sergeant Calder over in Hunslet?'

'I suppose so, sir.' He hesitated. 'They might want to know why, though.'

'Tell them you don't know, your superintendent requested it.'

'All right, sir.' He still sounded unsure.

*　*　*

By ten the folder was on his desk. Calder had been given three
commendations during his career, one of them for bravery. He
was a model copper. A widower with three children.

And carrying on with his late brother's wife. Both of them
were widowed now, so there was nothing wrong with that, except
that Calder was on duty according to the roster at the front of
the file.

He went back to the beginning and began to read again. Then
he saw it, jumping off the page at him and it all made sense.

Harper scribbled a note and handed it to a young lad
wearing a uniform too big for his scrawny body, with orders
to deliver it.

The woman was prepared for him now. She'd changed clothes,
putting on a sweeping burgundy skirt with a short, matching
jacket with leg-of-mutton sleeves, a little ruff of lace at the neck
of her blouse.

He tipped his hat as she opened the door. 'My apologies if I
called too early before.'

'I didn't have my wits about me.' Emmeline Calder gave him
a smile. 'I was hardly out of bed.'

In its own way that was true, but he didn't pursue it. She led
him through to the scullery, apologizing for the small size of the
house, the fact that she'd hardly unpacked and there was no
servant to help.

'Now,' she said brightly once they were seated, 'you said you
had a few more questions. How can I help you, Superintendent?'

He looked around the room before he spoke. Everything was
in order. He'd glanced into the parlour, with so many objects on
display that there was barely room to move.

'I was wondering if you'd discovered anything else your
husband might have left.'

'No,' she replied simply. Harper watched her. No widow's
weeds for her, no grief on her face. She wasn't a woman in
mourning.

'We've come across some valuable silver. It's an odd thing,
no one knows where it's come from. Very old.'

'I'm sorry,' Mrs Calder told him firmly. 'I don't know. Will
kept so much to himself.'

'Always worth asking. Has anyone been in contact with you about him?'

'Just with their condolences.' She paused, frowning. 'What exactly is it you want, Superintendent?'

The knock on the door came at the perfect moment.

'Some truth,' Harper said with a gentle smile. 'Nothing more than that.'

She eyed him curiously before she left. Urgent whispers at the door, too low for him to make out. Then she returned, Sergeant Calder trailing after her with his hat in his hands.

'You wanted me to meet you here, sir.'

'I did. Thank you. You found this house for your sister-in-law, didn't you?'

'That's right.' Calder glanced at the woman with a hint of worry. 'I've stopped by a couple of times to make sure she's settling in. After all, she's family.'

'Of course,' Harper agreed. 'I'm sure you're eager to see to her welfare.'

The sergeant reddened. 'Are you trying to imply something, sir?' His hair shone with pomade and his front teeth protruded slightly. Like the description they'd been given of the man walking with Henry White before he died. He'd never made the connection. Stupid, stupid.

'I don't need to, do I? I heard the pair of you earlier and I saw you try to leave without being spotted.'

'I know that was on police time, sir, but—'

'We'll talk about that later.' Harper turned to the woman. 'When did it all begin?'

'After I came out of Armley.' She was flustered, her face red. 'That's the truth. Nothing when Willie was alive.'

She sounded too earnest, too raw, for it to be a lie.

'Tell me, Mrs Calder, what sort of questions did the sergeant ask about your husband?'

She didn't understand. 'What? What do you mean?'

'Sergeant Calder,' Harper asked, 'what are your Christian names?'

The man blinked. 'John, sir.'

'John what?'

Calder took a deep breath. 'John David, sir.'

'J.D.' For a moment there was stunned silence, then he turned to the woman. 'Meet your lover,' he told her. 'The man who arranged your husband's murder.'

It happened too fast. He couldn't stop it. In a blur Mrs Calder turned and pulled a knife from the sink. She threw herself at the man, snarling, spitting, sinking the blade deep in his belly.

Harper vaulted the table and grabbed her hair. She screamed as he dragged her back. His fingers tightened around her wrist and shook the blade out of her hand, hearing it clatter on the floor. She struggled, kicking, shouting, screaming as he pushed her to the ground, face down. He forced the cuffs on to her wrists. For a second Harper glanced at Calder. The pool of blood was growing underneath him. No time.

He pulled the woman away and knelt by Calder. His hands were pressed tight over his bloody stomach, eyes closed. But he was still breathing. Harper put a fingertip on his neck; the pulse was strong.

'Don't you die, you bastard,' he hissed. 'Don't you bloody dare. I'm not letting you get away that easily.'

A last glance. Out in the street, Harper took his police whistle from his pocket and kept blowing until help came.

'I don't understand, sir,' Ash asked. They sat in the detectives' room, the door and windows open wide to let the warm air through. In the hallway the new plaster was already grubby, and the wood around the door looked darker, worn. Everything returning to the way it should be. 'How did you work out that Sergeant Calder was J.D.?'

'Luck,' the superintendent answered. The one thing they'd needed, and the one thing that had been in such short supply all the way through the case. 'Sheer luck. I stopped by to see his sister-in-law this morning and I heard two people arguing upstairs. I waited and saw Calder leave and I wondered how long the pair of them had been at it. When I took a look at his file and saw his full name was John David it all clicked into place.' He gave a helpless shrug. 'I hadn't banked on her attacking him, though.'

As soon as he saw the same, John David, J.D., he understood. Detective Sergeant John Calder was in the perfect position to arrange everything, to be the quiet mastermind. He could frighten

Henry White into keeping quiet, be his brother's silent partner, and know exactly what was going on in the investigation. And he was someone who could kill in cold, cold blood.

'He's going to live. We'll have him in the dock.'

'That's something,' he agreed. With four murders to his credit, one of them a copper, Calder would hang. No doubt about it. It was done, they had him.

After all the work, to solve it this way seemed like a let-down. It was too simple. Not detection, not police work, but luck.

Worst of all, the killer was one of their own.

The papers were already full of it, gloating. The chief constable had made his embarrassed statements. But the damage was done.

'Why do you think Calder did it, sir?' Ash asked.

So far the man had refused to answer any questions. The best Harper could do was guess.

'Greedy, maybe?' He shook his head. 'I'm not sure we'll ever know.'

When they'd searched the sergeant's house, they'd found three chests carefully hidden behind a false wall in the cellar. Good silver in two of them – part of the loot from old robberies – and money in the third, enough for anyone to pass the rest of his life in comfort.

Calder had used Henry White. He'd used his own damned brother. And what about Talbot, the guard at Armley? Probably he'd paid him then killed him. He wondered if they'd ever learn the full truth.

Then there was Conway. No one could forgive that. Nobody would try to explain it away. That had been an execution. Deliberate, cold, calculated. No lawyer would dare plead for mercy after that.

Moments came when he believed he understood why Calder had done it all. More often any sense behind it shredded like mist. Unless the man told them they'd never be certain.

So far he wasn't even showing any remorse.

The woman was back in Armley, remanded there until her trial started. Harper would be a witness for the defence, arguing for her release. She'd suffered enough.

There would be an enquiry into it all and he wouldn't come out of it well. Someone had to carry the blame and he was the new man, inexperienced at command. One of the councilmen on the watch committee had already taken him aside and suggested he should resign. But he wasn't going to give them that satisfaction. They'd promoted him, they'd wanted him in the job. If he was going to be their scapegoat, they could bloody well find the guts to sack him.

Harper had gone over it all, time and time again. Every moment of it, from waiting for Henry White outside Armley Jail to the knife in Calder's belly. No one could have solved it all sooner; he was absolutely, honestly convinced of it.

'What now, sir?'

'We're done on this. And Lester's dead, so the acid case is finished. Did Dr King ever give a cause of death for him?'

'It's what we thought, sir. Heart attack.'

The superintendent nodded. 'Why don't you go home? You've earned a rest.'

Ash snorted. 'See if Nancy remembers who I am. She might have moved her fancy man in by now.'

'Don't worry, we'll have other things to keep us busy in the morning.'

But that was tomorrow; he still had more to do today. Papers waited on his desk. Since he'd sent Calder off in the ambulance he'd spent most of his time here in the office. The hours and the days had passed slowly. Steadily. It came with the job.

TWENTY-SEVEN

He had the top hat and frock coat out again for Kendall's memorial service. The chief constable and some of the older members of the force read the lessons. Harper sat three rows from the front, in among the other division commanders. Olivia Kendall sat with her back straight and her head bowed, wearing a black velvet hat with a heavy veil.

Everyone who could be spared was there, men from the fire

brigade, too. He'd spotted Billy Reed in his best uniform, buttons and brass all polished.

The hymns, the sermon, they seemed to drone on for hours. When the final amen was spoken and he walked outside, it felt like sweet release. He'd said his farewell at the funeral.

'What did you think, sir?' Ash said.

'I think . . . it probably made the force happy,' he answered after a moment. 'A proper do.'

Two days earlier they'd worn the same formal clothes, going to a small church in Armley for Conway's funeral, with full police honours. He just hoped this was an end to it.

'I hear Sergeant Calder's in court tomorrow.'

'Yes,' Harper replied. He'd been transferred to the hospital wing of the jail. Able to stand and walk. And still refusing to answer any questions. The superintendent had been to see him twice. The man hadn't even acknowledged he was there. Simply stared off into space. The police had been building their case. It wasn't perfect, but more than enough to convict and put the noose round Calder's neck. For most people, the details of it all didn't matter. But he wanted to know the truth. 'As soon as we're done with that, we start dismantling Tosh Walker's little empire.'

'I'm looking forward to that,' Ash said with a broad grin. He put his top hat on his head. Together they walked down the path and through the lych gate to the road.

'So am I,' Harper told him. 'So am I.'

Leeds, May 1895

'Are you ready yet?'

'Almost.' Tom Harper slid the cutthroat razor down his cheek, one final stroke. He wiped the blade clean and splashed water from the basin over his face. A final adjustment to his tie and he was presentable.

'You scrub up halfway decent,' Annabelle said approvingly as she inspected him. She was dressed to the nines, a skirt and jacket in rich blue velvet, kid gloves, and a black hat with a silk band the colour of blood, set off by a single partridge feather. Mary's face and hands were freshly washed and she was wearing her new sailor suit dress, the cap set at a jaunty angle, a necklace of bright coral around her throat to keep her safe and healthy.

His eyes moved from one of them to the other, filled with pride and love. Sometimes it seemed as if he must have dreamed them both and all the happiness they brought him.

Annabelle refused to tell him where they were going. She pushed him out of the Victoria and up Roundhay Road, one arm linked through his, holding on to Mary with her other hand. Through the back streets, with hellos and how do you dos for everyone they met. The long spring was turning into an early summer, the weather already close, a Sunday sun peering through the haze.

From the direction he guessed they were heading towards Burmantofts, but he had no idea why. A surprise, she said, and he'd been content with that. Now, though, curiosity took over.

'Are you going to tell me where we're going?'

'No, I'm not,' she answered with a smile. 'You can hold your horses, Tom Harper. You'll see soon enough.'

'Where are we going, Mam?' Mary echoed, and he smirked.

'Like I told your da, you'll see.' She glanced down at the girl and sighed. 'How did you get that smudge on your dress? You haven't even done anything.' They halted while she brought a handkerchief from her sleeve, wet it with spit and cleaned the material. 'Honestly, you're a muck magnet, you are.'

Were they off to visit Billy Reed and Elizabeth? He hadn't seen the man since Kendall's memorial; there'd been no reason for their paths to cross. But Annabelle wouldn't make something like that into a secret, and they certainly wouldn't dress up for it. He was baffled.

At Beckett Street they crossed the road, and finally he understood. They were just one family among many visiting the cemetery on a Sunday afternoon. A flower-seller stood outside the gate. Annabelle looked at the selection, then up at him.

'The red roses,' she said and he nodded. 'A dozen of them, please.'

'Yes, missus,' the woman said, then took a daisy and handed it to Mary. 'A pretty flower for a pretty girl.'

'What do you say?' Annabelle asked her daughter.

'Thank you, miss.' Mary bobbed a small curtsey and he smiled.

Past the gates, Annabelle drew the notebook from her pocket. 'They told me where it was, but I thought I'd better write it down.' She gave a quick, embarrassed smile and laughed it off. 'I always seem to be at sixes and sevens these days. It's getting worse. I'd probably forget my head if it wasn't screwed on.'

A look and she was on her way, the pair of them in her wake. After a few yards she stopped and turned.

'There it is,' she said with pride. 'The subscription raised enough.'

A gravestone. Tom Maguire's gravestone. She'd put in the first money to make it happen, organized everything, and now it was here. Still new, shiny, the marks of the engraver's chisel clear and sharp.

Tom Maguire

Socialist

Born Dec 29 1865, Died March 9 1895

Bold, Cautious, True, And A

Loving Comrade.

He'd be remembered in Leeds; this would make sure of it. She'd needed to do it for the memory of all those years she'd known him.

'What do you think?' Annabelle asked.

'It's wonderful,' he told her and squeezed her hand.

'What do the words say, Mam?' Mary asked.

'You remember my friend Mr Maguire, the one who died?' The girl nodded her head. 'They're about him. That's where he's buried.'

Annabelle moved forward and placed the roses at the bottom of the gravestone. She stood with her head bowed then turned away, dabbing at her eyes.

'Right,' she said after a minute, trying to control her voice, 'Why don't we walk down to Harehills then catch the tram up to Roundhay Park? Make the day a treat, eh?'

He looked into her face. Sorrow, loss, maybe even joy. 1895 hadn't been a kind year. He leaned close to her.

'I love you, Mrs Harper,' he whispered, and saw her light up.

*   *   *

Maguire, Kendall, White, Calder, Talbot, Conway. The names seemed to give a rhythm to his footsteps as he strode through the Bank. Early still, the first day of the working week and men were moving grimly through the streets on the way to their jobs. No one even gave him a glance.

John David Calder had been found guilty of three murders. Set to hang next week, and still refusing to say a word about why he did it all. Too many mysteries would go to the grave with him. Too many questions without answers. At least Emmeline Calder had been released, back to live a small life in Holbeck, notorious now in her neighbourhood.

The story had filled the newspapers for a few days, the biggest scandal anyone could recall in Leeds. Then it had vanished, to be replaced by some newer outrage.

Harper turned on to Copper Street and stopped outside Henry White's old house. Where it had all begun. Maybe, if he hadn't been so cocky, some of those deaths might never have happened. But maybe and what if meant little as life unfolded.

He took a single red rose from his jacket pocket and placed it on the front doorstep. The people who lived here would wonder about it, discuss it for a day or two. And then it would all be forgotten. Like everything, it would pass.

AFTERWORD

Tom Maguire did die in 1895. Not even thirty years old, and pretty much in the circumstances described here – no heat, no food, no money. According to some, he'd been pushed away from the centre of politics in Leeds. His collection of poetry, *Machine-Room Chants*, was actually published posthumously. He was a vital figure in early socialism and working-class politics, and sadly far too few people know his name and achievements these days. He is buried at Beckett Street Cemetery, and hundreds did line the street for his funeral procession.

The moving pictures in a converted shop of Briggate were real, and Issott's Kinetoscope Parlour did remarkable business for a while, before it was replaced by something better, and better, until the full-length film became a reality. For anyone who knows Leeds, where it stood is now part of Marks and Spencer's.

The British Museum did send a collection of Cypriot artefacts to Nathan Bodington, head of Yorkshire College, now Leeds University. They ended up hidden away for decades in a basement. Thanks to Anna Reeve for the education on that.

My thanks, as always, to everyone at Severn House for believing in Tom and Annabelle, and for bringing this into your hands. To Lynne Patrick, the best editor a writer could want. And above all to you for reading it.